Down Along the Piney

THE RICHARD SULLIVAN PRIZE IN SHORT FICTION

Editors
William O'Rourke and Valerie Sayers

1996 *Acid*, Edward Falco

1998 *In the House of Blue Lights*, Susan Neville

2000 *Revenge of Underwater Man and Other Stories*,
      Jarda Cervenka

2002 *Do Not Forsake Me, Oh My Darling*, Maura Stanton

2004 *Solitude and Other Stories*, Arturo Vivante

2006 *The Irish Martyr*, Russell Working

2008 *Dinner with Osama*, Marilyn Krysl

2010 *In Envy Country*, Joan Frank

2012 *The Incurables*, Mark Brazaitis

2014 *What I Found Out About Her: Stories of Dreaming
      Americans*, Peter LaSalle

2017 *God, the Moon, and Other Megafauna*, Kellie Wells

2018 *Down Along the Piney: Ozarks Stories*, John Mort

DOWN

— ALONG THE —

PINEY

Ozarks Stories

JOHN MORT

University of Notre Dame Press

Notre Dame, Indiana

University of Notre Dame Press
Notre Dame, Indiana 46556
undpress.nd.edu

Published in the United States of America

Library of Congress Cataloging-in-Publication Data

Names: Mort, John, 1947– author.
Title: Down along the piney : Ozarks stories / John Mort.
Description: Notre Dame, Indiana : University of Notre Dame Press, 2018. |
  Series: The Richard Sullivan Prize in Short Fiction |
Identifiers: LCCN 2018021933 (print) | LCCN 2018023176 (ebook) | ISBN
  9780268104078 (pdf) | ISBN 9780268104085 (epub) | ISBN 9780268104054
  (hardback : alk. paper) | ISBN 0268104050 (hardback : alk. paper) | ISBN
  9780268104061 (pbk. : alk. paper) | ISBN 0268104069 (pbk. : alk. paper)
Classification: LCC PS3563.O88163 (ebook) | LCC PS3563.O88163 A6 2018 (print)
  | DDC 813/.54—dc23
LC record available at https://lccn.loc.gov/2018021933

∞This paper meets the requirements of ANSI/NISO Z39.48-1992
(Permanence of Paper).

In southern Missouri, the Big Piney flows from the hamlet
of Dunn northward for 110 miles, through pastures
and hilly national forests, until it reaches the larger
Gasconade River, which flows into the Missouri.

CONTENTS

Acknowledgments   ix

Pitchblende   3

The Hog Whisperer   13

Mission to Mars   29

Red Rock Valley   45

Home Place   57

Behind Enemy Lines   71

Blackberries   85

The Painter   95

The Truth   107

Take the Man Out and Shoot Him   115

The Book Club   165

Mariposa   179

The Hidden Kingdom   191

ACKNOWLEDGMENTS

Grateful acknowledgment is given to the publications in which these stories first appeared.

"Behind Enemy Lines": *Big Muddy*, reprinted in John Mort, *DONT MEAN NOTHIN: Vietnam War Stories* (Stockton Lake Publishers).

"Blackberries": *These and Other Lands: Stories from the Heartland* (Westphalia Press), reprinted in John Mort, *The Walnut King and Other Stories* (Woods Colt Press).

"The Book Club": *Sixfold*

"The Hidden Kingdom": *Arkansas Review*

"The Hog Whisperer": *Flint Hills Review*. Winner of the 2013 Spur Award for best short story from the Western Writers of America.

"Mariposa": *Big Muddy*

"Mission to Mars": *Printers Row Journal*

"Pitchblende": *Proud to Be: Writing by American Warriors*, vol. 2 (Southeast Missouri State University Press). Winner of the anthology's short story award.

"Red Rock Valley": *Sixfold*

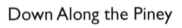

Down Along the Piney

Pitchblende

The last semester of my senior year, I signed up for industrial arts. That was fine with the Colonel, my father, who'd been off fighting wars most of my life and hardly knew me. My mother was another matter. "You're smarter than those other boys, Michael," she said. "You're not a thug."

Maybe it wasn't your future teachers or lawyers who took industrial arts. We were farm boys, mostly, and, when we graduated, became farmers ourselves, or joined the army. But we weren't thugs. We were the names you see on those brass plaques at the courthouse.

I suppose the idea originally was that you'd spend half a day in some factory, learning how to run a lathe or sweat fittings, so that when you graduated you'd have a trade. But I never heard of a kid who found a job because he—or she; we had two girls in the class—took industrial arts at Mountain Vale High School. You might get on with the county if your uncle worked there, but the factories had all moved to Mexico.

Mostly, we hung around smoking cigarettes and grab-assing. The shop teacher, old Dan Gooden, was asleep in the teachers' lounge half the time, and, when he did show up, he said, "This place is a mess. We're gonna clean it up, men!" The trade you learned in industrial arts was how to push a broom, and how to lean on one.

Fridays were the best days, when we cut all our classes and hauled the school's trash to the landfill. Little Joe Harpster, he's dead now, always drove, and the rest of us climbed behind the cab with the garbage, at the ready to whistle at girls. We took off our shirts and stood with our noses to the wind like hound dogs.

The county crew let the landfill mound up for a while, then bulldozed it flat, leaving a long, gradual hill with a drop-off like a cliff. You could see the water towers, gleaming like stars, of towns as far south as Arkansas. I liked to climb up there and roll a tractor tire off the edge. When it hit a rock or an old car it bounced high, scattered the turkey buzzards, and finally splashed in the putrid little creek.

If you looked back from the peak, the landfill was like a battlefield, strewn over with broken things, dotted with fires. I liked it. Wandering among the ruptured water heaters and stained mattresses, every now and then you found a treasure, a jar of pennies or a bundle of thirty-year-old love letters.

And I liked it because you could fire a weapon there. Little Joe had a Remington .22 semi-automatic that was cheap to shoot, and Sam Jablonski had that Springfield rifle he'd shot a fourteen-point buck with down by Gentryville. Sometimes, C. C. Cooper brought along his dad's banana clip and what he claimed was an AK-47. C. C. went into the army the week after graduation and got hit bad on Thanksgiving Day.

C. C. handed me the banana clip and I prowled the trash, eyes shifting, ears cocked for the rustling of a rat or 'possum, as Sam crept behind with a bucket of beer bottles. "VC, two o'clock," Sam yelled, and threw a bottle, and another one, and another one. I sprayed a dozen rounds, kicking the bottles along or shattering them first hit.

One time a car drew up and a beautiful woman stepped out. She wore a red suit, and there was something about the way she carried herself, so slender and graceful, that put you in your place. A professional woman, I thought, far off her route, and, even then, I wondered if anything so fine would ever come my way in life. She walked toward us, and, as if we'd been caught masturbating, we were shy little boys again.

Then I felt like crying, because the woman was my mother, and I hadn't recognized her. She had just bought the car. She'd had her hair done, and the red suit was new.

"Mike, that's your mom!" Little Joe said.

Her perfume smelled like crushed blackberries. I held her close and then stepped back, sad. C. C. and Sam and Little Joe stood a distance away, their rifle stocks propped on their hips, but I don't believe she even saw them. "I'm leaving the Colonel," she said.

I couldn't answer.

"It's not that he's cruel. Michael, he's—"

"Crazy?"

Her eyes glistened but she didn't cry. "I'll come back for your graduation," she said at last. "I can't take any more."

The Colonel was on the Cat, pushing blue clay and jagged hunks of limestone, when I drove up Bald Mountain. He threw me a mock salute like he always did.

I sat in her room for a long time, thinking I'd hear her call, then I lay across her bed and dreamed about her in the fine dress. When I woke the Colonel sat opposite me at her little writing table. "We got some adjustments to make," he said.

"Yeah," I said. "I guess we do."

He brought his fist down on the table. "Won't say a word against her. Only there ain't a goddamn thing to eat in this entire house."

We got in the pickup and drove to town. It was hot for March and I put my feet on the dash and leaned back drinking a Coke, thinking maybe I looked pretty cool alongside my military dad and would impress the girls when we passed the tennis courts.

At the IGA the Colonel threw potatoes and Spam and macaroni into the cart, not violently but absentmindedly, oblivious to the shoppers who stared. He was a local legend because of his attack on Bald Mountain. Bald Mountain was our farm, though all we had was a few goats, and they'd gone wild. People called the farm Bald Mountain because the Colonel had bulldozed half a dozen long trenches that rose up the grade like threads on a screw, and he'd knocked down every tree in the process. You could see it five miles off.

The Colonel paused before the ice cream. "How much can you eat?"

"I don't know," I said. Marybeth Baker passed by, smirking, or at least I thought so. I felt like a bug on the floor.

"Eat half a gallon?"

"Sure."

"What kind?"

"I don't care." The butcher, wiping his hands on his bloody apron, peered over his counter. He understood what fools we were.

"How about butter pecan?"

"That's fine," I said, knowing it was his favorite.

"A man's ice cream!"

Oh, he must have been joking! I didn't understand him at all. Why couldn't he get along with my mother? Why was he burrowing to the center of the earth?

We sat on the tailgate and he cut the butter pecan ice cream with his Case pocketknife, handing me half like he'd split a peach. "Suppertime, Mikey."

I hated to be called "Mikey," but there was no use protesting. "Thanks," I said, staring at Marybeth as she slid into her father's big Mercury. She wore a blouse that was the same red as my mother's suit. She didn't look at us, two thugs eating ice cream.

The Colonel pointed at a scrawny plum tree that hung on somehow in the wasteland between two parking lots. It was in bloom, and I could see bees working.

"By God, it's spring!" the Colonel said.

I don't know why she married him. Maybe he had some charm in those early days—a dashing officer. Maybe he didn't talk about Korea so much, or uranium.

I remember an apartment on Ft. Irwin, which is way out in the Mojave Desert, but a fine place if your passion is to shoot howitzers at big rocks. Some Mexican kids attended my school, and I thought it would be a fine thing to chop celery for a living, because then I could work alongside the darling of the third grade, Rebecca Bareiro. Of course, she was a brigadier's daughter, but I thought of her as one of Zane Grey's dark-eyed maidens in those novels my father left behind. I wanted to declare myself like a cowboy. "Reckon I love ya, little Becky."

California was all sunshine, with my pretty young mother coming and going in sandals and bright cotton dresses, driving me to school, twice a week leaving me with sitters so she could attend school herself, down in San Bernardino. Then a shadow fell: the Colonel came home.

He pounded the table. "We didn't have maps!" he said. "Christ, we couldn't get gasoline, what do you expect? And cold? Jesus Christ, I like to lost my toes."

It was as though a big dog sat at the table, dressed up in his greens and trying to act civilized, never quite mastering the trick of it. Sometimes, he drank, and looked at me blearily, no one else to talk to because Mom was away again in San Bernardino. "They're shafting me, Mikey," he said. "They want me out!"

In Korea he was a track commander. He took his battalion far north of the 38th parallel, rolling through those cold hills that look, in the pictures I've seen, like the hills around Mountain Vale. The Colonel saw no enemy but they were there, all right, mustering their forces, waiting. Waiting, as it turned out, for the Chinese to join them. When he was too far forward to call in artillery, they came out of the bleak woods and picked off the infantryman who brought up his rear. When his point track crested a ridge, they speared its belly with a rocket. When he tried to retreat, they mortared him in the tight little canyons.

"We froze to death!" the Colonel said. He lost half his men, as many of them to the cold as to munitions. So did other commanders in the Cav's retreat, and, like my father, most never found another true command. They taught ROTC at junior colleges, or inventoried blankets on those sleepy little forts left over from World War II.

Later, down in Panama, the Colonel read some old book about uranium. He'd been a young lieutenant in the Philippines when the Enola Gay flew and never got over the miracle of it. Atomic power was magical. Sure, you could blow up the earth, but also you could electrify it, power ships to Jupiter, bring humankind to the very throne of God. If he couldn't make full bird, the Colonel thought, maybe he could find uranium. The book claimed that all through the Ozarks, where in pioneer days they'd found lead and silver, there were rich pitchblende deposits just waiting for a clever prospector.

Mom was teaching college English when the big dog in greens came home to stay, talking crazy talk about the atomic age. Maybe she thought she owed him for all those years he'd left her to her own devices, paying for her keep while she picked up college degrees. She followed him to Mountain Vale, but the only work she found was waitressing, at which she lasted two weeks, and clerking at the supermarket, where she was fired for being too slow. She wasn't a churchgoing woman, and, in a little town like Mountain Vale, you don't have friends if you don't attend church.

Then an editor in Minneapolis bought her first novel, and I think from that moment she resolved to leave. Not long ago, I read her book. It's about a bulldozer operator who pushes up obstacles to his wife's career.

"There's no cupboards in this house," Mom said. "That carpet—they kept dogs in there."

"I'll buy a new carpet," the Colonel said, though he never did.

I'd leave the supper table and plop down in the living room to watch *Combat!* All I wanted was my driver's license. Like Mom, all I wanted was to leave.

"You think it was so goddamned nice in frontier times? I got work to do here, woman, I'm on a mission!"

"You used to talk about going back for your engineering degree. You have your pension. You have the G.I. Bill. Why are you digging your way to China?"

He grunted and scooted back from the table. "People made fun of Henry Ford."

"Henry Ford was a genius. You—"

I don't believe he heard her. He'd already pulled on his hat and coat and stalked into the living room. He gave me a nod, stomped out the door, and pretty soon the Cat choked to life again.

"What about me, Albert?" Mom murmured, looking through the window above the sink. "What am I supposed to do here in Hillbilly Heaven?"

Late at night, I'd hear the screen door swish shut and look up to see her, in her nightgown and sandals, headed for the abandoned chicken house that she'd turned into a study. She'd pump up two Coleman lanterns and sit between them, moths circling her head and bouncing off the globes.

In her way, she was as remote as the Colonel. Sometimes, I crept out and stood in the darkness outside the chicken house window, a foot or two from her face, her invisible son. She scribbled in a yellow pad, sighed, sipped mint tea. Then she hit that old Olympia again.

The Colonel didn't belong in the Ozarks, either. He knew nothing about cattle and couldn't have made a crop. He didn't cut wood or run hounds.

He did know about tanks, and, minus its howitzer, the Cat was a Sherman all over again. I grew so used to the sound of that big diesel that when it didn't run it seemed something must be wrong. It got so the Colonel didn't even come in at night, instead building a fire above his trench and sleeping on the ground. Unlike his wife, who stayed in bed until noon, he was working again at daylight.

Once, he dragged us down Bald Mountain and deep into the earth, where he'd exposed a long, black vein of rock, sticky to the touch. "Now," he said. "By God, *now!*"

But the county engineer took one look and knew better. "I only seen it once," the engineer said. "In Utah. This ain't it. It can be kind of cube-like, like lead only there's a soft, pitchy feel to it. And of course, your Geiger counter goes crazy. Don't you have a Geiger counter?"

"Damn thing never has worked right."

"That's because they ain't no uranium in Missouri." What the Colonel mistook for pitchblende was sticky and moist, but only because a spring seeped through it.

"This here's coal, Mister. Pitchblende would be somethin' to find, all right, but this is just that old soft coal you cain't sell. Blacksmiths used it, back in the day."

What if he had found pitchblende? He'd have been rich, of course, but, more important, he'd have mattered. Rather than a fool, he'd have been a hero, the bringer of jobs to a poor county. His wife, in her fine new house, would have stayed by his side, writing her romances in Missouri rather than Minnesota. And his son?

Who knows? Maybe I'd have gone to West Point.

One Saturday after Mom left I mowed around the house with the little Ford tractor. Looping downhill, I thought I spied a stump ahead and stepped down to inspect, but what I had seen was merely a rotten puffball. I kicked it and black powder, like an evil potion, sailed away on the breeze. When I turned, truly as if I had invoked a spell, a copperhead slithered ahead of me.

I think reptiles have next to no maternal instincts, but it's hard to account for how angry this snake was, unless it was a she and I had disturbed her nest. She darted her brown head right and left and flicked her tongue, slipping quickly over the ground toward the idling mower. She struck at one of the pulleys and then disappeared under the mower itself.

Bad move, Madame Copperhead, I thought, as I climbed back on the tractor and pulled the lever for the PTO. There was a thud and then snake guts spewed out the discharge. I cut the engine, and the air felt as it does before a thunderstorm, charged and reckless. Why do I feel so bad, I wondered, when I've killed something that could have killed me?

The Colonel stepped out of the house, calling me to supper. In her last months on Bald Mountain Mom hadn't cooked at all, so his efforts were an improvement, though all he knew how to make was chili and goulash and the like. This time it was fried potatoes, cheeseburgers, and the strong, gritty coffee he made in a saucepan simply by throwing in grounds and boiling them. I never drank it.

"Manjack wants me to dig him a lake. Up north along the Piney."

"What about the uranium?"

"Ain't no uranium in Missouri," he said, looking away.

My mother knew it, I knew it, everyone in Mountain Vale knew it including the county engineer, and now he knew it as well. I swallowed some of his bitter coffee.

"Goddamned big lake." The Colonel dropped a cheeseburger on my plate, then shoveled up potatoes. "We're talking about damming the whole valley. Take all summer, and you could be a big help to me, Mikey."

"Yessir."

"Pay you wages, of course. And you don't have to call me sir, hell no. We're just two old soldiers here, now that your mother's gone."

I wanted to tell him about the copperhead but I just listened, thinking that he'd finally found something real to hang onto. I wanted to tell him that I appreciated the meals he cooked and how he'd taught me to drive and bought me that Ford Falcon. But already he'd pulled on his coat and gone through the door. In the distance, I heard the Cat whir, then fire up in harsh, staccato gasps.

I followed him after a while and sat watching from above in the twilight, munching on one of his biscuits. I wondered why he searched for pitchblende when he had just acknowledged there was none to find. Or why it wasn't until Mom left that he concluded there wasn't any.

Then I was more puzzled than ever, thinking, *he knew it all along.*

I thought about Marybeth. I was slowly coming to the conclusion that she didn't regard me as a thug. Just that day she'd made eyes at me from across the cafeteria, and I tried to construct a scene in which I asked her for a date. I wondered if the Colonel could pass on his knowledge of such things, or if he had any knowledge. There must have been a time when Mom and he liked each other and fumbled about for things to say.

So suddenly I have never understood quite how it happened, the Cat flipped on its side, skidded on the frail dolomite, and flipped over. My father was somewhere underneath. "That's wrong," I thought, coming to my feet.

I stepped off the bank, lost one foot deep in the pink silt, caught my jeans on an oak root, and rolled to the bottom of the trough my father had made. Staring from upside down, I saw the Colonel right-side up, face in an uncharacteristic grin, eyes darting about, legs caught in some red, pulpy-looking thing.

"Mikey," he said. "I'm gonna need some help."

"Yessir."

He panted. I could hardly make out his words. "Quick, now. You go up to the house, call the fire department. Then, maybe. You bring around the Ford tractor and the winch."

Soon enough, a dozen men arrived, yelling and backing up vehicles and strapping chains, but they couldn't keep the gravel and clay from giving way, or pull out the Colonel before the Cat shifted again, and the broken tread flopped against his head like a hammer.

Darkness came. The little tractor ran and ran, and I remembered how proud the Colonel was of it, what a fine piece of machinery he thought it was, so versatile, so classic. Then someone shut it off, and I could hear the whippoorwills.

A tall man, I'd never seen him before, walked with me to the house, and he talked for a long time. He had a full, gray beard and pale blue eyes, and he'd lost his son in Vietnam. He said he couldn't make sense of it, and he didn't know why the Colonel died. He said you can't get through life without bad things happening, and all you can do is soldier on. You keep your eyes and ears open, and one day maybe you'll find what you're looking for. Maybe it's a woman, the tall man said. Maybe it's God.

Around ten, he called Mom.

She came down for the funeral and stayed another two months, until I graduated. She wanted me to go to college in Minnesota and I pretended I wanted to, but then in August I joined the army and learned to fly helicopters.

Out of my industrial arts class Sam, Little Joe, and three more were killed. C. C. Cooper died in the VA Hospital in Poplar Bluff just yesterday, his son told me. I went to see him once but he'd had a stroke. I could tell he knew what I said because his eyes lit up, but his speech was all jumbled and I couldn't understand him.

I was a warrant officer. I was a pilot, and twice I was shot down. Who knows why, but the bullets flew all around me, and I was never touched.

The Hog Whisperer

Carrie Kreider was raised on a three-hundred-acre farm in south-east Kansas where she showed a wondrous affinity with animals, winning three purple ribbons, once going to the state fair, with her hogs and goats. She kept guinea hens and always several dogs and once raised an orphan cardinal with her own secret formula. So perhaps it was inevitable, when her father sent her off to Kansas State, that she'd major in animal science.

Right away she declared she wanted to work with hogs. Hogs were pariahs—smelly, never perfectly tamed, misunderstood to the point that laypeople thought them mean or even satanic—and because she herself was a sort of pariah, Carrie sympathized. If she kept up a chatter, hogs grew calm around her, even affectionate in their fashion. Jokingly, but with admiration, a professor christened her "the hog whisperer."

Of course, Carrie didn't get the joke.

She didn't get a lot of things: men, for instance, when they were coming on to her, because it had happened so seldom she couldn't isolate the process; and women, when they competed with her by being catty and gossiping.

When she was a child she had no friends except for the imaginary kind. She talked to herself and made violent gestures, and the experts pronounced her retarded. Deeply shy might have been more accurate—and wild, because she'd run shirtless in the woods if you let her, looking for frogs and turtles. Her condition never had an official diagnosis, and maybe it wasn't even a condition. Maybe she was just a backward, and unusually large, country girl, hiding under the porch when the feed truck came. She learned to talk at a normal age, but forgot how at two, entering "her own little world"—the phrase she encountered when she was older, and read books trying to understand herself.

She was gifted, it turned out, and her giftedness—along with some good teachers and her widower dad's patience—earned her a full scholarship at K-State. She spent her time there reading—on the bus, in the woods, at the cafeteria. She would have earned straight As except for the occasional prejudiced instructor, usually female, who seemed offended by her oversized body, her mismatched sweaters, her thick glasses.

In her junior year she met a withdrawn young English major named Billy Mole. Everyone in the world knew Billy was gay except for his parents, Carrie, and Billy himself. Anyhow, they became fast friends, as shy people sometimes do when they discover another shy person. And they had no sexual issues until one night when they were walking back from a showing of *When Harry Met Sally*. From Carrie's point of view, a certain amount of data had been gathered, and experiments were in order. She said, "Let's have sex, Billy."

"I don't know how."

"Let's find out what it is. Let's get it over with."

For Carrie it was painful, and she had to comfort Billy when he cried, but still she wanted to try again. What good were experiments if you couldn't make them come out the same way twice; or vary them and predict the results? But Billy ran from her, and hid himself away, profoundly confusing Carrie. Nothing animals did quite matched this. Months later, she spied Billy with another young man, holding hands, and she struggled to assimilate this new data.

Simple by comparison was Carrie's master's thesis on how containment hog operations could become more humane. But she'd written exactly what they wanted to read at American Family Farms, a big and secretive firm where good publicity was scarce. American Family put Carrie to work in the Carolinas, Iowa, and Missouri, measuring square footage per hog, indoor particulates, and odor. Hey, bright girl! Can you make hog shit smell sweet?

At headquarters in Kansas City Carrie spent two years learning more chemistry, more physiology, and all about anaerobic digesters.

Then she was assigned several rather daunting projects and dispatched to the Texas Panhandle. That was four years ago, and—so it seemed even to someone as trusting and literal-minded as Carrie—the company had forgotten her.

In the Panhandle she at last understood that "hog whisperer" was an allusion to a movie called *The Horse Whisperer,* starring Robert Redford. She found the film at the Dalhart Public Library, enjoyed it because of its Montana scenery, and "got" what the character did when he communed with horses.

She still didn't get the humor in being called a hog whisperer, but she understood that no one was going to ascribe to hogs the nobility of horses. Still, Carrie thought it right and decent to minimize their miseries as they journeyed along the assembly line of their short lives, turning from pigs into sausage. A hog's only purpose was to be eaten, but that didn't give you license to be cruel.

Company policy strictly forbade it, in fact. Put it this way: cruelty was inefficient. One hog was a component of a great machine; abusing it made no more sense than taking a hammer to a balky diesel.

Still, there were always a few psychopaths, men who'd beat an animal as if on principle. And now Carrie had met such a man at American Family. She was more of a consultant than a supervisor, and she was down in the valley with the finish hogs, rather than up on Hog Heaven with the sows, where she usually worked, but she went immediately to Bud Varner, the foreman, and asked him to fire Dennis Woolsey.

"Whud he do?" Varner asked.

She said he'd abused a downer.

Several of the men, most of whom were Mexican, overheard just this much, and word leaped from barn to barn that a man was being fired for animal abuse.

Some of the men were embittered by the foul-smelling lives they led, and drank too much, and took their woes out on their wives with their fists. Such men found the concept of animal abuse a tricky one. Sometimes, you had to use prods when hogs knotted up at a narrow exit; sometimes, you kicked at them if they bit your knee or exposed hand. Was this abuse?

Relief passed among them when they learned that the abuser was Woolsey, a gringo. They knew he was crazy, and if it had come to a matter of testimony, they'd all have taken Carrie's side. She, too, was a little crazy, but she was also smart and hardworking and they held her in high esteem, hardly thinking of this tall, broad-shouldered personage in prescription goggles as a gringo, or even as a woman.

Woolsey had run the dead wagon down in the valley, servicing those thirteen 1200-head barns where shoats were finished into 250-pound hogs. The job was to cart away downers—hogs that went limp on the concrete slats of their cages, or developed tumors, which their brothers and sisters worried with their teeth. Eventually, the "technician" spotted the downers and wrestled them, dead or alive, onto the long center aisle.

Some downers burrowed into a corner like dogs, closed their eyes, and gulped at the steamy air as they awaited the end. Others squealed as the executioner neared, swinging his captive bolt gun.

All Woolsey was supposed to do was touch the captive bolt gun to the downer's forehead, or eye, or ear, and pull the trigger. Shoot the bolt; drag out the hog: that was all there was to it. If the hog was near market weight, you could find someone to help, or tip the carcass into a wheelbarrow. Not a pleasant job, but better than no job at all.

"Fucking pig!" Woolsey screamed, and kicked the hog in the ribs. It squealed in agony, and he kicked it again.

"You like that? You like that? I'll show you!" Now Woolsey hammered on the downer's snout with a length of pipe. It tried to stand, making two quivering steps, and then it hunched forward on its knees. Its squeal was more like a scream now. An almost human scream.

Why do such a thing? Who would be impressed?

Maybe the other hogs. They were screaming now in shrill protest.

Carrie, watching from the end of the barn, broke into a run down the aisle, never once thinking, I am a woman alone, and Woolsey is a strong man. Because she was no prairie flower. Back in Kansas City, coming out of the cafeteria, she'd overheard a woman whisper, "Hitch her to a plow." It took a while for the remark to sink in, but it hurt. She was six feet tall, plain as the Ukrainian Mennonites she was descended from, and could pick up a tractor tire if she had to and throw it into a pickup bed.

She spun Woolsey around, and his unsubtle face crowded with amazement. His eyes were blood red. "You . . . bitch . . ." he managed, and stopped.

She reached to grab the pipe. "If I ever see you treat an animal—"

Woolsey shot the captive bolt and the hog shuddered to its death. Then Woolsey yanked up the steel pipe, causing Carrie to stumble backward. He laughed at her. He threw down the pipe and brought a rope from his pocket. He bound the hog's hind legs and drew on the rope, pulling the hog toward the far end.

Carrie sighed. "I'm going to report him," she announced, speaking aloud as if to a companion. She turned, and twelve hundred pairs of eyes fastened on her, from up and down the aisle. For a long moment, the barn was silent, and she could hear that eternal Panhandle wind.

Varner banished Woolsey before the shift was done, and that should have ended the story. But several evenings later a stranger with heavy boots came up the steps of Carrie's deck and knocked on the trailer door.

She'd showered, pulled on a T-shirt and sweatpants, and turned up her air conditioning. She was eating a Lean Cuisine and some tasteless radishes she'd bought at Walmart and watching *Star Trek*. It was one of her favorite episodes, in which the humorless android Data, attempting to become more human, practiced telling jokes.

The man held his cap in his hands, thumbing the bill. He seemed shy, apologetic. He was slightly shorter than Carrie. "My name is Raúl Zamora. This is my first day. And they gave me—here in the colonia—"

Colonia was the name the Mexicans had assigned to American Family's company town. It was a trailer park.

"—the trailer of the man who left. Except—there's a big dog in there."

"Yes, he had a dog," Carrie said, and already she'd lost herself in Zamora's brown eyes. His face was sad, weathered, but kind.

Zamora smiled awkwardly. "Mr. Varner said you are the one to see about animal problems."

"Oh!" she said. "Of course." She reached for her scuffed leather bag, not exactly a vet's bag because she wasn't exactly a "vetinary," as they called them out in the middle of Kansas—Texas, too. Her bag was more like a toolbox, containing wrenches and pliers and duct tape, as well as antibiotics and packets of electrolyte powder for, perish the thought, bloody scours.

They walked to his trailer—one of the worst in the colonia, but company housing had its advantages. You didn't have to commute from Dalhart, burning all that gasoline. The rent was cheap and you could have a vegetable garden if you wanted. True, the hydrogen sulfide smell given off by manure was almost unbearable sometimes, made you cough, gave you headaches, secreted itself in your closets and lodged for weeks in your clothes. But the colonia was half a mile from the nearest barn, and most of the time the wind blew the other way.

Also, many of the families were illegal, and this farm was as remote as you could be east of the Rockies, north of the border.

"I thought he would take my hand off," Raúl said.

"You went inside?"

"I was reaching for the light switch. He leaped up and got my sleeve."

"How do you know it's a boy dog?"

"The neighbor called him 'Romeo.'"

They banged on the door as if the dog might bid them enter. With the air off, she thought, it was a wonder the dog wasn't dead. She stepped inside, bracing herself, but nothing happened. She fought for breath in the rank heat.

She turned on the living room light, revealing a psychotic mess of broken furniture, piled up dishes and spoiled food, and bright blue bags of trash. The smell was worse than a hog barn.

Raúl slowly smiled. "The first month is free."

She was halfway down the hall before she realized he'd made a joke. She turned with a belated smile and couldn't bear his curious eyes.

Romeo lay in the bathroom, a big, black mongrel with a big scrotum. Blood had caked in his nostrils, and he panted heavily, but she saw no evidence of internal damage. He was weak from several days without food, she reasoned, and the heat had worsened things. She wet a washcloth in the sink and daubed at the wounded nose. Romeo whimpered and pulled his head back. A lot of life left.

Raúl went through the trailer opening windows, and she heard a fan go on. He appeared in the bathroom door, and the dog growled, but calmed when she stroked its ribs.

"You have a touch," Raúl said. "Do you think I need to . . . take him to the back of the farm?"

"Shoot him?" she asked. "Oh, no. I'll take care of him."

"That's good," he said. "I don't think he likes me."

"Right now he thinks you're another Dennis Woolsey, whom no one liked. Buy him a package of bologna sometime."

He smiled. "Wish that were all it took with human beings."

She smiled up at him as she stroked Romeo. "Me, too."

Carrie's trailer had been installed on a grade, and its downhill side, shored up with cinder blocks, rose five feet above the ground. Over the next few days Raúl enclosed the area with wafer board and ran in a line to an automatic pig waterer. He made a door Romeo could nose open. Inside, he raked the dirt level and laid scrap carpeting. Carrie tested the dog lair herself, drawing in two worn blankets and sprawling in the darkness like some kid with a hiding place in the barn.

Immediately she missed Raúl. She schemed for some way to hold him near, but she'd never learned the set of skills having to do with flirting and enticement. She'd grown up without a mother or sisters, and in high school other girls ostracized her. For a time she'd bought those supermarket magazines, with their tips about coyness and how to please a man in bed, but they might as well have been written in German.

She thought she should have asked him to dinner. On television, couples always ate dinner right before they went to bed, and then the commercial came on. But when did you ask? And what could she manage to cook? She *preferred* TV dinners.

You couldn't come up on Romeo quickly, or he shrank and bared his teeth.

"I'm right here, boy," she said. "Things are gonna be all right. See what the nice man did? He built you a dog spa."

Not many days passed before Romeo wagged his tail when she came. A little kindness, she thought. The world was so full of cruelty that a little kindness was more powerful than the unleashed atom.

"Did I have a good day today?" she took to asking. "Well, yes, I did. And look what I brought home for you." She poured out half a pound of piglet testicles, and Romeo gulped them greedily.

By late fall his coat glowed from good health, and he whined happily whenever she was near, though he still growled at approaching men. She left him tied to her clothesline through the day, and in the evening she'd let him in and they watched *Star Trek*. She resolved to purchase the latest permutation of the series, *Enterprise*, because it featured a beagle.

In the crisp evenings she showered, put on fresh sweatpants, and walked past Raúl's trailer, but she never caught him home. Once, she passed him just as he was pointing his truck toward Dalhart. He smiled and waved.

She walked by his trailer at midnight, at three in the afternoon when she should have been working, and at 6:00 a.m. Deep in the night, she wrote him notes and taped them to his door—then ran back to snatch them up. I've never been like this, she thought.

She stood in the shadows, and the light above his kitchen sink came on. She shrank like Romeo when she saw, not Raúl, but a pretty Mexican girl. The girl lifted a glass to her lips, and looked through the window directly at Carrie. Carrie froze, but of course the girl stared at dark glass. She couldn't *see*.

Carrie worked fanatically, and in the bitter winter the first of her daunting projects—to make pig shit smell sweet—became viable.

American Family used a wave machine to wash out the barns every two hours, pushing water under the slatted floors of the pens and keeping flies and rats, and thus diseases, to a minimum. The periodic floods also did a great deal to reduce odor, but it was the bulk of manure that was the problem. The valley operation alone produced almost as much shit as the city of Amarillo.

You could spread some through your irrigation assemblies, absorbing it in corn and alfalfa, in effect feeding it back again, but the root systems of your crops, and the soil itself, rebelled from too much nitrogen, too many phosphates. Though it might not show up for years—until it percolated down—eventually manure poisoned the aquifer.

Lagoons were effective to a point, but didn't work fast enough to accommodate American Family's volume. They stank, of course, and drew vermin. And they seeped, no matter what company engineers told the state, and the weak county authority, and irate citizens.

And no matter where you disposed manure, flies gathered, endless flies, clots and gobs of flies, flies like thick black paint. Here was Carrie's approach:

1. Pump the hog water into a digester;
2. Let the solids settle;
3. Recirculate the water to the scrub system;
4. Heat up your solids, mixing in ammonia-eating polymers;
5. Bleed off the methane and run your generators;
6. Aerate the sludge;
7. Heat it slightly again and run it through a coarse sieve, making grub-sized pellets, and
8. Bag it—now odorless, black as buckyballs, and benign— as suburban fertilizer.

There had been times when she'd thought the brass in Kansas City had handed her an impossible project to be rid of her, parking their bleeding heart in that nascent desert called the High Plains. But with her team of good men—men who respected her, who enjoyed working for her—she'd done it. She'd filled a warehouse with the earth-friendly stuff, in green plastic bags, shrink-wrapped on four hundred pallets.

She'd sent email after email, proposal after proposal, to the CEO in Kansas City, to VPs in South Carolina and Iowa. For her friend, Janet Heinzman, head of development, she grabbed a bag of product and drove down to UPS. This is viable, she said, this is urgent! Finally, the company will look good. And we will make money!

If management was too stupid to respond, it wouldn't be the first time. Every two weeks her rather generous paychecks slipped into her account, even if she whiled away her days watching *Star Trek*. She never went anywhere, had no debts, spent hardly any money. She was damn near rich and could buy a ranch if she liked.

But she was restless. It was almost spring again, and she wanted something.

She could buy a better TV. She could ride a raft through the Grand Canyon. She could take a Caribbean cruise. She could trade in her Civic, still reliable all these years after grad school, for a fancy truck. But she didn't want a truck and knew how lonely she'd be on a cruise. She wanted someone to congratulate her—an admiring reporter, say, a young woman who saw her as a role model.

"They thought I'd never talk," she'd say. "Let alone solve the manure problem."

She drove into Dalhart. Yes, it was spring, but it had been another dry winter, and the ranches looked barren. American Family Farms, High Plains Division, was the only active business until you reached town.

She couldn't remember when she'd last had her hair done. Janet had taken her to that place in Crown Center; when was that? And working with hogs, what was the point? When her hair grew long enough to annoy her, she snipped it off.

The Vietnamese girl held up several pictures of movie stars.

"That one," Carrie said.

"The blonde? She so cute."

She bought some checkered slacks at Walmart and a tall woman's pink blouse and a wide sunbonnet similar to one her grandmother had worn, tending her garden. Such clothing didn't appeal to her; therefore, she'd try it. It looked fine on other women.

And sturdy shoes. She knew how to buy those, at least.

How could an afternoon in May be so hot? She walked slowly, staying within the shadows of the escarpment that stretched into New Mexico, following Romeo's trail. Wherefore was that dog? Whenever she took him from the colonia he became a greyhound of the purple sage. He always came home, but she worried about a lady coyote over the rocks somewhere, luring the big fool toward her craven brothers.

The escarpment twisted west, and she sat drinking water, admiring the sun on the yellow and purplish rocks. The Panhandle was almost desert. Still, more moisture was available than your average midwesterner might think, and in many summers the rains had a way of arriving exactly when they were needed. For an hour she climbed through the rocks, along a crooked path probably made by the Kiowa. Down her back trail, lights were coming on in the colonia. She'd be walking home in the dark, but she'd never encountered rattlesnakes here, and the moon would be full.

She sat on a crumbly expanse of limestone facing southwest, laughing as a roadrunner danced clownishly to distract Carrie from her nest. Carrie took off her sunbonnet and shook her new hair. In the mirror she'd thought it looked all right, more or less a restoration of her grad school do. She patted it absently, thinking about Raúl—and squinting. She'd put aside her old reliable goggles for contact lenses.

She reached the uneven ground between four crop circles. It made a sort of square, but with parabolas for sides, of perhaps six acres—three atop the escarpment and three some thirty feet below—at the edge of the valley floor. A creek, spring-fed but dry through the summer, ran down the middle, dropping off the escarpment into a murky pool that would evaporate by August. Someone had carved out two small fields next to the company's circles, each carefully terraced and ditched backward toward the pool, the idea being to capture runoff from the irrigated crop circles—and then pump from the pool again.

She knew who this experimental farmer was, of course. She'd seen his truck shimmering in the dry air, headed for the back country. And now she heard his tractor atop the escarpment.

At last the Kiowa path leveled out and she reached the top, where she spied Raúl on a small Yanmar diesel, a gray market relic without a roll bar, pulling what looked to be a disc designed for a team of horses. As she'd surmised, there were another two fields here, each devised to capture water from the crop circles. She stood staring, half in amusement, half in admiration, and then he cut the engine.

He didn't see her and despite the failing light grabbed a hoe: already he had crops above ground. Carrie, the farm girl, came down to his makeshift toolshed and grabbed another hoe. Following him, she saw that he'd channeled the creek as well, pushing it into a pool under an overhanging rock—where it would be slow to evaporate. Using gasoline pumps, siphons, and drip lines looped around stems, Raúl might nurse his crops through August if one or two rains fell to help, and if the spring held up through June.

"This is amazing," she called out.

He turned, recognized her, and smiled.

"What's your new field going to be?"

"Watermelons."

"And you'll drip them."

"Yes. Everything."

They hoed all that he had planted. She could just make out the sprouts in the moonlight, though the drip line, like a long black snake, was harder to see. They stopped simultaneously, knowing it was long past time to quit.

"Smart," she said.

He shrugged. "It might not work. And next year, maybe there won't be even this much water. But it's what I've always wanted to do."

"Really?"

"Since I was a kid. My father had a little place, not even this big, though water wasn't such a problem." He stared at her. "I'll sell what I raise in the colonia."

"Very smart. The women won't have to drive to town for that crap at Walmart. How will you kill the weeds?"

"Well, in country so dry, if you just drip the vegetables, you starve out the weeds."

"Not the stubborn ones. Listen, there's an old rototiller in the blue barn. I think it still runs."

He didn't answer immediately. "You're right, Carrie. I could put that to good use."

"Can I help you? With hoeing? Setting up a stand?"

He didn't answer.

"It's what *I've* always wanted to do. You wouldn't have to pay me. Except in tomatoes, maybe."

He laughed. "We'll see what your attitude is in July."

They walked slowly toward his truck, once brushing against each other, and she summoned all her courage. "Mr. Zamora," she began.

He laughed again. "Carrie, it's Raúl. We're friends."

They both turned toward the creek, where a black shape raced toward them.

"What is it?" Raúl asked. "Carrie, get behind me, I'll—"

She laughed. Romeo ran up between them and shook himself, raining all over them. He'd found the pool. Before she could scold him, he barked once and jumped into Raúl's pickup bed—at last showing some good manners.

Raúl covered his tractor with a tarp, and they slid into his pickup and jostled along the company road in second gear. Carrie went careening back to those days when she'd come in from the field with her father. Sometimes, even though it was past her bedtime, he'd surprise her by driving on to the Dairy Queen.

Her heart pounded and she began burping. She hadn't done that since college. It was embarrassing. She rolled down the window and gulped the cool night air.

"Are you all right?"

"Yes!" She pounded her chest with a fist. To be so like an animal. To be so . . . coarse. But he hadn't mocked her, like the kids at school used to. Slowly, as she regained her breath, it occurred to her that her new look had been wasted. Sweat had plastered her hair to her skull, and it was dark now anyhow. Even so, she was going to say it. "Raúl, would you like to come to dinner sometime?"

"Of course, Carrie," he said. "Let me bring a dish."

Three days later, after a trip to the Dalhart library for cookbooks—Italian, Chinese, Mexican, Texan, Mennonite—she came home to a message from Kansas City.

"Girl," Janet said. "Call me soon. We've got a preliminary launch next Thursday in the boardroom. The big boardroom—you remember! Congratulations, old pal out in the boondocks, you've split the atom. Your manure *does* smell sweet."

Product launch, Janet meant. For an instant, she'd visualized a rocket taking off.

Almost as an afterthought, Janet said that Carrie had been named employee of the year—no small thing, in a company with four thousand workers. She might take a train, she might take a plane, but Carrie had to be in Kansas City to receive the award in two weeks. She went out into the night again and turned round and round under the Panhandle stars. What great good fortune! She was *so* happy. She almost waltzed toward Raúl's trailer.

And jerked to a stop. It was that Mexican girl again, sitting with a drink on his steps, her long, slender legs akimbo. Raúl sat above her, smoking a cigar.

Carrie ran a few steps, her big feet falling flat, and slowed to a walk. She began to belch uncontrollably and hit at her chest with a fist. She took deep breaths and rushed to her outdoor spigot for a drink. Romeo came out of his spa, crawling on his belly, whining.

Friends, Raúl had called them. Maybe that's all the Mexican girl was. A friend who showed up every other weekend and spent the night. She couldn't compete with a friend like that. "What am I gonna do, Romeo?" she asked, and the dog whined sympathetically, but offered no advice.

She folded her big hands over his muzzle and stroked his temple with her thumbs. She looked into his inky eyes, into his doggy soul. It was a simple place, but sorrowful. Like poor Romeo, she could have turned her head to the moon and howled in pain. She was in love, God help her, and it seemed fatal.

Mission to Mars

Just before midnight, with the full moon lighting his steps, Brad kicked off his shoes and walked across the sand to the pier at New Smyrna. He'd driven all the way from Missouri and had no place to sleep, but wanted to stand for a few moments above the glistening sea. Immersed in the starlight that bounced all around him, making even his clothing glow, it seemed he had reached another planet.

Ashore, two men and a woman got out of a battered Dodge pickup with a camper on the back and walked a little way onto the pier. They carried plastic buckets and a mass of equipment that Brad couldn't distinguish in the soft light, and for an instant he panicked, thinking these interlopers, at this evil hour, must be up to no good. They were drug smugglers, here to rendezvous with a fast boat. They'd kill him, a stranger, and make off with his four hundred dollars. He glanced at the dark beams below and considered jumping.

But the visitors paid no attention to him. Their voices carried, informing Brad of the nocturnal behavior of Florida's most endangered species, the cracker. They belonged to the same declining family that half of Missouri did. He walked slowly toward them and nodded hello.

They were an old man, a stout, middle-aged woman, and a huge young fellow in bib overalls and no shirt, who grinned perpetually and rolled his eyes at whatever was said. The old man squatted, sucking on a cigarette as he studied the sparkling water. "How are *you*, sir, this beautiful night?"

"Pretty fair," Brad said. It occurred to him that he hadn't really spoken to anyone for almost a week. "Are you fishing?"

"Mean to if we can," the old man said. He motioned to the woman, who didn't acknowledge Brad with so much as a glance, and to the simple fellow, who kept grinning. "Name's Rudy House-holder. That's my wife, Ann, and this here's her son, Georgie."

"Brad Naylor," he said and nodded to the big man. "Hello."

"Georgie cain't talk," Rudy said. "Here they coming, Annie!"

Ann and Georgie picked up the long, weighted net that they'd already unraveled on the pier. Rudy stood, squinting, hunched for-ward as if he were about to dive. "See 'em?"

Ann spoke for the first time. "Oh fudge, fudge, fudge, that's a boatload."

"Bust the springs on the truck."

"What?" Brad said.

"Mullet. Kinda like a shadow."

Brad stared but saw nothing. Ann and her silent son stood poised with the net now, while Rudy paced the pier, puffing on his cigarette. "We gonna make some *real* money."

"Wait'll I tell you, Georgie," Ann said. "Don't drop it too quick."

And now Brad saw it, not so much a shadow as a black space across the ubiquitous glistening, a patch darting left and right, ex-actly as a fish swims, maybe fifty feet from the shore. As the patch drew nearer, he could make out the fish one by one, black, straight strips leaping along the silver surface.

"Georgie!" Ann shouted, and she and her son dropped the net. Georgie hung low off the pier as Ann jumped into the water, splash-ing heavily, losing her balance, and bobbing up waist-deep. The two let the net sag and then as it tightened pulled back in unison. Ann flipped it on its side, Georgie pulled hard, and Ann handed up two loops to Rudy. Georgie started to lift up the net, but Rudy called out to Brad. "Mister, if ya'll don't mind—"

Brad jumped to his side, they pulled the net to the pier, and shortly the big fish flopped about. Ann, unable to climb onto the pier, walked to shore and back again, and then all of them set about catching mullet with their hands and throwing them into buckets. One squirmed upward in its final leap, coming down not into the sea but inside Georgie's overalls. "Wo . . . wo . . . wo," he said, his grin intact, still, but with his cheeks sucked in.

Brad tried not to laugh. "I think it's stuck."

"Can you reach down in there and get that fish, boy?" Rudy asked. "Your mama's gonna have to undress you, if you don't."

The fish bulged at Georgie's crotch. He stood perfectly still, then dropped a massive fist on the invader.

"Son!" Ann said, with great seriousness. "Don't hit yourself!"

Georgie bent double, but just as quickly stood erect. He reached carefully inside his overalls, and proudly held up the fish.

"Big one, Georgie!" Ann said.

"Wo."

Brad loaded eight bucketsful of mullet into his Chevy and followed Rudy and Ann home to Titusville. They ran a diner by the water in a square, cement building that looked like a garage but supported, out front, the roost for a neon flamingo. By now he felt so weary that the words from conversations seemed to hang in the air, awaiting his ability to process them. Nonetheless, he pitched in to clean the mullet, some of which Rudy stored in a freezer and some of which he packed tightly in his smoker, a filthy-looking apparatus welded together from scrap iron and two steel barrels. Rudy built a fire from pin oak chips, painted the fish with a mysterious dark liquid, then choked off the air supply.

Georgie crawled into the camper and in moments dropped into a loud, fitful snore. His bare feet dangled over the bumper and his great, soft belly shook periodically. Ann drew a blanket over him, cooing as if he were a baby, still, and went off for her shower.

Rudy worked tirelessly, humming "Just a Closer Walk with Thee," but once breaking into the chorus of "Born to Be Wild." "You can still find mullet," he said. "Though they ain't so plentiful as they was. Only people used to eat mullet was the colored and poor folks such as the man you're looking at, but you smoke it and the Yankees make out like it's blue fin tuna. They used to be crabs and you could find 'em all along the shore, but where them marshes was ain't nothin' but mud now, all kindsa trash in it."

"Ah huh," Brad said, snapping awake.

"'Let it be, dear Lord, let it be.' Well, they build their houses out on the water, they pump up the bottom of the river and divide it into lots. I just don't get it. You'd think the gov'ment would step in. When I was a boy, you could still find sea turtles, and the gov'ment fin'ly started protectin' 'em, only good luck findin' one to protect. Appreciate your lendin' a hand, my friend."

"I better quit. I'm really tired," Brad said. As if to prove his point, he held up a cut finger.

"Damn," Rudy said. "Let me put something on that."

Ann emerged, wearing a cavernous housecoat and shower sandals. Her great toes spread over the sandals and dug into the sand. She rubbed behind an ear with her towel and, for the first time, looked at Brad directly, her eyes glistening shrewdly. "You in some kinda trouble, Mr. Naylor?"

"Trouble," he murmured drowsily. "Why you think?"

"Young man, dresses neat, very polite. But here he shows up at midnight in this ratty old car, don't add up. We thought you was one a them druggies and then I said to Rudy, 'He's runnin' from something.' Is there a woman somewheres having a hard time on account a you?"

"I'm exhausted, that's all. Drove—"

"Why come here?"

For an instant, his fatigue fell away. "I—nobody believes me. It sounds strange, but I wanted to be close to the rockets. I've never been anywhere, see? I was always Mr. Solid Citizen, but down deep I *wasn't*. I wanted to see the world. You understand? I came here for the experience."

Ann stared at him as if he were a visitor from space, but her massive breasts shook with laughter. "It's another one of those fellas looking for experience, Rudy."

Brad laughed, too. He knew he made no sense.

She shrugged. "There is a job here if you want it. If you are a reliable man in no trouble with the police."

"No . . . police." Brad leaned against the old truck. The smoke from Rudy's contraption made him nauseous. "A job?"

"Minimum wage and meals. That's if you know how to cook, but if you don't, I'll teach you."

What a strange night this had been! And who was this woman addressing him, with her tiny head and scraggly hair, on a body like a manatee's? "Thank you," he managed. "Thank you very much, Ann."

The police weren't after him, though they might have been. He'd stolen from his employer, a small-town bank—moving money from a school fund to make a mortgage payment they'd been three times late on. Julie, out of work for two years, had just begun at Walmart, and when her pay became numbers in their account, he moved the stolen money back.

Only ten days passed, but it was a serious matter. And unnecessary. They could have gone begging to Julie's dad, the pastor at the Assembly of God, but Brad couldn't bear to face the man yet again. With her father, failure couldn't be separated from sin.

Of course, old Fred Tappett caught the transfer. And forgave it, if Brad agreed to leave the bank. And no one, Julie assured him, knew what he'd done, but Brad doubted you could keep secrets in such a little town. He sank into depression and seldom left the house. Until—this was how Julie thought—God intervened.

Brad's dad died, and the three brothers sold the farm to Tyson Foods. Brad was still out of work, but had enough to pay off the mortgage and a little besides.

Of course, that wasn't all of it.

So long ago he could hardly remember, he'd been the smartest kid in high school, a natural in physics and any kind of math you threw at him. He started the astronomy club and convinced the school board to mount a telescope on a light-free hill south of town. He didn't earn a scholarship, but surely, despite the poor family he came from, was college bound. Surely, if a kid worked hard enough and could think fast enough, he'd succeed. But a kid couldn't think at all, and story of his life, Brad tripped himself up. He got a scared little Christian girl pregnant.

She *was* cute. Wore those short skirts. They set themselves up in a rented trailer, and saved for a house, and tried, and tried, and tried, to join the middle class.

He never made it to college. He didn't join the air force, or take a long trip through the West. In his thirty-two years, he'd been to St. Louis exactly four times—twice on bank business. He knew everybody in town, and everybody liked him because he and Julie had worked so hard, crawling from under a hard place.

Maybe he stole the money to force a change. Maybe he knew Old Man Tappett wouldn't prosecute. Maybe he wanted Julie, preacher's daughter, to throw him out.

Up at four and walk to the diner, turn on the lights and air conditioner, brew coffee, tune the radio to a classical station from Gainesville, bring in the deliveries of bananas and orange juice and bread and ground beef, stir some eggs for scrambling and omelettes, bring down the ancient waffle iron, turn on the grill. Fix himself bacon and eggs and grapefruit, sit with strong, sugared coffee, read the *Orlando Sentinel* and the *Miami Herald*, carefully fold them and put them on the counter along with the *Toronto Daily Mail* and the *New York Times.* Plug in his laptop and send a message to his son: *Doing fine, sending you some money for your grades. The air force put up a satellite yesterday, what a big firecracker! Say hello to your mother.*

Switch the radio to country and western from Orlando.

Open the door.

Ted the Bum came first, promptly at six, but then he'd been up all night and breakfast was his reward to himself. That he'd reached yet another sunrise was reason enough to celebrate, but he was sober in the mornings, clear-eyed for a few hours. Though he came day after day, so regularly that if he hadn't come Brad would have worried about him, he hadn't learned Brad's name and Brad had learned his only because of Ann. Ted the Bum nodded hello and muttered his order, then headed for the diner's bathroom to brush his teeth and shave. He was neat about it, and so Brad never said anything, though he knew Ann didn't approve.

Ted emerged wearing his greasy suit coat and with his thin hair slicked back, and by then Brad had cooked his western omelette and poured his coffee. Ted nodded thanks and retreated to a corner booth, where he perused the *Wall Street Journal* until seven fifteen, when he retired for the day to whatever palmetto glade he slept in, whatever abandoned car or packing crate or culvert.

After Ted the Bum came Katherine the Great, a diminutive widow from Hamilton, Ontario, who'd outlived three husbands but was open to the prospect of another, depending on his investment portfolio. She always ordered an English muffin and half a grapefruit, then demanded her 10 percent seniors' discount. "So what's a nice-looking young man such as yourself doing in a dingy little place like this? You know?"

"I'm studying for the priesthood."

"Begging your pardon?"

"This is my penance."

Katherine the Great batted her extraordinarily long lashes. "You have nice buns, Mister. You know?"

"Thank you," Brad said.

After Katherine's reign the counter grew more hectic. Claudia, waitress for the morning hours, and herself a card-carrying AARP member, showed up at seven thirty to complain of the indigestion she'd suffered from the carrots and meatloaf served at the rest home where she lived with her much-less-ambulatory husband. When she arrived, Brad disappeared into the kitchen and sweated over the grill through the lunch hour, when Ann took over. Brad saw little of Rudy except for when they went after mullet; other nights, the old man pushed a broom for NASA.

After lunch, Brad liked to stuff a paperback in his pocket and borrow the bicycle—a Christmas gift for Georgie, but Georgie had never learned to ride it—to pedal along the Indian River. Then the rainy season commenced, and he spent his drowsy afternoons at the library, reading about a subject until he could find nothing more written about it—reading about Central America. Costa Rica might be his next stop.

At nine, when the library closed, he returned to his kitchenette, ate his meager supper, and slept. This *is* the priesthood, he thought. I am a monk. He tunneled off into sleep, and just as soon as he did, the alarm sounded. He dropped to the floor for sit-ups and pushups, showered, and went to work again.

The rains ceased, and what passed for winter in these regions began. He drove to Canaveral National Seashore and hid himself away, lying between dunes, listening to the wind overhead, and watching the waves sweep monotonously in. He read from a novel, *The Razor's Edge,* that the librarian had recommended.

Dozing, he dreamed of the bank. This time, Old Man Tappett hovered near even as Brad shifted his crooked figures. Tappett shook his head tragically, as if Brad were his son, and picked up the phone to call the police. Brad moved numbers frantically, to make his sins go away even as sirens wailed.

He woke to the screeching of gulls, outraged when a big cormorant landed, and attempted to drag away their dead grouper. The cormorant wasn't strong enough, but it raked open the grouper's abdomen with its beak and flew off with a long strip of flesh. Then an entire flock of gulls settled like flies. *Where am I?* Brad thought.

He lay near the Cape, and it grew dark. The Mars launch was only three days away, and tonight the Coast Guard would enforce a curfew for all this area. He had to get back to his Chevy and head for the motel.

The Mars launch was a private effort, not entirely sanctioned by NASA, but they needed the cash. A man and a woman had trained for two years for the journey—which itself lasted two years. Mars and Venus plunging into space, the two unacquainted before the rigorous process of their selection.

Both NASA and the private company were mum about the prospect of sex, but certainly the cable channels speculated. How could sex be avoided? How could a man and woman travel so unimaginably far, in so tight a space, through utter darkness, and not go mad? Not kill each other? Sex might go a ways to keep you sane, if it didn't turn plumb weird. Anyhow, the company claimed that a man and woman stood a better chance than two men or two women. Was their prognosis truly scientific or just politically correct? Perhaps it was mythic—not Mars and Venus, but Adam and Eve.

The scientific press loved the mission, but was also dubious, because the astronauts wouldn't even land on Mars. They'd loop around it, snapping pictures—a robot could do it. Still, Brad wished he could be on that rocket. The brave couple, if they made it back, would make space travel sexy again.

He pulled on a sweatshirt, tucked the novel under his arm, and began running, scattering the gulls. Craft in the Indian River, returning to the marina, had turned on their running lights. He ran at surf's edge, letting the water bounce off his ankles, dancing around once like a boxer in training, shouting at the pale moon. Then he dropped into an even stride, dipping his legs into the thick evening air, and breathing in the salt. He felt young and weightless, as if the long line of light the setting sun lay down were a path and he could run along it, toward that gleaming rocket over on Merritt Island, toward the sun itself.

He crested another dune and looked down on his Chevy a quarter mile onward. Now he thought of the stew he'd warm on the hot plate, and the homegrown tomatoes he'd slice. He'd fall asleep watching some old movie and rise at four in the deep silence of his anonymous new life.

Then he saw them: his wife, Julie, behind the wheel, and his son, Seth. He wound down his pace and came to a dumbfounded stop. Unconsciously, he swatted at the hordes of tiny grasshoppers that leapt out of the sea oats and banged against his bare legs. Briefly, he was enraged. But he came forth from the twilight like a fugitive surrendering to authority, bravely meaning to shout out his presence and take command of the consequences. At the same time he was stricken with shyness, so that in moments he stood mute by the door of his five-year-old Buick and the side of his wife of fifteen years.

Julie had fallen asleep, resting her head on a blanket folded over the window. He murmured her name but she didn't awaken, and the longer the moment endured, the less familiar she seemed. She was quite beautiful, a woman who would have intrigued him were she truly a stranger. As the absurdity of this thought sank upon him, he reached out to touch her.

"Dad!" Seth came running, and Brad braced himself, not quite sure of the role he needed to play. He had not abandoned the boy. They exchanged emails every day; Brad even knew the names of his school friends.

"Dad!" Seth said. "Is the launch on?"

"Sure! Day after tomorrow, bright and early."

"Great—great to *see* you."

"I'm glad to see you. Really glad, son." He was near to crying. Only a fool would leave this strapping son and this fine woman. Yes, but he *was* a fool.

"Oh, my God," said Julie. "Brad!"

She stepped from the car, brushing at imaginary sand on her blouse and jeans. She was barefooted, and her long, black hair aroused him. He wished they'd met for the first time on the beach, both of them eighteen. He reached for her, but she didn't come into his arms immediately, not as if she were showing her independence, but as if she were afraid. Seth sat on the Buick's fender now, lifting his eyes nervously toward Brad. I'll explain it to him, Brad thought. Fathers are supposed to explain things.

"We'll get some supper," Brad said. He had just enough in his billfold to pay for it. "Hungry, Seth?"

The boy shrugged and looked toward the sand dunes.

"He's starved," Julie said.

Pelicans cruised low over the calm water. They sat behind the diner, facing Merritt Island. Far off, you could see the big rocket, lights playing on it dramatically.

"This is a wonderful place, Brad," Julie said, lowering her eyes as if she were on a date. For possibly the third time in her life, she ordered a glass of wine. He was about to explain that the diner had no liquor license but Ann, waiting on them reverentially, put a finger to her lips and nodded.

"See those gantries, Seth—those towers? Way out there? That's all that remains of Apollo."

"Cool," Seth said.

A breeze rose. Julie turned her chair away from the lights and sipped her wine. Brad stood at her side, watching his son and Georgie toss a Frisbee.

"His grades are good," Brad said.

"Oh, he's a good boy, Brad. We're very lucky."

Ann returned from the kitchen and sat heavily near Julie. "We like your husband," she said.

"I like him, too," Julie said, looking up with moist eyes. She stroked his arm but he stood rigidly, suspicious of affection, like the little boy Seth had been not long ago. Julie reached again for her wine and threw herself into conversation with Ann, while Brad gathered up the dishes and fled to the kitchen.

Julie was glorious in bed. He was swept along and yet it seemed too athletic, as if she'd attended some workshop to improve her technique. It hadn't been so good since high school, down by the Piney River in that old station wagon, when everything was mysterious and new.

"There's a Loretta Lynn song about all the ceilings she's stared at," Julie said. "I've only stared at one."

He laughed.

"One *man*." She sat up, clutching the sheets to her breasts, her black hair trailing against her pillows. "Wasn't I a good wife?"

"Of course," he managed.

"What am I supposed to *do*? All the years we've put in! Don't you think I've had some dreams, too?"

"Pursue them," he said. "Please."

She began to cry. He reached for her hand, but she tore away, and he pulled on his jeans and sat in the broken chair by the television. Headlights from the street pierced the front window, illuminating the room, leaving it dark again.

"Working as a *fry* cook. The smartest man I ever knew."

"I like it. I get most of my food, and there's money for the rent and gas and a movie once in a while. All I want to do is read, Julie. Read and read."

"What do you read about?"

"Mars."

"Is that your next destination?"

He looked away. "I *had* to do this, Julie."

"Jesus!" she said, but then her voice grew soft. "Had to do *what*, sweetheart?"

He sighed. "Every day when I get off work, I go to the library."

"There's a library in Mountain Vale."

He shook his head. "Day after day, I sit reading about why they shut down the Space Shuttle, and why the space station should have been a moon base, about different kinds of rockets, and the moons of Jupiter, and how habitats might work. I get on the internet and look at pictures of Mars. We can go there, Julie! We just need to *want* to. I read until the rain stops and walk home and go to bed and never speak to anyone except Ann and old Rudy. But one day this very nice lady, this librarian—"

"How old?"

He grinned. "Seventy, Julie. At least. She comes over to me when I'm just sitting and watching the rain, and she says, 'Can I help you, sir?' 'What?' I say. 'It's none of my business,' she says. 'It's just that you were looking kind of lost. I wondered if I could help you find what you're looking for.'

"I guess I was tired. Irritable, and I snapped at her. I said, 'I'm looking for the meaning of life.' It didn't faze her a bit. She just said, 'Try *Webster's Third*.'"

Julie laughed. "Librarians are very practical."

"But when I said it, I knew it was true. That's it, Julie, stupid as it sounds. The meaning of life."

"The meaning of life is your family, Brad. What about Seth? He worships you!"

He nodded. "Yes."

"And me. We took *vows*. I love you!"

"I love you, Julie. It's just—that stifling little town—"

"Only for a while, sweetheart. Two years—do you understand? Then Seth's on his way to college. Then we can move—Tulsa, maybe."

He nodded. "Arlene's there."

"Yes. And for now, just a little longer—you remember Pete Logan?"

"Sure. Our pitiful little astronomy club."

"I think he has a job for you."

"At the lumber yard?" Brad laughed again. "Not keeping the books, I'll bet."

He hurried to the jalousie window. Was a gray dawn rising over the gray sea? Would the launch be postponed? No: every star shone. The day would be clear, and windless.

He stood above his wife, who slept on her back, legs spread wide. For fifteen years, she'd slept on her stomach. In no time at all, he thought, we are revealed as imposters. "Julie," he whispered.

"Five o'clock?" Her eyes snapped open, pure fire.

He staggered back. "Yes."

"You and Seth go."

"Julie—"

"You two need to talk. And when you come back, *I* want an answer."

Outside, a neon light came on, and myriad colors rolled across her face. She turned over. Her legs gleamed dully.

How would they manage it, Mars and Venus? Two years in the darkness?

"Okay," he murmured. He went into the front room. Living here alone, he'd thought the kitchenette to be the definition of freedom, but in the presence of his family it became the worn, tacky place it truly was. He stepped to the pallet in the corner, knelt, and shook Seth's shoulder. "Wake up, son."

"What?"

"It's time."

Near the water the streets were deserted. "I want an answer" kept repeating itself in his head, but Brad couldn't have answered a phone, he was so sleepy. Seth, too, stared glassily at the damp streets.

"I need coffee," Brad said. "You want coffee, Seth?"

"I saw burritos on the menu."

He braked sharply to avoid a meandering dog that shrank into the night, scooting under a wooden fence and into a junkyard. They pulled up at the diner just as Ted the Bum left, grunting hello to Brad, probably displeased by the service he got from Ann.

"Your day off, Mister!" Ann called out.

"We need coffee and four burritos. Going to see the launch!"

Maybe it was mistake to stop.

"We won't make it, Dad," Seth said, finally awake. "We'll be late."

"We're all right." Brad thought of that hillside south of town, out there with Pete and the old telescope at four in the morning when the coyotes yipped, and they danced about to keep warm.

Ann kept turning, and staring, but he couldn't meet her eyes, even when she brought coffee and food. "Thank you, Ann," he managed, but his voice seemed phony. He found it strange to observe her at the grill, doing what he usually did. He'd been pushed once more into irrelevancy.

"You like the rockets, Seth?" Ann asked.

"Sure," he said. He'd wrapped his burritos in a napkin and half-stood.

"You and your dad," Ann said.

Brad dropped money on the table, and they hurried to the Chevy. Yes, Seth and his dad. What else mattered? Put another way, who else, besides Seth and Julie, gave a damn what he did? He stepped through the door again. "I don't know what to say, Ann."

"Don't say anything. Don't miss the launch."

"I've been happy here for the first time in years. You, and Rudy, and Georgie—"

From the back room, Georgie's head poked out, grinning as always.

Ann's round face broke into a smile. "You have a very nice family, Brad."

In half a mile cars crowded around them. Hawkers strode down the dividing lines, selling Chinese replicas of the Mars rocket, the Shuttle, Apollo. They turned through the gate and followed the flashlights, finally squeezing into a tight space. They sat on the hood, silent as they watched the bright rocket, and then the red sun rising from the water.

"NASA has a plan to send a drone to Mars," Brad said. "You read about that, Seth? I mean, it's not so dramatic—"

"But it makes more sense," Seth said. "The drone sits there and makes fuel for the manned ship that comes later."

"Cuts down on weight. Makes the project more affordable. You know, people will go there and live in your lifetime, Seth. When you're my age—"

"I'll never be *that* old."

When he's my age, Brad thought, I hope he loves his work. I hope he gets an education. I hope he sees the big cities and the wonders of the world in South America and Greece.

"Dad! Dad! Look!"

But just as there was ignition, just as flame spewed and baked the sand and the clouds of poisonous smoke rolled out in great banks of gray and black, Brad fell back and closed his eyes. A mammoth weight pressed down on him, all his body shook, and he couldn't breathe. In the distance he heard his son shouting, but then even the roar of the crowd was lost in the shrieking that had taken over the atmosphere, a sound so maddening, so revolutionary, that he wanted to run into the swamp. Oh lift me, lift me *up,* he thought. Take me up!

He sat, smiling at his son. Seth grinned back.

"One-two-*Now!*" someone sang out above the roar. They waited. No one talked—not that you could have heard them. But there would always be this suspense, because, not so many years before, rockets had exploded on the pad. Some with people in them, but not today. Today there was liftoff. Today a man and a woman began their long, improbable, possibly homicidal trip to Mars. Brad came up behind his son, patted his shoulder, and they joined the chorus: *"Go! Go! Go! Go!"*

Red Rock Valley

It was 1:00 a.m., twenty-five outside, and Donald Stone hadn't slept on the flight from Miami, but he chose the train from O'Hare, rather than a taxi. The train took two hours, a taxi twenty minutes, but his per diem covered cab fares, and he could claim the difference on his expense report. Every penny counted. He was saving for his retirement—as a relatively youthful *pensionado* in Costa Rica.

He knew there was no such thing as paradise, but when Greg and he had gone there Costa Rica had seemed close. At least it had for Donald. Greg's appreciation of nature stopped with viewing sunsets from the balcony at the Hyatt, perhaps while sipping a piña colada. But Donald talked him into a canoe trip down the Río Pacuare, with the argument that they had become so domesticated they needed an adventure they could talk about in their golden years. They tapped into their credit cards for a guide and canoe and muddled their way, with their dubious Spanish, to the put-in.

The rapids were tame, or they might have drowned. Downstream ten miles they paddled into the stinking effluent of a coffee mill; the muck splashed up and seemed to invade everything in their craft. Filthy, high on caffeine, and cold, they made port in a low canyon, by calm water on a red rock shoal. They built a fire, then stripped and washed out their clothes and hung them to dry. For a while they lay together, resting.

Donald rose, at last, and drew on his stiffened clothing, but as he looked down on his sleeping partner felt alienated from him, as if their life together were an accident, or that they each, for the other, had been less a choice than a capitulation. He turned, strode the rock face, and looked upstream, past the wild undergrowth and the dazzling flowers and the palms sticking up like tall men in a crowd, toward the ramshackle mill. He thought of the creek in Arkansas, on his parents' farm—the place he liked most when he was a child.

The top of the shoal split and dropped down a path between two great boulders. Surely, Donald thought, no place on earth was unknown, but he felt something new here and followed the trail as it wound, first narrow then wide, toward a spring clear as the one in Arkansas. He knelt to drink. The water was cool and invigorating, and he imagined that it was the stuff Ponce de León had looked for. Ah, *sí!* In the dark green glade Mayans had camped, and after them, the clumsy Spaniards. They'd washed their jungle sores, drunk the magic water, and grown young again.

Donald waded the water to a pool where bass darted among submerged red rocks. He looked out upon a valley where, instead of forest, there was lush, bluish-green grass that stretched for five acres or so until it met the opposite face of rock. Like a sign, two white horses appeared on the red rock and seemed to eye Donald over the distance, before they turned and fled.

He returned to the Pacuare, where Greg had awakened, and looked about impatiently. Greg was weary of their middle-aged adventure and wanted to embark immediately for the take-out, thinking they could return to the hotel, and a magnificent meal, that evening. They would visit San José's famous orchid gardens in the morning, then catch their plane.

Donald never told Greg about the valley. He never told anyone. But he thought about it at every conference his company sent him to and every time he rode the train. He thought of it now, eying the snow as it swirled down the Kennedy and Chicago's back streets. These were the resting hours for the homeless, shifting trains through the night to escape the cold. Most slept, but a little woman at the end of the car had vomited all her insides over two seats and the center aisle.

As the years passed, Donald sometimes wondered if he had truly seen the horses, or if he had imagined them out of a need to visualize perfection. But he came to think of the valley as the one place on earth where he could find peace. He'd live out his days in

San José, eating wonderful food and mastering Spanish, making new friends in a place where your past didn't matter. When it was time to die, he'd travel to the valley, stretch out in the sun, and wait for the horses.

Donald got off at Washington, shouldering his baggage for the walk, like a portage, through the tunnel to the Howard Line. It was an effect of the cold, perhaps, but the odor of wine and urine was not so sharp this morning, and the haggard black man at the center of the tunnel, pounding out a rhythm on his conga drums, seemed brave and admirable, to be at his work so early. Donald stopped, shifted his luggage, and threw the drummer what change he had. The man smiled faintly, the nearest thing to a welcome Chicago ever offered.

Once upon a time, he'd enjoyed his work. He took cabs every-where, ate at fine restaurants, and spent every penny of his per diem. He was a fine salesman, after all, and deserved his little rewards. But over time the hotel food all seemed stale, and even the quaint ethnic restaurants lost their charm. Greg was sick and couldn't come along any longer. Donald came to prefer Wendy's, or even to eat cold food in his room.

They got through Greg's illness somehow, with not much help from either of their employers. As a couple it was a final humili-ation, little assuaged by the few who came to the memorial. In the end, Donald wasn't a widower, but a confirmed bachelor—or, in the minds of his co-workers, an aging homosexual.

The new car was deserted and Donald closed his eyes briefly. The train rolled from underground into the stormy dawn, but he was out of the weather by four—home, it was called. Always a sur-prise to greet your former self, and discover he was a pig. But Don-ald had no visitors and saw little point in housekeeping. He had sold his car, most of his furniture and dishes, and even his books, strip-ping down to the severest efficiency. He lived here not half the time, and anyhow decor had been Greg's department.

He turned up the thermostat and watered a spiky houseplant that was one of the few things that he still kept of Greg's and that no amount of neglect had been sufficient to kill. He went through his mail—bills, frequent flier statements, catalogues. After his nap, he thought, he'd allow himself a small treat and go out for Thai food.

His cell was for business, the landline for personal calls, but he so seldom had a message, even when gone for a week, that sometimes he forgot to check. Lately, he'd thought of ending the service. He'd put on Brahms's *Ein Deutsches Requiem* and settled into his recliner with an afghan when he noticed the blinking light.

"Donald . . . this is Mom. It's Saturday night, about ten, I guess, I'm at Lakeland General Hospital. We're staying at the Flamingo Motel. It's your father, Donald . . . he had a heart attack. I think he . . . the doctor, he's from some African country, he says it's very serious."

Donald called the motel and then the hospital but couldn't run her down. He pictured her, sleepless and frail, collapsed at the foot of his father's bed.

He left a message for work and then booked a flight to the other coast of Florida.

Long before, his parents held the usual hopes that Donald would find a nice girl and father children. Donald, too, had entertained the notion—down in Conway, he'd gone for a while with a Brenda, a Mary, and an Arlene. Each was attractive enough, but Brenda and Arlene had been so bland that Donald could no longer separate them in his memory, although he'd seen them through the years, when he returned for visits. He didn't suppose he'd have made them any more miserable than the men they married.

Mary, the only one of his ancient loves with a wit, had affectionately rejected Donald, complaining that his testosterone level was too low. "I thought that was what I wanted in a man," she said. "But it isn't."

Donald liked Mary; he'd have gone to dental school for her, and they could have built a house on one corner of the farm. Far better than what he had done, which was simply to drift. Truth was, he was a remote sort with men and women alike, and only Greg had been able to break through. It didn't have much to do with sex. Donald was asexual—like a character out of Henry James, he fancied.

He hadn't visited his parents for seven years, but that was because of his father's disdain for Greg. Not for Greg himself so much as the *fact* of Greg. His mother always kept in touch and even stayed with them once, when she came to Chicago for a church conference. Greg was gravely courteous, fixing buckwheat cakes and sausages for her breakfast, because Donald told him this would please her.

Yet even if his father had been more accommodating, he wouldn't have visited often. The farm near Conway had charm, but his old friends had grown distant, and the martyr's religion his mother practiced tried his patience. More: when he went back he was forced to confront the fact he hadn't gone anywhere. If not a dentist for Mary, then why hadn't he become a teacher, a county engineer, perhaps a farmer?

He might even have been like Orville Bledsoe, who, as he grew older, Donald more and more admired. Bledsoe was a cheerful, wizened immigrant from Missouri who made his living pumping out septic tanks, but he sent three daughters through college. That was a life worth living, Donald thought. Never a lover, he could have been a devoted father.

He slept all the way to Tampa, then rented a small Toyota for the drive to Lakeland. He scarcely noticed North Tampa; it looked like Los Angeles, or Houston. But heading east, distracted as he was, he caught a flavor of the down-at-the-heels cracker Florida his folks had been so fond of. Not so different, Donald suddenly realized, than his obsession with that valley in Costa Rica.

His father, Alvin, had somewhere got the idea that prosperous Arkansas farmers should go to Florida in the winter. He and Donald's mother would find some beat-up kitchenette left over from one of Florida's boom-and-bust cycles, then live for six weeks on mullet, dented canned food, and Ruskin tomatoes. For recreation they sought out flea markets and vintage attractions such as Weeki Wachee Springs or Parrot Jungle. There was church, of course, which Alvin tolerated in his old age. Sometimes, Alvin struck off inland in search of abandoned farmsteads and free tangerines.

Once, when Donald was ten, his father and he waded a swamp and cut three cypress knees. That wasn't legal anymore. It wasn't approved of even when crackers were king. Back in Conway, his father boiled away the bark, dried the knees, and made lamps. The lamps were a low art, a stolen art, and after a while Donald wished that they could be restored to the swamp. Even so, the lore of it all had provided good moments with his father.

"He was skilled with tools," Donald announced, as he drew into the hospital parking lot.

He checked in at the nurses station and saw the doctor—a tall, grave Kenyan he could barely understand—the one time he would. "Alvin does not like the catheter. He fights, and he is a very old man."

"He was never in a hospital. Will he get through this?"

The doctor shrugged almost contemptuously and then caught himself, as if, in the past, he'd been criticized for his insensitivity. He shook his head. "What we can, we do."

So, Donald thought. My father is a dead man, and that is why I am here.

His mother sat crumpled like a pile of laundry, but without her presence, Donald would not have known that this naked, emaciated old man was his father. Alvin Stone's eyes were closed. His hands kept traveling down to yank at the yellowish catheter—hovering, pulling back. Greg fought the same battle. The enemy was not death but plastic tubing.

The walls were off-white and bare. A curtain separated Donald's little family from a haggard middle-aged man who stared off vaguely and every so often cried out, "Fooch!" Across from Alvin's bed, placed so that he must have memorized every detail these past three days, was a painting of a generic Florida scene: live oaks draped with Spanish moss, a lake, a setting sun, behind them.

Donald grasped his mother's shoulder. "Have you eaten, Mom?"

"Donald!"

His job was to remain calm. That poor soul on the bed was dying, but it was his mother who needed to be shielded. She'd grieve and contend with endless, narrowing loneliness. Soon, perhaps, Donald would be driving down to Conway for her funeral.

"He's been asking for you."

"Can he . . . hear me?"

Incredibly, the old man sat up. His eyes were fierce, startling Donald: they held the same fury as Greg's toward the end. His hand hovered above the catheter again, then reached weakly for the wadded-up sheet in a gesture toward modesty.

"Dad?"

"Alvin?" Donald's mother stood quickly and grasped the bed rail. "Alvin? It's Donald!"

"Jesus Christ, I know that."

"Come to take you home, Dad."

"Naw." He fell back and studied the ceiling. "Thinking of Yellowstone."

"Yellowstone . . . National Park?"

"Mom and I—"

"My mother. Eileen. Your wife."

"Listen! We drove *out* there."

"Five years ago," Donald's mother said. "He means—"

"Naw, naw, naw. Donnie was eight. You don't remember."

"Yes, I do, Dad. You didn't even have to reserve a campsite back then. Just us and the bears. We went fishing."

"They pulled the fish out of the lake there and plopped it right in the hot spring. How they cooked it."

"The Indians," Donald murmured.

"You liked them camping trips, Donnie."

"Well, Dad. Let's go camping."

The old man closed his eyes. He didn't speak for a long time.

"He has diabetes," Donald's mother, Eileen, whispered. "We didn't know. He'll be on a very restricted diet."

"This!"

"Alvin—" Eileen moved closer to the bedside.

"I bought four quarts of oil and a filter."

His wife seemed to chide him. "Alvin."

"Donnie knows how—"

"I can change it, Dad. Sure."

"You *do* it," he said, his last words for Donald—or anyone.

Alvin Stone fell back into sleep, and his heart rate seemed steady, so Donald checked in with the nurse and then chaperoned his mother to the cafeteria. She had half of a Cuban sandwich and pecked at a Jello salad. Donald ate what the hospital's food service was pleased to call Key lime pie.

"Did you have a good winter down here? Before—?"

She grew angry. "We should never have come. He's been sick; he couldn't drive. And Florida's *changed.*"

"If he should die, Mom. Have you—?"

"He won't die."

"Even—even if he's laid up for a while, can you—?"

"Could you drive us home?"

"Sure."

"This must be strange for you. You and Greg . . . we haven't been a family in so long."

He sighed. "Always a family, Mom."

"We've been talking about selling the farm. Conway's grown right next door; it's worth money. Oh, it's just a shame, all the little farms disappearing."

"It is. And it's not like life in the city is so grand. Hard to understand, really."

She brightened. "You could have the farm if you wanted it, Donald. Your father—he would like that."

He began to shake his head, but stopped. The offer was oddly tempting. Of course, in Costa Rica, he might enjoy living again. It was a place with mysteries such as the hidden valley, while Conway lay in the known world. "I'll think about it. You—"

"You wouldn't have to farm. You could sell off a little chunk of land for houses and live like a king. You have this fantasy, that place down in South America, but Donald, you won't know a soul there."

He could keep peacocks and goats, species as odd as he was, and he could raise some good tomatoes, which you couldn't buy in the city. He had ten vigorous years, still. His costs would be minimal. Of course, if he kept livestock, he couldn't really travel, but he'd traveled enough.

"The grass is never greener, Donald. Look at your father, always coming to Florida, never finding what he wanted."

"Mom," he said, trying again to prepare her. "I know you and Dad had a good life on the farm—"

"We had a *real* life," she said, dry-eyed. "Your father was faithful. There was always plenty to eat. But he wasn't . . . a Christian man, Donald."

Donald nodded abruptly. He didn't want to hurt this old woman. "I'm sorry, Mom."

"And he was mean to you, Donald."

He slid back from the table. His lack of sleep had caught up with him, and he fought against an unseemly yawn. "Not mean, exactly. He never really said *anything.* He just couldn't take it in, Greg and me."

She nodded. "'My own son,' he said. 'My only son.'"

"It's so long ago, Mom."

"I'm sad for you, Donald. You're a *good* man. If you only—"

Patience, he thought.

"—had Jesus in your life. You don't want to . . . *die,* oh Donald you don't want to go through eternity—"

Over the intercom, right on cue, eternity summoned them to the bedside of Alvin Stone.

"He can still hear you," the nurse, a Jamaican woman, whispered. "Talk to him. Tell him you love him."

"I love you, Alvin," Eileen said. "Donald and I are here. You're going to a better place."

What was the best advice, Donald wondered, for a man experiencing his last seconds? Pointless, harmful, to say what he truly thought, that sheer nothingness was a better place than a hospital bed. His father lay motionless, but there was the color of life about him still, even though his heartbeat was fading and his breathing indiscernible. His mother fell back to her chair as if some force propelled her. She cried softly.

Donald took his father's wrist. He could have told him he loved him; he had told Greg that. He spied a western novel on the bed stand and thought that if there had been anything romantic in Alvin Stone's nature, any longing to escape from his hard and mundane life, it had been in how he'd loved the West. His mother was a little wrong. Alvin Stone came to Florida, but he longed for the West. The fabled West of lone gunmen and glorious sunsets.

"There's a man on a horse," Donald said, and as he spoke a deep cold passed beneath his fingers, out of his father's hand and through his wrist. "He's an old soldier, looking for the place where he grew up. He's tired, he's fought in a hundred campaigns, and now all he wants is peace.

"Nothing looks the same to him at first. The soldier scouts with his horse all day long. Finally, late in the afternoon, he finds the trail he's looking for."

The cold spread up his father's arm. Donald stared at the old man's lips but they didn't move; they were blue. His eyelids were still. Maybe he could hear.

"The trail climbs a mountain. It's a faint trail and part of the way the soldier travels over rock. All he can do is follow the chinks in the granite that the Sioux made many years ago.

"But he remembers where he's going now. He leads his horse over the crest and follows a draw down between two sheer, red cliffs. The sun is setting, and it catches the red rock and makes it glow. From one of the cliffs a spring flows. The soldier stoops to drink: it's sweet water."

The cold traveled through his father's shoulder and perhaps found his heart. The nurse had come to the foot of the bed, but Donald wasn't watching the monitor.

"The soldier follows the stream and comes into a beautiful valley. There are tall pines, and trout in the stream, and a meadow full of blue-green grass. Far off, wild horses run. The soldier dismounts his horse and sets her free to join the remuda. He walks through the grass and sits with his back against a big pine. 'I will make a garden here,' he says. 'I will build a house.'"

The nurse nodded. Donald put his arm around his mother and escorted her into the corridor.

"He's so sick," Eileen said.

"He's gone, Mom."

"Oh," she said.

Nurses ran in and out of his father's room with a theatrical commotion. He sat with his mother on plastic chairs. After a while he took a call from the Kenyan doctor, but could not understand what the man said.

Donald wanted to believe that his voice had reached his father's brain before the cold had. And he would have told him one more thing if he could have. He'd have told him that he changed the oil and drove his mother home to Conway.

Home Place

The storm raged on, and everywhere water flowed. Wayne Dietrich slowed to twenty, then ten, then three to ford a low-water bridge where the stream slushed almost to his front bumper. He climbed again, with not three miles to go.

In the good old days, those gas-guzzling days when they drank and smoked marijuana and chased girls, when their strength was endless and their stupidity boundless, Wayne and his pals topped the last ridge at ninety, attempting to fly. Fortunately, you landed on a straightaway and didn't need to brake until you saw the bicycle reflector Wayne had nailed to the mailbox.

Hillbillies. So full of fun.

In the rain he topped the ridge at thirty-five, and the mailbox itself was gone. He spied the lane only when he passed next to it: a length of dark water stretching uphill, shimmering when lightning flashed. Wary of the shoulders, he turned at the next crossroads, making a wide circle as if steering a boat. The exhaust echoed dully.

Creeping off the flooded road, he crossed his father's railroad-tie bridge over Plunge Creek. Navigating by memory, he thought of his mother's favorite quotation: "Faith is the substance of things hoped for, the evidence of things not seen." Where was that from? Corinthians? Hebrews?

The tires slapped against the planks and gripped the invisible lane again. Now he made out the outline of the house, but the storm had brought down a cottonwood directly ahead.

"That's all right," he announced, grateful for something physical to do, for a task that didn't require wit or clever retorts, fake sympathy or pandering. He reached over the seat for a wadded-up windbreaker, grabbed a flashlight from the glove box, and dove into the rain. He found the back door key atop the propane tank, taped under the regulator hood, and shoved open the back door. He moved the light around, a little frightened—mice, certainly, but maybe also a raccoon.

Henry and Louise sold most of their furniture at auction but the wood range, heavy as ten dead men, remained in the kitchen. The firebox was clean; Wayne held a distinct memory of scattering the ashes. He opened the damper and lit a fire with kindling his father had split so long before some of it had dry-rotted and added oak slats from a broken pallet. The chimney drew strongly, and he pulled a can of soup from his backpack and poured it into a saucepan.

Shivering, he stalked the house, finding the rollaway bed in his childhood closet, some ragged blankets, and a limp pillow. He pushed them all into a corner of the kitchen and went out into the yard again to rescue a plastic lawn chair.

In winter, late at night after Henry and Louise had gone to bed, he liked to prop his bare feet on the oven door, shifting them as they toasted. He read Jack London's Klondike stories here, as the wind howled out of the woods and slapped snow against the kitchen windows, and the imperfectly dried slab wood his father bought from the sawmill shrilled with escaping steam. He heated cocoa, solved his algebra problems, and fretted whether girls named Susan and Miranda and Meg would go out with him.

"Where are they now?" he murmured, sipping soup as if it would restore life. He visualized each teenaged girl even though they all were in their thirties now, married and divorced and married again. The smart ones, the pretty ones, all left for the city and never returned. You couldn't make a living in Texas County.

He remembered Miranda eying him sorrowfully on her last day in town. So naive. So sweet. So silly, he thought, crawling under the blankets, doubling them over his cold feet, to remember a twenty-year-old glance across a room.

He was a romantic. That's why he pursued a degree in English, rather than math or computer science. You had to find a dream somewhere if you worked in the car business and went home every night to rich, dull West County. High culture out there. Too high to feed the soul.

He sank in his chair and thought of beautiful women customers, their long legs tilting into Mercedes and Audis, their eyes drifting lustfully up. Wayne never strayed. He wouldn't allow Ruth the moral triumph. He kept his mouth shut, his eyes on the prize, and he earned the degree. He had his life back.

The woods dripped and steamed, bees moaned overhead, and up above a woodpecker banged its head against a dead sycamore. Wayne carried his father's double-edged axe and bucksaw down the lane, filling with joy as he walked. He imagined himself a pioneer clearing a homestead claim: self-sufficient, alone, pure.

As he chopped the fallen cottonwood, he sang his mother's favorite hymns, "Wonderful Words of Life" and "In Canaan's Land I'm Camping," and felt her presence and that of his father, the two standing on the bridge, beaming with pride for their strong young son.

He slid back the door to the machine shed and sat in the semi-darkness, opposite the Ford 700 that still had the sickle bar attached. The tractor would run. It had to, but he'd need to buy a battery at the least and baby the thing along until he'd worked through its hibernation kinks. He used to come here when he was small and Henry had gone on a plumbing job. The tractor with its high, muddy wheels and the lengths of chain and rope and oakum and wire that hung higher still were more mysterious than church.

A bench grinder, a drill press, a wood lathe. An electric welder. A cutting torch. Junction boxes, outlets, and switches. Faucets, nipples, unions, and a pipe threader. End wrenches, socket wrenches, pipe wrenches. Assortments of screws, bolts, washers—which Henry, not known for neatness, had sorted according to type and size and meticulously labeled. Cans of paint, mineral spirits, linseed oil that he'd have to dispose of. An elegant ash level inlaid with brass. Atkins and Disston handsaws with apple handles.

He saw the old man crouched above the vise, drawing a file over the tiny saw teeth, playing with perfect rhythm his melody of screeches.

Wayne couldn't catch his breath. Dust lay everywhere, decades of dust. He staggered into the sunshine, his lungs pulling hard, his heart thumping. One, two, three, he said to himself. Go into Mountain Vale and turn on the electricity. See the man about the propane. Apply at the school.

More than once, after Henry and Louise died, he picked up the phone to list the farm for sale.

"Hold onto it," said Ruth, the ex-wife who despised the place. "You might need it some day."

Maude Townley, who'd been the school secretary since the War of 1812, remembered him as Wistful Wayne. He never knew who labeled his picture in the school annual. The sobriquet made him still more wistful in the old days, but seemed beneficial now. "Look at old Wistful Wayne. Never thought he'd amount to—"

Pick your cliché: hill of beans, pig in a poke, diddly-squat, zilch.

"Shouldn't mention this," Maude said. "But I happen to know Jane Harpster's four months along."

Wayne knew the name Harpster, but not Jane. He gathered she taught English, and smiled wistfully.

Maude lowered her voice. "I'm thinking, along about March."

"Wow," Wayne said. "Thanks for—"

"And you'll be substituting by the end of the month. We can pull you in for History, too. Ever coach volleyball?"

He hadn't been in the teaching racket long, but knew you had to be on the good side of the secretary. That went for car dealerships, too. You couldn't go trysting with a customer, dump her, and expect to survive the month.

Not that he'd gone trysting. Not wistful old Wayne.

He drove to Red Buck, too, but the secretary had the day off and the place was chaos. A pretty math teacher, Abbie Ferguson, took pity on him. She set him down at a computer and found the application site.

Abbie was too friendly. Wayne divined how miserable Abbie was, how much she wanted to return to Kansas City or at least Wichita. Small towns were hell on teachers if they couldn't adjust their thinking and worse for a single woman than a man. Good old boys and good old gals, themselves morally bankrupt, held exalted notions of teachers. Abbie couldn't buy a bottle of wine at the supermarket without it being all over the county that she drank. No amount of churchgoing would absolve her of an overnight liaison. Abbie should dress like a nun and seek out bird-watchers, or amateur astronomers, or local history buffs.

Abbie had that fish-out-of-the-big-city look. Wayne wanted Abbie, with her big, sad eyes. But while it didn't seem possible, she was lonelier than he was. And she'd establish the record for rebound. The little hand pointed to one. He'd been divorced exactly three days.

He caught the principal on his way out, a doggedly cheerful fellow with girls and boys climbing all over him, all wanting favors, all with hopeful faces. Hopeful faces were the best thing about teaching. You'd do anything to keep from dashing those hopes.

"Next year, who knows?" the principal said. "But I'll call you for a substitute."

Back in Mountain Vale, he bought a battery for the tractor and then cruised the square. A woman wearing jeans and a western shirt smiled at him and disappeared inside of Louie's for a long night of drinking. Something else you could do in a small town, other than church. Or drugs.

He found a corner booth at Sarah's Home Cooking, which had been professionally countrified with crosscut saws, horse harnesses, and paintings of old barns. On Wednesdays, Sarah's hosted a tea room. They couldn't be far from serving sushi.

"Everything all right?" asked the waitress. Rhiannon, her name tag announced. She shook her thick black hair, revealing turquoise earrings in the shape of stars.

"Great," he said, pulling back from the spell she cast. The food hadn't changed: a green salad, mashed potatoes, beef and noodles, and blackberry pie with ice cream!

"I picked those blackberries," Rhiannon announced, leaning near to refill his iced tea. She smelled of vanilla extract, inspiring a memory. His mother dabbed it on when she went to town.

"Where?"

"Along the Piney. You know that bridge under Highway 63?"

He smiled. "My dad took me fishing there."

She smiled, too. "Haven't seen you before."

"I've been working up in St. Louis. Have a little farm down here, belonged to my folks."

"Wish *I* had a farm."

He didn't know any women for whom farm was a magic word, rather than a synonym for coarse or dumb, or at least hard work. Maybe the waitress was the horse-loving type—plenty of those in West County, Ruth among them. Hook up with Rhiannon, and he'd be chauffeuring quarter horses all over the Midwest. Vet bills, fees for shows, a big truck to haul them around in, and horses ate—well, like horses.

Rhiannon glided off to the kitchen, and he couldn't think straight. As with Abbie in Red Buck, his idiotic penis volunteered for service. Three days! What a damn goat! Let some time pass, the counselor said. You'll keep telling yourself you're all right, but you won't be. You're emotionally frail, Wayne.

He was probably a year from a steady job. He liked the prospect of filling that year with hard work and reading. He'd grow a beard. Maybe he'd try to write a little, nature stuff like Wendell Berry, or in-your-face poetry like Walt Whitman.

"How are the beef tips?" Rhiannon asked.

"Wonderful," he said, and they were. He tried to keep his eyes neutral as he met hers. He tried not to think of sex. He couldn't understand why, in his time of noble celibacy, the universe brought such lovely women into view. It defied demographics. How many beautiful, single, interesting women could there be in this podunk county?

Three days, but it wasn't as though Ruth and he had been having sex. He couldn't remember the last time. "This farm you wish you had," he said. "What would you do with it?"

"I'd put a lot of it in easy vegetables."

"Such as?"

"Potatoes, bok choy, green beans. Rows and rows of them, a week apart."

"Yeah, pretty easy. For the farmers' markets?"

"Yes. Also restaurants. And I'd make wine."

He sat back. His lust fled as he contemplated the amount of work her notions would entail. "Take a while to set that up. And in this country, you can't grow anything but Concord."

"Concord's fine. I think muscadine, too. And blueberries—of course, you'd have some expenses getting the pH right. And I'd raise goats."

"Goats!"

"With all the Middle Easterners in the cities now, there's a big market."

"St. Louis," he murmured, thinking, where do they live? Not in West County.

"Maybe Louisville."

Now he wanted to talk, but Rhiannon glided toward the window, where she poured coffee for an old couple. Then she disappeared through the swinging doors that led to the kitchen. At the last moment, she threw him a thoughtful glance.

He left a big tip.

He woke at five in the morning, staring at the ceiling light. He didn't know where he was, but wait. The lights were on!

He plugged in the coffee pot, then went out to the machine shed. The tractor engine fired immediately, but spluttered and died—as he'd expected. He held a vague memory about the gas line and unbolted it. Warily, he plugged in the air compressor, but it ran without complaint except for the wheeze it gave off even when he was a kid. He blew out the line, bolted it back on, and shot the carburetor some ether. The tractor belched fire, then ran like it had a brain and remembered when it was new.

By noon he'd mowed the lane and around the house, dragged off the cottonwood limbs, and cut a path circling the one tillable field. Walnuts had sprouted all along the woodline and needed thinning. Once there were nearly fifty great trees, ancestors of these saplings. When he was a kid Wayne picked up the nuts and sold them. In a few years he'd do so again. Not a lot of money, but that's what you did in Texas County, assemble an income.

Henry sold the big trees to pay for space in Beulah Land, a Baptist retirement home where meals and maid service were provided, but you could retain much of your independence. Louise was so arthritic she could hardly walk.

Or do the laundry, Wayne thought, skimming beggar's lice from his jeans with a pocketknife as he turned his attentions to the summer kitchen, which Henry and he had converted to a laundry room. He had to shove open the door with his shoulder, but yes, the washer and dryer were there. He supposed the dryer would function, but when he pulled out the washer he saw where the pipes had frozen. So much trouble for nothing.

Wayne sat on a stool, crying. That emotionally frail thing the counselor mentioned. He might as well cry. If a man cries in the forest, does anyone hear?

Louise claimed the old Maytag wringer washer aggravated her arthritis. Henry installed it where the burst automatic stood now, around the time of the Korean War, and Louise became the envy of every neighbor woman. Few farms had electricity then, and plumbing was far from universal. But the Maytag grew old, and Louise grew old, and her hands ached when she ran Henry's overalls through the rollers.

The Maytag outraged Ruth. "Is an automatic washer too complicated for your father—the *plumber*—to install?"

Wayne sighed. "He installs them, but doesn't approve."

"Because they make life easier?"

"He thinks they're designed to fail and that you can't fix them."

"*He* can't fix them."

"Nobody can. The circuit board dies, you have to go to China to find a new one, and it costs more than the unit."

Ruth nodded. "Sounds like a car."

"The old Maytags never went bad, and if they did, the parts were simple." Wayne paused to see if the ecological argument had had an effect. "It's Mom, too," he added. "She'll tell you clothes don't get as clean with an automatic."

"Nonsense. Imagine doing diapers in a wringer washer."

Ruth was pregnant. To Wayne it seemed like immaculate conception, since they so seldom slept together. And they were drifting apart over Wayne's insistence on his impractical English degree and arguments with her father over just about everything. But perhaps a baby would keep them together, and somehow Ruth linked it to buying Louise a new washer. "I don't believe your mother said such a thing. If she did, it's because she doesn't want to make Henry mad. He is absolutely primitive."

"They can't afford—"

"*We* can."

You can, Wayne thought. You and your dad and your show room full of BMWs.

"You're right," he said at last. "But they'll be in a rest home soon. Dad's got along all these years by fixing things anybody else would say was junk. They grew up in the Depression. I'm afraid you'll—we'll—make them mad."

"*Talk* to Henry. Tell him it's a Christmas present."

"And you'll talk to Mom, I suppose."

"I already have."

That afternoon the women drove to Mountain Vale, and Wayne was faced not just with having to sell his father on the virtues of an automatic washer but with announcing that one shortly would be delivered. Wayne wasn't much of a salesman. He'd already demonstrated he couldn't sell fancy German cars, and anyhow moral outrage was at work. Henry was a cave man and had to be disciplined.

"It'll be a lot better for Mom," he said.

Henry shrugged.

A truck arrived bearing not just a washer but a matching dryer. Hanging out the wash, opening clothespins, aggravated Louise's arthritis, too.

"I wouldn't a bought GE," Henry said.

"Maybe she got a deal."

"We coulda gone after it ourselves, saved a little money there."

"Part of the price, I suppose."

"You notice she didn't hire nobody to put it in. She knows that I know water runs downhill. We come up to visit, you'll have to point out the door where I come in."

Wayne fell into the stooge's role his father had assigned him when he was ten—hustling off to the truck for a hose clamp or pipe wrench, holding the flashlight while Henry bored a hole or probed for a wire between studs. But installing the washer was simple. They had no drains to dig. They needed only to haul out the Maytag and stick the modern machine in its place. They ran a new gas line for the dryer and cut a hole for a vent.

They were both lying on the concrete floor, working the vent through the wall, when the women returned. Louise's thick legs appeared like hickory posts in the door. Ruth clomped across the linoleum with her heavy heels.

"They're here!" she said in a little girl's voice.

"It's a Christmas present, Henry," Louise chimed in. "Isn't that nice?"

"Generous."

Ruth maintained the phony voice. "Is GE a good brand, Mr. Dietrich?"

Henry grunted as he tightened a fitting. "It'll outlast me."

At dinner Henry waxed philosophical about the days after World War II, when every farm wife decided she needed indoor plumbing. "Old farmers didn't care," he said. "Andy Hoskins, he lived there on the outskirts of Red Buck, had fifty acres down along the Piney. City come around and made him put in a bathroom. He done it and went right on using the outhouse."

Hard to know what that meant, but it seemed conciliatory. Louise, after gleefully doing her first load of laundry, fell asleep in her chair. Ruth also was quiet.

In the morning Ruth, dressed nicely as if to sell cars, came out the back door and stood by the cistern. She waited for Louise, having announced she'd drive her to church.

"Four years ago," Wayne murmured, as he backed the ruined washer out of the machine shed with a dolly. It hardly mattered, but he could just fit it into the Buick trunk and haul it to the salvage yard. He was headed to town, anyhow, to buy a TV. Not five days divorced, and the silence drove him crazy.

Henry always claimed that it was an accident, that he'd meant to make a joke. Wayne stood where his father had, trying to envision Ruth. Just like that Sunday morning, the wind caught the screen door and slammed it shut; all that was missing was the click of Ruth's heels on the walk.

"She was trying to be a good wife," he murmured. Yet her motives weren't pure, and he saw what his father had seen again and again: an affluent, suburban woman, putting him in his place with her checkbook.

Long before, Henry had placed a plastic drum under a downspout from the summer kitchen, mounting it atop a platform to gain some pressure; during dry periods, he'd drain the water onto his tomatoes. Ruth took five of her bold steps, and Henry turned over fifty gallons of water at her feet. She shrieked and stumbled off the walk. Her heels sank into the wet grass and she fell to one knee, then onto her stomach. Mud streaked her skirt and stockings.

Hardly an accident. Fifty gallons of water was four hundred pounds, and you couldn't dislodge it without a mighty, deliberate effort.

Hearing a scream, Wayne hurried out of the summer kitchen and saw his wife flopping about in the muddy yard, his bewildered mother leaning down. Wayne ran to help his wife but she tore away and stumbled indoors.

Rough country humor? Only cruel Henry laughed, and Wayne had never seen his mother so angry. "Didn't mean to cause a fuss," Henry said sweetly. "Guess I kinda overdone it!"

Later, Wayne analyzed the scene again and again. This was the spot where his marriage ended, but maybe that part of things wasn't his father's fault. He simply added gasoline.

Ruth changed and drove Louise to church, but never again spoke to Henry, nor was it part of the old man's psychology to apologize. Ruth didn't return even for Louise's funeral.

And she miscarried. Something else might have brought it on, but Ruth didn't think so. They would have been combative parents, which didn't matter, either. In Ruth's mind that savage old man, Henry Dietrich, killed her baby.

In that last year Wayne himself joined his mother in the argument for Beulah Land. Louise would have almost no work to do and could spend her last days talking about Jesus with her old friends. Henry never liked church, and round-the-clock church was even less appealing.

"We didn't hardly even make a garden last year," Louise said. "Henry wants me to put up beets and soup mix, but I just cain't no more. We don't need the farm now we get Social Security." She sighed. "I'll miss the place."

"You're gonna want the farm some day, Wayne," Henry said.

"Not likely," Wayne said. Instantly, he regretted the sadness in his father's eyes.

Surprising them both, his father found another way: he sold the walnut trees. A veneering mill bought them, but some of the lumber made its way to the Amana Colonies in Iowa, becoming grandfather clocks and rocking chairs.

One year after the washer and dryer episode, his mother and father moved into their apartment. Wayne visited regularly and tried to bring Henry out to the farm. He imagined the two of them overhauling a lawn mower, or sculpting hammer handles with a spoke shave, but Henry wasn't interested. He was re-reading his twenty-odd Tarzan stories and seldom lifted his head from the page.

Louise, in a wheelchair now, seemed happy enough. Giggling, she told how the widows chased Beulah Land's few bachelors— most of whom just wanted to go fishing. After two blissful years, she died.

"Wanta move back to the farm?" Wayne asked his dad.

"Lonely out there," the old man said. "Wouldn't be no point to it without Louise."

Wayne knew it was futile to ask his father to come to St. Louis, nor would Ruth have tolerated him, but he wondered about a trip to Florida. "You always liked Panama City. You always wanted to go deep sea fishing."

Henry nodded. "Winter sets in, maybe so."

In December, on a night when ten inches of snow fell, the old man disappeared. His truck was gone but he wasn't at the farm or anywhere in town. At first the people at Beulah Land surmised that Henry had, indeed, gone to Florida. It was only later that they discovered Henry sold his truck the week after Louise died.

A utility crew found his body in February, in the woods five hundred feet behind Beulah Land. Henry wore the blue corduroy jacket he'd worn for chores. He sat with his back against a white pine on a three-legged, black walnut stool he'd made himself.

According to Louise's young minister, Henry Dietrich was inconsolable after his wife's death, although he had developed "a good relationship with Jesus." Distraught and not quite rational, he wandered into the woods and, in the blizzard, lost his bearings." He's with Sister Louise now," the minister said.

Wayne knew better. There was the empty bottle of vodka by the body, for instance, and the old man never drank. He knew what his father had done because it was something he himself might do. His father had quite deliberately walked into the woods and found himself a place out of the howling wind. He sipped the vodka. He grew colder than he'd ever been crawling under houses, but the vodka numbed him, and in the end he felt warm again. All in all, it was a practical way to die.

Wayne sawed wood until four, when he hit a rock and dulled his last chain. He was too exhausted even to read and didn't want to cook, so he drove to Mountain Vale.

He hadn't foreseen the problem of loneliness. His theory about celibacy, that you wore yourself out with work and dropped off to sleep immediately, needed adjustment. If he were Catholic, he might have asked a priest about it. Maybe there were books.

Ruth all but shrank from his touch. With sex gone, they didn't have a damn thing, not even arguments in the end. But you've been through this, Wayne told himself. With Ruth, with the counselor. The marriage wasn't a true partnership. She had the money. Her dad held the cards. And finally, Wayne escaped.

He took a bath, shaved, and pulled on his last clean shirt. He might drive up to Springfield in a day or two. He needed a washing machine.

He dropped off his saw chains at the small engine shop and tried to make conversation with the owner, but the man was duller than the chains.

Go home; read a book. That's what he should do, but he couldn't calm himself. Thirty-five miles to the nearest movie theater. There was probably a cornball dance, a country show, if he knew where.

He found himself circling the square. He had to eat; why not at Sarah's Home Cooking, when the alternative was McDonald's? But the restaurant's lights flipped off even as he cut the Buick engine.

Worse, it began to rain.

He stepped out of the Buick and stood wiping his face with a shop rag. And now the waitress named Rhiannon ran across the street, the scarf over her hair making her look old-fashioned. In the half-light of the square, her eyes swept over him, and he thought he saw her lips move. Then she slid into her Toyota and started the engine.

But the click engaging the transmission never came.

Just five days, Wayne. You're crazy.

She has a history, too. Who says it even works out?

He ran across the street and tapped on the waitress's window. "Miss! Rhiannon!"

Behind Enemy Lines

"Oh," Killer murmured, and clutched at his jaw, because his teeth hurt. The pain had awakened him. He'd had a bad dream, too, but couldn't remember what about. He'd had many bad dreams lately. His teeth hurt him in his sleep and caused his mind to conjure horrible things.

He dropped his feet to the floor. He knew where he was: in the bus, on the island, in the river. "Wolf!" he called, and from beneath the metal floor he heard a growl.

Killer stepped outside, naked except for his shoes and ragged shorts. He reached into his mouth with a thumb and forefinger and pressed on a molar. Eat something, get busy, and he'd forget his pain.

He filled the coffee pot, then dropped potatoes and onions in a kettle. He hung both pot and kettle over his cooking pit and built a fire. He headed for the river, carrying his .22 rifle, swatting at mosquitoes. Bullfrogs croaked out a full chorus—their farewell until another nightfall.

Wolf crept from behind and gently caught Killer's shin with his teeth. "Think maybe I'll make some wolf stew," Killer said, and the animal whimpered, and rolled in the grass, before slipping into the brush.

Killer reached the gravel bar at the head of the island. Rain had to be falling upcountry because the water was high. Ordinarily in summer he could have walked five hundred feet farther, casting lines, without getting his feet wet.

He plunged off the submerged bar and wriggled down in the muddy water to his fish trap, but he had no fish today. He broke the surface and swam a few strokes, drifting with the curls of fog that still caressed the water. A red-tailed hawk sailed low, gliding just above the surface before powering upward again to cruise at treetop level above the swamp. Killer dropped his feet to the slimy bottom, fearful of leeches. They lived in water like this. He eased forward, goop squeezing between his toes, until he found gravel.

Wolf lay in a first patch of sun. He'd sniffed out a nest of young cottontails and, when they panicked, tracked them each down their little tunnels under the matted grass. He trapped one, snapped its back in his teeth, and sucked the steaming meat from its skin. Now he opened his eyes and growled low.

Not fifty feet away, across the channel on the Missouri side, the doe's ears flicked from out of the brown and green oak leaves. She darted her head about, nudged the open air as if it were palpable, and then quickly, delicately, stepped to the water.

Killer sat on a rickety dinette chair he'd brought back from the Platte County Landfill. He pulled on his socks. He heard Wolf growling and then saw the doe drinking. He shot her through the eye.

It took him half the morning to butcher the doe, but the work kept him so busy he didn't think about how much his teeth hurt. He threw the entrails to the fish and cut out the haunches and all the lean meat and threw the remainder into the brush for the coons. Blood soaked into the muddy bank but the river still rose. In a few days the blood and stench would be washed clean, and deer would come again.

He loaded the meat into his canoe and paddled around the head of the island. A barge carrying scrap iron chugged upstream, and on the Kansas side a farmer walked along the top of the dike, looking out. The farmer waved at a man on the barge but neither of them noticed Killer, who guided the canoe in among a stand of sycamores and began carrying the venison to his camp.

Killer knew there were such things as licenses and hunting seasons but the state couldn't catch you unless you went to a processing station, and they couldn't catch you, either, if they didn't know you were alive. Barge workers and fishermen saw him occasionally, but there wasn't much to see. He had thin hair and a matted beard and he was brown like the river. The island looked like more of the swamp, rather than an island, and you wouldn't have thought anyone could live on it, or want to. Even in the winter the high ground where Killer's bus sat was hard to see.

Every time he killed a deer he had trouble with Wolf, who tried to rip open the abdomen for the liver, or throw dirt on the carcass, or urinate on the meat after he'd gorged himself. So Killer coaxed the animal into the pen he'd made out of chain-link that had come drifting downriver atop a broken shed. Wolf growled and clawed at the fence as Killer brought up the pieces of deer. "Shut up," Killer said, and the animal stared at him with his yellow eyes. Killer threw him a foreleg.

He salted the rest of the meat and strung it on greasy wires inside a metal feed hopper. Then he connected some thirty feet of pipe back to his stove. He shoveled up coals, covered them with chunks of hickory, and closed the damper. He'd keep a low fire for several days.

He opened the pen and Wolf walked out with an aggrieved air. Killer stood astride of him and kneaded his ribs and the animal caught Killer's wrist in his mouth, then rolled over and lay near the cooking pit.

Wolf was truly a wolf, orphaned from a pack that had wandered down the river bottom all the way from the Dakotas. They'd ranged in the swamp for nearly a year, preying on highland sheep and poultry, until farmers shot them. Killer found Wolf, clumsy and not yet weaned, floundering by the water. He scared the pup; it ran into the water and nearly drowned.

As for whether Killer was truly a killer, he himself couldn't have said. He was christened when he bought his .22 at a garage sale in Platte City. "This gun shoot straight?" he asked. "I want to kill deer with it. They get in my garden."

"Shoot a deer with a .22?" the woman asked. "What a killer!"

He liked what the woman said, and afterwards thought of himself as Killer, though if you had asked him directly he would have told you his name was Robert Coogan.

"*Hush.*"

He sat up. All was black. "What?"

"They're coming."

They lay inside a thicket of bamboo, waiting for the major. Tiny boats drifted by, their lanterns flickering, on a river so broad you couldn't see across it. In the dark he couldn't tell the difference between land and water, because both places were wet. It had rained for as long as he could remember.

"Take the Claymore."

The man thrust the little generator into Killer's hand and rolled over to prop himself behind the machine gun. Killer's eyes stung from the rain and he didn't know which way to look. It was always raining and it was always dark.

"Now. You hear?"

He brought the halves of the generator together and an arc of light lit up the river and six men on the trail. Behind them, around them, the eyes of animals stared, before the eerie light went out and a soldier screamed and a fish plopped on Killer's head. Killer screamed, too, as the man beside him opened up with the machine gun, firing at the image of men still imprinted on the air, on his and Killer's eyes, and then at the blackness.

"Lincoln," Killer murmured, remembering his companion's name for the first time in a long while, though he'd had the dream before. More a memory than a dream, perhaps, and he lay without moving in the dark, panting a little, trying to figure things out. The rain pounded against the bus. It was that darkest time of the morning when the birds and insects don't sing and no dog howls.

His teeth ached fiercely and he stumbled about with his flashlight, searching for aspirin. He turned on the radio just to hear a voice, but the batteries were dead. He could tell by the silence in the woods that it was not quite five o'clock.

"Jesus!" he shouted, as the pain shot through his eyes.

He staggered outside. Pools of water stood around the cooking pit, and rain fell steadily. He sat beside the sputtering coals, holding his jaw. For years there had been a dull pain, but now a wild animal was inside his mouth. He clinched his teeth and beat on his mandible with a fist.

He built up the fire, made coffee, ladled out stew. He stoked the stove again. Yellow eyes glinted in the woods, and Wolf materialized. Killer fed him, saw that he had water, and shut him in the chain-link pen. Otherwise, the animal would follow him into Platte City.

Killer couldn't have a timber wolf at his heels. He caused enough of a stir all by himself.

Halfway to Platte City stood a store where you could buy bait and beer and snack food. Killer rose from the swamp and came around the corner abruptly, almost stumbling over two young women sitting with sodas. They weren't local. They had fancy bicycles and wore tight, short pants and odd-looking helmets. "Ex*cuse* me," said one, drawing up her legs, and then she just stared.

"God," murmured the other, as Killer went in the door. "Are we in the sticks, or what?"

The man behind the counter grunted hello. He'd tried to strike up a conversation once or twice but Killer didn't understand him very well. Killer couldn't think of anything to say, but liked the man because he never tried to run him off.

Killer bought aspirin and a can of peaches. Plastic spoons were free and he took six. He went out to the picnic table and sat washing down aspirin with peach nectar. The peaches stung his teeth but he didn't have to chew them. He also liked the peaches in green cans. Apricots were even better but there weren't as many in a case.

The women didn't look at Killer now. They put on their backpacks and strange helmets and pedaled away in the drizzle. They were from Mars.

He walked along the interstate, then crossed a fence and began thinning Jordan Prescott's apples. Killer liked the work because it went on hard and monotonously for a month or so and then was done. He liked that Jordan was a bachelor and didn't talk much. In October Killer returned to pick the apples and Jordan always gave him two bushels of Jonathans besides paying in cash. Killer hated checks because without a driver's license no one would cash them.

Three years before, in a winter when the channel ran dry and the swamp froze over, Jordan gave Killer the school bus. It ran just enough for Killer to drive it to the island. He'd been living in a lean-to covered over with sheet iron and dirt.

It was all right to thin apples in the rain because you stayed cool. But Killer's teeth started hurting again. Jordan found him sitting at the top of a picking ladder, thumb and index finger pressing hard on the roof of his mouth. "Bobby! Go to a dentist!"

"No money."

"Can't you go to the VA, across the river?"

Killer considered. "Yes," he said. "I know where that is."

"I got business in Saint Joe. Take you to the crossroads. Poor day to work, anyhow."

Killer stared out the pickup as they passed the women on bicycles. He'd known a woman who looked like the one riding in front. That was when he lived in the city. Louise. She lived up above.

"Going cross-country, I spose," Jordan said.

"Yeah."

Jordan pulled over. "Feel bad not taking you all the way."

Killer nodded.

"Got to get some spray for the beetles. It's such a wet year I can't hardly keep up. Don't know *what* kinda crop I'm gonna have." Jordan pulled out his worn billfold. "Can I give you something for a haircut?"

Killer held the money. It was more than he would have made if he'd worked all morning.

Jordan eased out the clutch. "Little trim wouldn't hurt. Beard, too, Bobby."

Killer walked along the highway to Leavenworth through the low ground. The ditches were filled with water and pools stood in the soybeans. The sun came out briefly and he began sweating. The women on bicycles swished by, and Killer dropped his head.

"Hi, how are you?" Louise asked, and Killer waved and smiled. He liked Louise. He knew he had done something to make her unhappy in the city but it was long ago.

"*Boy*friend," the woman behind her called.

"Jan, the poor thing."

"Romance on the *prairie*."

Killer had forgotten about women. He didn't dream of them anymore. In Platte City they paid no attention to him, but he could tell that the woman on the bicycle meant to be nice. She wasn't really Louise, however. Where had he known Louise?

It began raining again. He stood on the bridge to Leavenworth, watching the water churn. Ten miles to the south was his island, and Wolf. He'd never seen the river so high.

The women were gone forever.

It was Monday and the barbershop was closed. He didn't want to go to a barber, anyhow. He didn't care about the top of his head. It was his teeth that needed fixing.

He walked past the guard station, expecting to be hailed, but no one was on duty. A green truck swished by in the mist and he stepped off the road, climbed a spongy bank, and disappeared inside a willow grove, where he surprised a flock of Canadian geese. They hissed at him and he ran into the cemetery, where the rows of white markers marched down to the river. He came to the water. He couldn't see where the river ended and Missouri began. Great trees floated by and a dead pig on a raft.

He turned on heel and walked straight for a massive, brick building that must have squatted here through a dozen wars. He found an entrance and sloshed across a marble floor; to his left and right were offices. Ahead, blocking access to a long, dim corridor, stood a big man in whites. A guard, Killer thought. He sought out an old man who pushed a laundry hamper.

"What?" The old man stared at Killer. He wore thick glasses that magnified his eyes.

"I need to get my teeth fixed."

"Oh." The old man pointed across the hall, where several men waited in a row of chairs.

Killer walked along the edge of the marble so that he could see inside the office, where three women worked at computers. He studied them for a long time and stared at himself reflected on a stainless steel post. He combed his hair back with his fingers and tugged at his gray beard. His teeth were black. Did that mean that they would soon fall out, because they were dead? But they weren't dead, or they wouldn't hurt him so.

He charged the office like it was high ground but then stopped abruptly and sat.

"Brother," said the man next to him. "Who you with over there?"

Killer's legs were shaking but he leaped up and went through the door. He stood before the first desk, not knowing what to say.

"Sir?" The woman didn't look up. She had red fingernails that were so long it didn't look like she'd be able to type, but her fingers kept moving.

"I have to get my teeth fixed," Killer managed. He swept back his hair again. A pool formed under his shoes.

"You're a patient here?"

"I live by myself. Wolf and me."

The woman still didn't look up. "Name?"

He told her. She began tapping rapidly, looking up at him once, and blinking, then back at her screen. "Still raining out there?"

"Raining like crazy."

"They're evacuating some of the low areas." She shook her head. "No record of you, sir."

"I just want to get my teeth fixed."

"You may need to contact a private practitioner. At this time the Veterans Department does not offer outpatient dental care."

Killer stared. "I was with the Cav."

"Sir, you can't just walk in and get your teeth worked on. You will need to go to a civilian facility."

Killer propped a hand on the woman's desk and bent near her, so that she had to look at him. "I don't have any money. Jordon said you have dentists here."

The woman swallowed. Her eyes widened. She scooted her chair to the wall. "The Veterans Department does not offer out-patient dental care at this time. Sir."

Killer sat on the steps, watching the rain blow across the great parking lot and toward the river. It would never stop, he thought. And he had to go out in it, back through the town and across the bridge and downriver ten miles. He would be long after dark arriving. Wolf would be crazy.

"Goddamn monsoon out there." Leaning against the wall was a tall, lean man with closely cropped black hair. He had a brown face stained almost black from his heavy beard. He wore an earring. It was the man who had called him brother.

He offered Killer a cigarette, which Killer took even though he didn't smoke. The man struck a light and they stood blowing smoke into the rain. "John Oglethorpe," the man said.

"They call me Killer."

"Unfucking real, man. I was in the Cav, too. When you there?"

Killer concentrated. "I don't know. I was in the delta, and then I . . . went back."

"You done two tours? No wonder you're so fucked up."

"I—"

"Hey, no sweat. I'm a sick man myself. Why else would I be hanging out at the VA?"

Killer flipped the cigarette away. It gave him a headache. "I just wanted to get my teeth fixed."

"Heard the entire sad story. Here's a man don't have a nickel, coulda got blowed away in the service of his country, they won't even fix his teeth. See, you can't be a patient unless you already *are* one. Heard that before? I mean, it ain't the army but it's damn close. What you need to do, I'm telling you because I *been* there, man, is get drunk. Totally, stinking, dog rotten, dead drunk. Then you can check into detox 'cause you have an alcohol problem, and they'll fix your teeth. You copy, brother?"

Killer shook his head. "I got to get back to Wolf."

"Ah." Oglethorpe laughed. "You're a married man."

They sat drinking in Oglethorpe's camper. They were parked on a knoll in the graveyard looking down on the river. It kept raining and it was so dark Killer thought that the day must be done, but Oglethorpe told him it was only three thirty. By four Killer's head was spinning. "I'm worried about Wolf," he said, and reached for the door, but then Oglethorpe handed him another plastic cup filled with fire.

"I am a fucked-up individual," Oglethorpe explained. "There is agreement on that point. The question is whether I am 100 percent fucked up or only maybe 40 percent. If I was 100 percent I could get my own place."

"I live in a bus," Killer announced.

"On an island. With this big dog looks like a wolf."

"*Is* a wolf."

"Can't be no wolf, man. They killed all the wolves. I got to piss."

So did Killer. He staggered across the asphalt and fell down in the grass by a white marker. The river covered the entire world. It wasn't brown anymore. It was black.

Oglethorpe urinated on one of the stones. "*Pissing* in the rain," he sang.

"Not right," Killer said.

"It's a fucking major, son. Who cares about a goddam dead major?"

"Officers—" But Killer was confused. An entire house floated by. He should climb onto the house and float down to Wolf. He threw a bottle at a window and fell backward and rain poured into his mouth. He closed his eyes and rolled over in the mud and then he heard gunfire. Oglethorpe was shooting an M-16 at a cat sailing by on a door.

Killer didn't want the cat to die. "Give me that gun!"

"Fuck you, dude!"

Killer tried to grab the rifle but Oglethorpe twisted it away and brought the stock down in Killer's stomach. Killer dropped into a pool and then struggled to his knees. He vomited.

Oglethorpe opened up again on the cat but all his rounds fell short. Killer lay in the water and thought, they're coming for me, I'm dead. Then he rushed Oglethorpe from behind and clubbed him with his clenched hands and tore away the rifle. He sprayed the water, emptying out the magazine, and as he did a green truck drew near, lights on. Two MPs got out and stood in their gray slickers.

"He's crazy!" Oglethorpe screamed. "He's back in Nam!"

"Easy," one of the MPs said. "Throw down your weapon."

Killer dropped the rifle in the mud. He raised his hands high.

"Go for it, brother," Oglethorpe said, and threw a wild swing. Killer stumbled after him, blinded by the rain and the headlights, and an MP coldcocked him.

"Your history," the woman said.

There was a black man in the group, Howard, whom Killer thought he knew from somewhere. There were two white men who grinned, nodded, but never spoke. There was John Oglethorpe, who talked too much. And there was this woman who kept asking questions. "Robert," she said quietly. "Do you want to give us your history today?"

"I don't know much about history," he said.

"She mean your life story," Howard said. "Before you was a hopeless drunk."

"I am not a drunk."

"Just hopeless, then."

"You know about the flood, don't you, Robert?" the woman said. "You know that your dog drowned."

He nodded but didn't believe her. Wolf was smart. Wolf would swim until the water rose to the top of the fence.

"Do you feel that you have a problem with alcohol?" the woman asked.

Killer looked at Oglethorpe. "I do," he said, nodding.

"But you just told Howard that you don't drink."

"He was in denial!" Oglethorpe said.

"John," the woman said. "Let Robert answer for himself."

"In the city," Killer said, and maybe it was true, because he didn't remember. "I'd drink all day and then I'd pass out."

"I see," the woman said, as if she weren't convinced. She glanced at her notes and then at Oglethorpe. "How do your teeth fit, Robert?"

"Good!"

"I understand they're serving corn on the cob tonight." She smiled. "What do you think?"

"I grow corn on the island," Killer said. "Only the coons come after it."

"Shit," Howard said. "Doc made a joke. Where they find this hillbilly dude?"

"Man's a hero, fucker," Oglethorpe said. "Saw some serious shit in Laos."

Howard threw his hands out expansively. "Shittin' me, motherfucker."

"Goddam Silver Star!"

"Okay, okay," the doctor said. "Robert is giving his history. We need to respect each other here. Do you recall getting the medal, Robert?"

He didn't know the name of the village. He didn't know the name of the river. It was raining and he couldn't see and the pilot kept talking crazy talk. The pilot had black splotches on his face and puckering cuts. He looked like a monster in the movies.

"They beat the man," Oglethorpe said. "But you got there, Bobby. You found him!"

Rifle fire popped out of the trees behind the wharf and the major went down. He couldn't move. His legs quivered and melted together in the mud. You couldn't tell what was legs and what was mud and what was water. "Shoot me!" he screamed. "I'm dead, shoot me!"

Killer crawled in the weeds by the river. He sank in the mud and clawed his way up again frantically, looking for Lincoln. But Lincoln was hit. He fell without a sound. He lay in the water staring at Killer, and the pilot went on blubbering, and the major screamed for Killer to shoot him.

"Jesus H. Christ!" Howard said. "What you do?"

Killer shook his head. "I killed them."

The doctor was alarmed. "The major!"

"I killed *them!*"

"He mean the bad dudes," Howard said. "Ones fucked over the aviator."

Killer pointed angrily at a tall old window. "They were two of them. They came from the village where the pilot was. I saw them."

"You killed them," the doctor said. "You remember."

"*Got* to kill them," Oglethorpe said, shaking his head.

One of the grinning, silent men spoke. "*Got* to."

"And then, Robert?" the woman asked. "You're doing just fine. Then?"

He shut his eyes. "I went out on the dock and—and there was a boat. I went to the pilot because they were all dead. I shook him real hard. He crawled in, and then I got the major. He—he was—"

"In shock," the doctor said. "He was in shock."

"I just dragged him over. He was all covered with—"

"What about the village?" Oglethorpe asked. "Were they coming from the village?"

"I . . . couldn't see. Rain everywhere." Killer shook his head. "I got Lincoln and put him in the bottom except I knew he was dead. There was a little motor on the boat. The pilot, he—"

"How'd you know which way to go?"

"I went . . . *somewhere*. Off in the rain. And they found us."

"The navy?"

"The . . . the Thais."

"The Thais!" Oglethorpe said. "But how?"

"That's fine," the doctor said. She smiled again. "We'll talk more about this at our appointment, that's fine. Good, Robert."

"Good?" Oglethorpe said. "I guess so!"

"Damn good," Howard said.

It was good to eat food with teeth that didn't hurt. It was good to play ping-pong. It was good to go to the PX. It was good to listen to the radio. It was good to watch a movie. It was good to stare down upon the swollen river from this dry place.

It was good to lie on his bunk and look up at the rain bleeding down the skylight; he watched the rain hour after hour, imagining Wolf swimming in the rising water. He lay with his arms outstretched, perfectly still, but in his mind he moved his hands and swam just as Wolf swam, floating on the flood that slowly rose beneath him, never panicking, conserving his strength until the moment of escape. He seemed to burst through the skylight just as Wolf clambered over the fence.

Maybe Wolf would find his way to the Dakotas. Somewhere there were other wolves. He'd look down on the river from a high, sunny slope and not even remember where he'd been.

"Disability," Oglethorpe announced. They wouldn't let you smoke in your bunk anymore so he always sat on the rear steps by the fire bucket. "No way they'll turn you down. You're a lucky sonuvabitch! One hundred percent!"

"Oh," Killer said, leaning back on his hands and closing his eyes, thinking how odd it was to talk to people, to listen, to reply. "That's good."

"Money for nothing? Hell, yes, that's good." Oglethorpe laughed and flipped his cigarette into the drizzle. "Good as it gets."

Blackberries

One Saturday in July, just before dawn, Ivan Lotus was cooking breakfast. He took a step or two and then slid from the stove to the refrigerator to the table, one hand high in a flourish, the other carrying bacon or toast. He felt as though there were a news crew nearby, eager to film this extraordinary young man.

He splashed grease over the eggs until they were hard, as his mother had shown him, as his father liked. Ivan had in mind to take up the eggs in one neat, quick motion; but grease splattered on his wrist and he dropped the skillet lid. He pounced on it before it could bang into the refrigerator, but still the sound had been loud. He sucked in a breath and listened: no stirring beyond her door.

Ivan had looked forward to this day. His father, Jasper, and he were going far back in the hills to finish wiring a house for a woman. Jasper figured to be done by noon, and they'd go to town for groceries, electrical supplies, books for Ivan's mother. They'd eat at the cafe on the square, and Ivan, tall as his father now, would sense the camera on him again as he sat at the counter with the other men. He'd order chili and a grilled cheese. He'd drink a lemon-lime, taking it with him across the square, sucking ice. No doubt, Melinda Heinz, whose parents ran the cafe, would glide by in her shorts and halter top. How could she help but admire his muscles, his tan? Yet she always spoke to his father rather than to him. No question, Ivan needed to be an older man. Next October he'd be sixteen and could go to town on his own, in his own car if he could talk Jasper into it.

His father came in from chores, walking softly as anyone could hope in those heavy boots, across the oak floor. He nodded, but they ate in silence, both sensing, perhaps, that there would be more freedom to talk on the road. At last Ivan, who was proud of what he'd learned about cooking and had even been thinking about baking a pie, couldn't contain himself. "Well?"

Jasper seemed to pull himself from far away. "Good. Sure is, son." He grinned. "You'd make somebody—"

"Don't say it. Don't you—"

"—a good little wife."

Ivan rose, slammed dishes into the sink, threw the silverware on top. "Nobody even cares."

"Sure they do, son. *I* do."

"You don't, either. I been working really hard, and you don't even see. You treat me like a little kid."

"I don't mean to, Ivan."

"I'd like to see you get the meals around here. You, you—"

"You'll wake your mother."

Yes. Ivan hurried through the dark living room, trying to calm himself. It was humiliating how close to tears he'd been. Everyone treated him like an adult except Jasper. "Bastard," he muttered. He stood on the porch. The birds sang in the silver maples, and somehow they reassured him, how they always awoke at once, as if from some collective dream. He took out his grandfather's pocketknife and ran his thumb along the edge. When Ivan was small, his grandfather, dying of brown lung, used to slice off a piece of chewing tobacco and offer it to Ivan. Ivan would back away, frightened. "Dad!" Ivan's mother would say, as the old man broke into a prolonged, rasping laughter that ended with his terrible cough.

She must have awakened after all. Ivan couldn't make out the words but heard a murmuring from the bedroom, another of the house's night sounds.

He walked toward the truck, a bold silhouette for the cameras. The maples rustled. With first light, each leaf moved as if caught in a stroboscope. Every color had washed out overnight. So, too, the garage, the barn, the garden were colorless in the steadying light. Ivan sat in the pickup, thinking of his mother.

In a few moments Jasper slid behind the wheel, ground the starter, pulled back the shift. They headed east where the night sky and the outline of hills split crudely apart, as though scrawled with an orange crayon. Jasper drove a little faster than usual, and his eyes bulged.

"What is it?" asked Ivan.

"Son, I—" Jasper reached to the dash for a piece of butterscotch candy. "Her hair's all gone."

They left the state highway to follow a narrower road, marked "MM," down to Horseshoe Bend. Far across the hills, Ivan saw the gleam of a water tower, like a star. They climbed again. Here the way had been chiseled out of rock; his father downshifted to second. "Damn roads."

"Real pretty here, though. Maybe we could go fishing sometime." Ivan wore his good jeans, which he hoped to keep clean for town. He rested his arm on the truck window so that his biceps bulged. "Maybe I'll come down here by myself."

"Rocks just eat your tires *up*. That LaRue Hill recommends me for jobs like this while he sits on his ass in the coffee shop. Plus, he cheats on his copper."

"Yeah." Ivan looked at the Piney River below, tucking itself around the hills, gleaming. Here and there were deep pools in the rock. Perch, he thought. Lineside bass. "He cheats on his copper?"

"Him or me, we'll pay sixty dollars a box for romex, wholesale, what's that? That's—"

Ivan sighed dramatically. "Sixty cents a foot, Dad."

"You know what Hill charges?"

"I don't know."

"Make a guess. Just . . . guess."

"Seventy-five cents."

"A buck a foot, you believe that? Cheats these poor folks! Then turns around and sells the old wire."

"*We* do that."

"Huh?" They reached the crest, where the road was smoother, and gained some speed. To the south, the land was rolling and partly open. Half a mile onward, a white house caught the sun's glare. "That's her," said Jasper.

"The woman?"

"Not a bad old house. No insulation. He's gone most of the time, works on the highway. Felt kinda sorry for her, way out here, tiny baby. Man shouldn't do that."

"Shouldn't do what?"

"Leave her, leave her. Asking for trouble."

"You mean, like escaped convicts?"

"I bet it was one helluva winter. No juice!"

"Mom wouldn't put up with that."

Jasper hunched toward the wheel. "What?"

"No electricity."

Jasper slid back, brought a foot to the brake. "No. No, she wouldn't, son."

Something thudded within. Jasper shrugged and looked off across the pasture, as if in contempt for anyone who hadn't done half a day's work by now. Ivan stood where a path had been worn and the form for a sidewalk laid down; along the form were planted plastic zinnias and tulips. He tried to adopt the same pose as his father: stern, but receptive to the customer.

The woman opened the door and stood behind the screen; she murmured something and reached clumsily for the latch. She dipped into the sunlight. Her hair was disheveled, and a button of her dress was missing, or perhaps her sleepy fingers passed it over. "Jasper," she whispered.

"Brought my boy along."

She withdrew into shadow. She held open the screen so that Jasper and Ivan bent under her arm as they entered. The three stood awkwardly in a short hall. "This is Ivan," explained Jasper.

The woman smiled. "Heard so much about you. Would you like some coffee?"

"Wanted to get right to work, ma'am," Jasper said. "We have to get on to town."

"I'd like some coffee," Ivan announced.

His father frowned. "You get my plastic tape and my needle-nose pliers. And that long screwdriver."

The woman yawned. "He could have some *cof*fee, Jasper."

"Ah huh."

She laughed. "You don't drink coffee, do you? Or smoke—"

"You mean the red screwdriver?" asked Ivan. He didn't want it to seem that he had to have his father's permission to drink coffee, with the whole world out there not only drinking coffee but smoking cigarettes, having social drinks—wild parties, too.

"Blue one. Get the red one for yourself."

Ivan had maneuvered himself to the woman's side. Looking down at her, he tried to seem wise and mature, tolerant where his father was intolerant, while at the same time seeking out the unfastened button. The woman's eyes were wary. He saw a hint of Melinda Heinz there, not quite prepared to dismiss him. Then suddenly she smiled, with the sort of smile reserved for children and failing old people, and Ivan knew he'd been found out. He turned sharply, too precisely, but managed not to stumble into anything.

Still, when he had his car, he might just happen this way again, and if the woman were home . . . he pictured them walking across the pasture, hand in hand, toward the Piney. He sat across from her, sipping coffee and sampling a stale roll. "Must have been a rough winter."

"God." She lit a cigarette, which surprised him. "I wouldn't go through it again, not for anybody."

"I only got four more faceplates to do," Ivan said. He could hear his father downstairs, grunting occasionally as he wrestled with the wires in the breaker box. Ivan hoped the woman didn't realize what a simple job he'd been given. Errand boy, that's all he was. Jasper wouldn't give him a chance. Yet around home, who did the cooking, the laundry, even paid the bills?

"Oh, yes. I can't believe I'll finally have . . . what does Jasper, what does your father say?"

"Juice?"

"Juice. The dumb stove's been sitting there for six months."

Ivan stared, unable to speak.

She brought a hand to her throat. "Your father says you're a very good student."

"I guess so."

She snuffed out her cigarette and then lit another. "Are you going to college?"

"I don't know, ma'am."

She leaned forward suddenly, startling him. "Do you want a cigarette, Ivan?"

"Oh, no."

"I won't tell Jasper. It's just that you were staring—"

He was frightened enough to be reckless. "You're so pretty, to smoke—"

She exhaled violently. "What's *that* got to do with it?"

"My mom smokes. Used to . . . as long as I can remember."

She seemed to collapse. She crushed her cigarette. "I'm *so* sorry, Ivan. You've had your hands full, haven't you? You know . . . your father loves you very much."

He stared at her with alarm. She should remain a stranger, merely pretty. How could she know? Jasper was so remote . . . how could he even talk of such matters outside his home?

She placed a hand lightly on his. He stiffened. "Ivan," she said. "People shouldn't have to bear it alone. You know? If you see someone who's hurting . . . you should help. Don't you think so, Ivan?"

"I don't know, ma'am," he said. He pulled his hand away.

"Patricia. Please."

"Patricia."

"Ah. Was that so hard?"

"No, ma'am." He was sweating. He rose to finish the faceplates and looked up at her desperately. "You ever . . . go swimming?"

But she moved away, out of the kitchen. She turned, her smile distanced now. "The baby."

"Oh." He'd forgotten about the baby. It compromised her, put her beyond his understanding, as though she herself were done for, dying. Patricia opened the bedroom door. The baby cried, ceased crying. Ivan picked up two of Patricia's cigarettes: elegant things, to be so deadly. He returned to the faceplates.

Jasper came in. "You done?"

"Two more, I—"

"It's my fault, Jasper," Patricia said. She emerged with the baby, now paced with it against her chest, and patted its back. It burped and opened its eyes. It stared at Jasper. "We just got to talking," Patricia explained. "Is it ready?"

"Not quite. I'll crawl up on the roof and tape the entrance, that spot I missed. Then yeah, flip on your meter, throw your mains."

"*Good* boy. Good, good boy," Patricia said, low to the baby. She glanced up at Jasper. "I'll have juice?"

"Power to spare."

"*Won*derful. Now, now. You wanta sleep some more?"

"I'll set the ladder," Ivan said.

"No." His father shook his head vigorously. "Want you to pick some blackberries."

Ivan was amazed. "Dad? What?"

"For your mother," Jasper said quickly. "You remember this morning I went in, and you know how she talks, just blurts out things; she asked me if the blackberries was ready, and I said I thought so. 'You pick some, I'll make you a cobbler,' she said."

"But she can't—"

Patricia crept back to the bedroom, holding the baby carefully. "That would be *nice,*" she murmured.

Jasper nodded. "We try to take care of her. I thought . . . you and me could make it, Ivan. You think?"

"She can't *eat* that, Dad."

"Maybe. Maybe she can."

"There's a pan under the sink," Patricia called back. "That's really sweet."

If his mother truly wanted a cobbler, why not pick berries in the morning when the juice mixed with the dew, on their own land where he knew every bush? That was how Jasper was: logical, and shrewd, about some things, and quirky, even downright ignorant, about others. You couldn't reason with him. One of these days Ivan would have a car and Jasper could pick his own berries. Or by God *pay* him to do it. Was he some kind of slave?

Ivan stayed with it until he had nearly a gallon, then walked to the river to sit cross-legged on a gravel shoal. On the opposite side, swallows flew in and out of holes in the watered limestone, seemingly at full speed. He debated a quick swim, but the water was slow here, murky, and he was fearful of water moccasins. He took out one of Patricia's cigarettes, rolled it between his fingers, stripped it. The paper and curls of tobacco floated away.

As Ivan climbed the bank to return, a flatbed truck rattled over the wooden bridge; dust sifted to the water through the boards. On the road, crowded in by oaks and grapevines, Ivan was a lonely man, with great sorrow in his past and sacrifices; the camera would catch the noble lines in his face. In moments, though, he was soaking in sweat, irritable, and no fit subject for a camera. He came upon the flatbed trailer again, parked in the yard of a double-wide trailer.

On the steps, made of cinder blocks, sat a girl dressed in jeans and man's shirt. Inside, a woman yelled, and something crashed. Ivan knew the girl, her face at least, from school. "Hi," he said, but with a voice too weak to travel, so he waved. The girl turned sideways and stared intently down the road, with the absurd pretense she hadn't seen him. He saw that she'd been crying and hurried past, like a man detouring a cross dog.

At last he rounded the curve to Patricia's house, holding the berries already bruised with heat. The ladder was back on the truck. The job was done. Jasper sat on the steps with Patricia, a check in his hands. The baby, on a blanket in a piece of shade, crawled like an insect. Patricia reached in the air behind Jasper's thick neck, stretching, saying something; Jasper smiled. Then she saw Ivan, and her gesture became an awkward wave. She'd combed her hair and changed to shorts. "Hello, stranger," she said, reaching for a cigarette. "Did you find any?"

Ivan tilted the bowl slightly for them to see, but moved no closer.

"Those are nice," she said. "I should pick some, too."

Jasper stood. "We better get on down the road. Want me to look into it, about that air conditioner? You got no shade. It'll get hot out here."

"If you *want* to, Jasper."

"Okay, I'll—"

There must have been something almost violent in the way Ivan jerked up his head, or shifted his weight, or brought the berries to his chest. His father and Patricia turned almost as one. Their eyes held the same, quickly subdued, alarm.

"My mother's *dying*," Ivan said.

They took the back way to town, past the double-wide and over the wooden bridge. The road meandered but cut off ten miles. Two deer, browsing in lespedeza, darted away quick as current, leapt a fence. Ivan sat rigidly, the bowl of berries jiggling on his knees.

"You don't have to make that cobbler, Ivan. We'll just eat 'em, cream and sugar."

He didn't answer. For weeks now, he'd brought her books she couldn't read, cooked her food she couldn't eat. In his dreams, she leaned on him, as he helped her down the hospital corridor, the endless corridor, toward Radiation. And if he had done this, no matter what some doctor said, shouldn't she live? How could it be so futile?

"What's the matter, son?"

"I want some money. Some regular money."

"Sure. Listen. It's been a burden, I know that, and I—maybe I coulda helped out better. But somebody has to make a living, Ivan. And there's just no way for a man to act, situation like this. Nothing to do. Your mother, she's a fine woman, and—"

"Don't you talk about my mother!"

Jasper stopped the truck. They were at the crest of a hill, and Ivan could see the town below, the crooked, white-capped Piney River. As his father spoke, Ivan felt his anger subside, though not in forgiveness. It didn't matter exactly, about his father.

"I never had friends, Ivan." His father was eating the black-berries, one at a time. "I just would do my work and come home to your mom and work some more. All I ever done was work. And you know, you'll be going off to school here, 'fore you know it. I'll be out there all by my lonesome. You ain't lived as long as me, Ivan. You don't know."

Slowly, Ivan grew conscious they'd been sitting in the sun, neither of them speaking, for a long time. A Corvette rolled up behind them, swerved, honked, and sped toward the town.

"Ivan," his father said. "Ivan, you wanna drive?"

Ivan didn't answer. He looked out the window and refused to cry. Blood thumped in his ears. At last his father pushed in the clutch and started the engine.

The Painter

Mavis and I did not have any money when we first married, and we had to live in an old apartment house where you couldn't shut out the cold and the big trucks went by rattling the windows. This was in Springfield, which was the Big City for us. I had been in the United States Army, but really we were just farm kids.

I drove a forklift for a catalogue printer, working the graveyard shift. I would unload rolls of newsprint from the railcars and stack them high in the warehouse, bring them down again, and deliver them to the web presses. I made decent wages, and with what Mavis brought home from waiting tables, we were able to save some. Still, we were unhappy in our jobs, knowing that we had not found our true vocations before the Lord.

Around three in the morning work slowed down, and the men wanted to play poker. I learned in the United States Army that there is a time and place for the Lord's witness. I did not try to tell them that it was wrong to gamble, but I could not remain in the room with them while they smoked and took the Lord's name in vain.

So I took my New Testament out to the delivery bays where the empty railcars sat. When I need strength I always turn to the Beatitudes. *Blessed are the poor, and blessed are ye when men do revile and persecute you.*

But it was a cold night, and I could not sit still to read. I paced along the concrete dock, staring at the dark hills to the south. The starlight was magical, and the moon hung low and red, like some sort of sign if only I could interpret it. Suddenly, I stopped walking. I thought I'd seen something scurry and run into one of the cars. It might have been anything: a piece of brush the wind had dropped, an armadillo, or one of my co-workers, playing a trick on me.

But somehow, I felt that the Lord was testing me, and I tried not to be afraid. I walked to the very last car, where shadows swallowed the starlight. I stared into the void of the railcar. And a great force pushed me to my knees.

"You!" a voice said. "Thomas Hovey!"

"Yes, Lord." I could not breathe. "I'm here, Lord."

I cannot say if there was a physical presence in that boxcar. The voice boomed like some big gun, but perhaps only in my head. That did not make the moment less real. The time has come, Thomas Hovey, the voice said. Find a church, bring the gospel, and help the poor.

God delivered us a church deep in the Ozark Mountains, down by the Piney River, in the town of Red Buck. In the old downtown, near the railroad, we found a great cinder block building that once had been a farm implement garage. The long pit for working under trucks remained, as well as a continuous table, built into the walls and covered with broken tractor parts. Everywhere you looked, on the floor and settled on the ceiling beams, lay half an inch of oily dirt.

In the back, long before, someone had built an apartment. It had electricity and running water, but Mavis did not want to live there.

"It's the Lord's will," I told her.

She found a job right away at the aluminum plant. Not out on the floor, but in the front office, which meant she had to dress well. Of course, for a bathroom, we had nothing but the stool and a sink streaked brown from the parts washer, so I installed a new sink and hung a mirror above it and constructed some shelves from particle board. Mavis complained that she had no privacy, and so I hung a curtain.

I almost didn't recognize her when she left in the mornings. She looked like one of those women on magazine covers.

I scrubbed the apartment floor to ceiling and found a man to bring a new electrical service from the pole. Then I ran wire through the building, all in conduit just as the city told me. I installed a new tub and shower. I laid tile in the kitchen and hooked up a second-hand washer and dryer. Mavis complained there were no closets for her new clothes, so I built her two.

All of that took me three months, and I had not begun with the church. Sometimes, God seemed far away, and I doubted my purpose.

I hauled trash from the garage for a week. I took a high-pressure gun to the beams and then to the floor, to knock away those years of grease. I scrubbed it all down, disinfected it, and sprayed it white.

I made a platform in front and some altars from pine packing boards that I sanded and filled. I drove back to Springfield, where a Catholic church had closed, and bought a podium, pews, and folding chairs. I asked Mavis to help with the windows, but she could not find time, so I made curtains myself from white muslin.

I placed an ad in the paper and a sign on the street. On our fifteenth Sunday in Red Buck, Mavis and I stood out front of the newest church in America, hoping someone would come.

Twenty good folk straggled in, the wretched of Red Buck. They were the panhandlers and the drunks and the mental cases. If their eyes were not glazed over, they were hostile.

"Jesus told the rich man to give all his money to the poor," I told them. "It was the one thing he could not do."

"Amen," an old woman said.

"But, dear friends, none of us here today has that rich man's problem."

"No-o-o-o," came a chorus. And everyone laughed.

"We have a place to meet. We serve the Lord. We have riches greater than earthly treasures!"

"Praise the Lord!"

They had not among them enough money to pay the church's electric bill. Prosperous folks attend prosperous churches. A prosperous church must keep the poor at a certain distance, or its congregation will go elsewhere.

Mavis understood this, and to my sorrow I began to lose her. Or, to be perfectly honest, I had probably lost her long before.

She could have dealt with our situation had she thought that one day we would own a beautiful home and a fine car. Instead, it seemed that I had doomed us to the same, eternal poverty that our followers knew. And that both of us had grown up with—in her case, on a little hilltop ranch, with a drunkard for a father. I did not drink, but I couldn't offer the escape she hoped for.

"Maybe God didn't lead us here at all," she said. "Maybe you just *thought* he did."

"I heard a voice."

"You heard a voice. Did you ask this voice about your wife? Did your voice say anything about living in this dump?" She paused. "I'm sorry, Tom, but that's what it is."

"There's not much more I can do with it, Mavis."

"You've done everything a man could. We need a real home, Tom. Could we bring a child into the world here? Would the Lord— would the Lord *want* that, Tom?"

She had been riding to work with her boss, which seemed kind of him, but now I understood that it was more than kind. She filed for divorce, and soon after that, married the man. Seven months after moving out, she bore his daughter.

In the summer I hired on to make hay, and later to run a big John Deere corn picker, all to support the church. I would not enjoy such a life on a permanent basis, but I was still young, and it was good to work long hours under the sun.

Sometimes, I saw Mavis downtown. What a lovely, worldly woman, I thought, then realized that I had been married to her. At first, she smiled awkwardly, and we exchanged a few words like distant cousins. Later, I ducked from sight before we could meet—and I believe she did, too.

I knew that we had married too young, and that we were not suited. True, both of us were raised on farms, but her ambitions were different than mine. I rushed into my church for the poor, and perhaps, if I had waited, and found a building not quite so run down, she could have risen to the same call. Often, thinking of her, I was beset with doubt, and lonely. I wondered if this path the Lord had taken me down could content any woman. Paul said that it is better to marry than to burn, and without Mavis my nights were long, and I burned.

My little community rallied around me. The women—sad widows of broken men, and retirees whose government checks never stretched far enough—took my part, and I was not noble enough to dispute their opinion of Mavis.

In winter I shifted from the fields to a lumberyard, but there were weeks when the church almost supported itself. A reporter from West Plains wrote about us, saying how the clothes on your back were just fine in this particular house of God, and how some newly homeless family could spend the night, and how the big churches sent us their destitute—and sometimes, their checks.

Four years passed, and Mavis moved to a fine new house in Poplar Bluff—and bore a son. Then the painter came.

His name was Abraham Sawyer, and when he shook my hand and said hello I felt I knew him somehow, that he was my lost brother or even a kind of father. He had just returned from a trip across Montana and down through the Dakotas to Iowa, where he was raised.

We were tacking on a new roof and painting the exterior. The women scraped and filled the big metal windows and scrubbed the cinder blocks while the men tore off the roll roofing and laid new tar paper. Some were sick or old and worked only an hour before having to stop. Others could manage no more than to make sandwiches and lemonade.

But Abraham arrived at dawn and worked all day. He outpaced me, and I was thirty years younger. He repaired the soffits and painted the high, difficult places. You could tell that he had done this kind of work all his life.

He had retired from the aluminum plant the year before. "When I came home from Vietnam I settled right here in Red Buck," he said. "They made me a welder. It ain't easy to weld aluminum, but I was good at it."

He married the first girl he saw and never lived a happy day. His wife bore him a son with Down syndrome, and the years of coping with the boy sapped her energies. When the child died, at sixteen, she took to her bed and didn't leave it again, living out her days in a fog of alcohol, antidepressants, and soap operas. "'Get up!' I'd tell her," Abraham said. "'Woman, where is our life?'"

An outdoorsman, he spent many days away from Red Buck, camping along the Piney River, and in Idaho, he'd tried to find the same wilderness Lewis and Clark had. I think that many times his loneliness nearly drove him insane.

He'd found no solace touring his origins in Iowa. The farmhouse where he grew up had been gutted and abandoned. He did not recognize the town where he had gone to school, and the school itself was gone. His relatives were dead except for cousins and their children, and they did not know his name. The beautiful girl he almost married before the war had made a bad marriage, divorced, and fled to California.

Abraham took me to his house one night and it was like entering a museum, with all the bucks and bighorns he'd mounted and rifles bristling on the walls. He hadn't touched his wife's things. He lived between the kitchen and the living room, where he watched television, ate, and slept.

Abraham brewed coffee and we sat, two lonely men, talking until midnight. "I'd take the boy with me sometimes because he liked the outdoors," he said. "He'd sit by the fire and sing Beatles songs."

I wondered how many times he'd had this conversation with himself, blaming himself for his dead family. "I wanted him to be strong, to stand on his own two feet! I made him try to fire the rifle, but he couldn't even hold it right. And he couldn't take the kick." He stared at me angrily. "Reverend, I screamed at him. I said he was a runt—and an idiot."

My own father, who died when I was a child, would have been Abraham's age. It was odd to counsel an older man. "We are not saints," I told him. "You should not—"

He drew a rifle from the rack. "I shoved this against his shoulder and I said, 'Don't you cry! Don't you cry!' And he didn't. He held it like this. He held it *right!*" Abraham shouldered the rifle and aimed toward a window. I was afraid that he'd fire it.

"I meant to tell him, I meant to say rest it on a tree limb if it's too heavy, and then you breathe in, and breathe out, and hold your breath, and squeeze the trigger. But it went off! I don't know if somehow he brushed the trigger, but it went off, and he fell down backwards kind of, and hit his head on a tent peg. He never woke up."

Sometimes men bear such awful burdens that nothing you can say is adequate. Perhaps it helped simply to tell his story. Weeks passed, and I grew used to finding him sitting in the darkened church, reading the Bible. He wanted to know of prophecy.

"When the Rapture comes, Reverend, and some don't go. Do you read that those who hold to the faith can still be saved?"

"Yes." It was a strange question, though I appreciated his interest in religion. "But it will be a terrible time."

Abraham made a steeple from cypress he had planned to use for still another gun rack. I sat watching as he angled the boards with his table saw, then hand sanded the edges until you couldn't see the cracks. It was the last thing needed to make the garage look like a church. "Amazing work," I told him.

"I could have been an artist."

The steeple was too heavy for one man, so two of our old men cranked it to the roof with a come-along, careful not to damage it. Abraham and I carried it to the apex, because I was fearful those old fellows would take a fall. The air was pure up there. You could see all the way to the countryside.

"Thank you, Brother Abraham," I said, as we bolted the steeple down. "An artist is exactly what you are."

"This is just cabinet work, Reverend. I could have been a real artist. A *painter*. I was accepted at the Kansas City Art Institute."

I didn't know if this was impressive or not. "What happened?"

"My dad wouldn't let me go. He needed me on the farm, and he thought drawing pictures was a lot of foolishness. I stayed home for two years and then run off to the army."

"Well, you have done the Lord's work, Abraham. It's a beautiful steeple."

We climbed down and the four of us contemplated the steeple. It sat straight and reached up a respectable twelve feet. It didn't shine in the sun or light up at night. It was humble, like our church.

One of the old men said, "That's awright, Brother Abraham."

Abraham looked up, too. "Yes," he said. "I think it will do."

And then he was gone. He had no phone; I dropped by his house, looking for his truck, but found no sign of him. Down along the Piney, I thought, fishing. Or maybe he'd gone to West Texas, where I believe he had a friend from the war. I left a note on his door: "Everyone at Red Buck Full Gospel loves your steeple. We miss you at service! Pastor Tom Hovey."

And then I had no time to be lonely, for someone else took over my thoughts. A dark-haired woman in expensive clothes began attending, and I am not so dense about these matters that I could not understand why. It was the pastor who interested her, not his sermons.

Dear Lord, I was vulnerable. I still thought about Mavis, and sometimes I found myself staring at women on the streets. They'd stare back in amusement, occasionally in outrage—bringing me to my senses. I must be above this, I told myself. I am not a priest, but I am a man of God.

Melinda attended faithfully for six weeks, but I might never have said more to her than "Good morning, Sister." One Sunday as I stood beneath Abraham's steeple, shaking hands, she leaned near enough I could smell her perfume. She pressed a note into my hand: "Come to dinner Tuesday."

And soon, it was dinner every night. She was a lawyer's ex-wife, and I did not know what she saw in me, unless it was that our church had begun to succeed, and she admired our work. She lived on a high hill above the river, and you could see all the town. We sat on a patio beside the sunken hot tub the lawyer had installed.

"This fall I'll be teaching school again," she said.

"That's good, Melinda!"

"Yes. I don't want to waste any more time, you know, *acquiring* things. I want to give something back. And I look at those poor women—the ones you help, Tom—"

"You help just by coming, Melinda."

"Excuse me for a moment," she said, and slipped into the dim interior of her house, while I sat contemplating the sunset, grateful for this lovely woman's fellowship.

She returned wearing a robe. She let it fall, startling me with her nakedness, and then slipped into the tub.

"Melinda! This is—!"

"Sin?"

I could barely speak. "I . . . think so."

"Then you'll have to marry me, Pastor Hovey."

"Oh," I said, nodding. I rose and looked down on her there in the water. It had been quite some time since my divorce.

One night as my new wife and I were returning from dinner I saw a light in the church. "Stay in the car," I told her, but she was right behind me.

I entered through the abandoned apartment—which we'd transformed to a daycare center—so that I could creep up on the intruder. I crawled behind the pulpit, feeling like an intruder myself.

But we had no reason to call the police. It was Abraham, his shadow dancing down the long wall that I had painstakingly scrubbed and painted. He'd trained a floodlight stage center, where he had painted our Lord and Savior. To the left and right of Jesus, the twelve disciples sat at a long table, exactly like Leonardo da Vinci's original except that Abraham's painting was fourteen feet high and almost forty long.

I walked among the pews, angry, but for the moment unable to speak. Melinda—who had kicked off her shoes and seemed quite short, suddenly—slipped from behind and put an arm around me.

I had some idea, of course, what my poor friend had been through. "Abraham is crazy," I whispered. "We can . . . paint over it."

"Paint over it!"

"This is God's house, Melinda."

"And isn't that—that wonderful painting—an act of worship?"

Yes. Yes, it was. The painting was only a copy of a great idea, and Abraham was an amateur, though the way he'd mixed colors was startling, and the expressions on faces were, well, like the expressions you'd see on the streets of Red Buck. His Jesus wasn't Leonardo da Vinci's Jesus. A man of many burdens, surely, but an ordinary man with gray hair.

He had been painting for three days. He did not see us; he did not see anything but his work. He held up his hands like claws in the harsh light and made a devilish shadow.

It became clear why the Lord spoke to me that night by the railcars. Our little church of the homeless was famous. Abraham's painting interested not just the local paper but papers across the Ozarks and a network television show. As if I had something to do with it, I was interviewed again and again.

The church was full every Sunday, and donations come in so heavily that we bought another abandoned building and refurbished it into apartments for the poor. Melinda showed great ability with our finances, and we looked for new church sites in West Plains, Poplar Bluff, and finally even Springfield.

And yet there was no end to sadness, because Abraham had disappeared yet again. Every day I drove by his house, but only God could say where he had gone.

Eight months after Abraham finished his painting, I had a call from Sergeant Giles Moore of the Red Buck police. Abraham had been arrested for driving on the wrong side of the road. He was sober and yet insisted that the wrong side was the right side. Some weeks before, the sergeant said, Abraham had called to complain that he had a prowler and that the prowler had discharged a firearm. But a neighbor had seen Abraham carrying a rifle and breaking into his own house, in which he had not lived for months. He had been sleeping in his truck in a campsite on the Piney—living on the fish he caught. Probably cold weather drove him to town.

I could understand why, in Abraham's mind, he was an intruder in his own home. "He's so lonely," I told the sergeant. "So lonely he doesn't know who he is."

I went down to the station but Abraham could not speak. In the weeks afterwards I visited him at the veterans home and couldn't be sure that he knew me. I left him my New Testament and the Barry Sadler novels from his house, but I doubt that he could read them.

He died in January, and when I preached his funeral I finally allowed myself to see, from the way the light filtered down out of the beams cut from those old trees, that the Judas in the painting resembled Abraham. "Jesus and Judas," I said suddenly, interrupting my eulogy, but the congregation, which included every minister in town, the city council, and a reporter from St. Louis, did not notice that I had paused, or see what I saw.

The Truth

Kimberly Kells accepted the Lord Jesus Christ as her personal savior at the age of eleven, the Sunday after what she thought of as her drunken Saturday night revel, when she drank three beers at her friend Trudy's house during a sleepover. Trudy, more daring, got into her father's whiskey and grew quite jolly and mad until she vomited over her grandmother's quilt. Trudy promptly passed out, leaving Kim to scrub the quilt and meditate upon the broad path that leadeth to destruction.

Kim stepped forward at the Sunday evening service, cried softly, hopelessly, lovingly that she was a black-hearted sinner in general, then later, to the wide-eyed youth pastor, confessed her specific sins. She drank three beers. She'd ridiculed chubby Erica Sizemore's attempts at running during gym class. She'd stolen a bottle of nail polish from Trudy while Trudy slept off the whiskey. Oh, to be free of the burden of sin!

Jesus, his eyes on the sparrow, forgave her. His love washed over Kim, and she resolved to serve Him, and try to be worthy, until that day when every Christian was called home.

And yet, how did one live? Of course, you studied the Scriptures, and listened to pastors and teachers, but Kim needed a guiding principle. In ninth grade she found one, in the words of Jesus in John 8:32: "Ye shall know the truth, and the truth shall make you free." At first Kim thought this meant she should blurt out that her father had atrocious table manners, chewing with his mouth open, spilling soup on his shirt; and that she'd seen Judy Bender, the algebra teacher, kissing pot-bellied Coach Hazeltine; and that once when she tried to sell Girl Scout cookies to Miriam Frears, the bachelorette who lived two houses down, the woman came to the door half-naked and, well, *not* drunk. Stoned. Kim hardly knew what "stoned" meant, but somehow the word popped into her head when Miriam bought nine boxes of Peanut Butter Patties.

Kim soon discovered that pointing out such truths made people angry with her, causing them to point out *her* faults, such as that she was rude, and vengeful, and much, much too young to understand. You had to be careful with the truth. It was dynamite. Kim needed a corollary and had only to turn to Jesus: "Judge not, that ye be not judged."

Once she ceased to judge, Kim acquired the reputation of a genuine, "nice" girl. Other girls brought her their troubles, and Kim offered advice—and Bible verses—upon request. More often, she simply listened—uncomprehending, even dumbfounded, but she appeared wise for not talking. Kim's devotion to the truth, and refusal to judge, worked well as guiding principles until she reached college—and met Blake Lee.

Blake played shortstop on a scholarship and told Kim right away that he was "all field, no hit." He was an acrobat across the infield, but couldn't hit breaking balls. He managed an even .270 for their Christian college team, mastering bunts and almost delicately dropping in singles off the league's fastballs. Pretty clearly—Blake held no illusions—he'd never turn pro.

But Blake enjoyed hanging out with the guys, tossing back a beer or two, schmoozing—you had to, really, if you wanted to get along in the world. His dad, Eli, was a schmoozer, too, a CPA well connected with his Chamber of Commerce, a forward-looking man, Eli insisted, though rock-solid when it came to basic American values. Eli was a bore and a boor, and his example wasn't enough for Blake, who was idealistic. He wanted "to work with young people," which meant he'd coach, and teach American history, if he were doomed to a high school job.

Certainly, Blake was a Christian—he could not have qualified as Kim's boyfriend otherwise. And her parents approved of him, though once she overheard her father say to her mother, "Too good to be true."

Blake's parents approved of Kim as well, Blake's dad even making a pass one lively, loose Saturday night down in a basin by the Piney River, under the rustling cottonwoods near the end of a dry spell, couples drifting along, schmoozing, at the edge of firelight. "You're awright," Eli said, pressing against her suddenly, unbuttoning two buttons of her blouse so quickly she didn't resist. Then Kim ran up the hill, sat in the car, locked the doors, while the coyotes howled out their woes like a Greek chorus on the lone prair-ree.

Kim didn't believe in sex before marriage and neither did Blake, but they were young. After many fumbling, futile episodes, during which Kim's tugging those shortstop hands away from her breasts became a kind of caress, Blake pulled down his sweatpants. Kim couldn't help but look, because she'd never seen a man's genitals, but then turned her head. She wasn't sure if she felt excited or nauseated.

"Put your hand on it."

She had never truly encountered evil, but now maybe she had. "Blake, this isn't you. This isn't us. We—"

For an instant, he subdued his panting. "We're getting married, aren't we?"

"But *before* we're married—"

"It's not sex, Kim. It's foreplay. Bible don't say a thing about foreplay."

There was something in the Old Testament about onanism, and maybe that's what this was, but anyhow they weren't struck dead. Unskilled at first, she soon found "the right angle," as Blake put it, and he writhed on the bucket seat, or couch, or bed, before collapsing.

"Aw, I'm sorry," Blake said. "You're such a nice girl, and I'm *not* nice. I'm really bad."

Kim knew she'd become a fallen woman, but wasn't it all out of love? Her doubts subsided in June, after graduation, when they were married. A storybook marriage. Kim found work teaching second grade at a Christian school in Bentonville, Arkansas, while Blake secured a more prestigious job: assistant women's volleyball coach at the university.

Married, Kim lost her fear of showing herself naked, of intimacy—and really, the act of sex didn't amount to much. She just lay there, relaxed, while Blake thrust his hairy body above her, until he fell away in a stupor. Nothing more required of her, Kim went off to the bathroom to stare into the mirror.

As if on a timetable, their couplings resulted in a pregnancy, and Kim, after the normal joys and travails, gave birth to a seven-pound, six-ounce little girl they named Esther. Esther learned to walk when she was supposed to, learned to talk when she was supposed to, and knew how to read as she began kindergarten—this last, no doubt, because of Kim's devotion.

Kim loved to dress Esther in white or yellow dresses, white stockings, and black buckle shoes. As a family, going up the church steps hand in hand, they made a beautiful picture. Like some old painting, she thought.

She wanted a second child, perhaps a boy this time, but Blake no longer seemed interested in sex. Kim supposed this was what happened to old marrieds, and she led an idyllic life in most respects.

Kim hardly saw her husband during volleyball season, and her evenings stretched out with only the TV for company. Once Esther had fallen peacefully to sleep, she indulged herself with a bottle of wine and a weepy movie. The King James Bible said, "Drink no longer water, but use a little wine for thy stomach's sake and thine often infirmities." Kim was never sick, but the verse was widely thought to be a blessing on wine for straight-laced Christians, really a harmless vice, if vice at all.

Blake bought a motorcycle, touting its gas mileage and how its small size meant that he could park outside his campus office. Kim rode behind him once, but hated it. Motorcycles were dirty, noisy, barely short of violent, and she preferred the comfortable hum of her Camry. Certainly, Blake could have a motorcycle if he wanted. Kim didn't want to be one of *those* wives. As her colleagues at the school said, men needed their toys.

After Blake became head coach he was gone even more. His games and recruiting duties took him all over Oklahoma and Texas. He was an important man and Kim was proud of him.

Kim loved her daughter, she loved her little students, and she loved her church, but sometimes, she wondered if there was more in life. A Christian needed to give something back, and perhaps in the process spread the gospel word.

She learned of a program for homeless teens, signed up for training, and joined with other well-meaning folks to provide hot meals, conversation, and board games on Thursday nights. She held high the thought that they'd all been abused and that with quiet encouragement, with tutoring, that at least some of them could find their way back into the mainstream. If she could guide just one troubled soul out of darkness!

Most, however, seemed unaware of their predicament. They flitted between programs, interested only in handouts. Kim heard several compare the meals offered by the Catholics versus other denominations. The consensus was that the evangelicals brought better food, but the Catholics hassled you less about Jesus.

One of the Catholics was a seminary student named Austin, a gentle, earnest, dreamy young man she assumed was gay. Austin was easy to talk to. The kids liked him, while they never warmed to Kim no matter what she tried. She knew they thought she was a Goody Two-Shoes from the suburbs, while Austin seemed one of them, almost. He'll make a good priest, Kim thought.

One night when they were near to closing—only Austin and Kim remained—she discovered Heather Briggs on the floor of the girls' bathroom. Heather was covered with tattoos and piercings and was ordinarily a snarling beast of a girl, but now she lay comatose. Kim screamed, and as Austin came running, Heather began to convulse, beating her head on the concrete.

Austin tossed her his phone. "Call 911!"

As Kim did, Austin knelt by Heather's side, cupped her head in a palm, and reached into her mouth to pull out her tongue. "Could you find a pillow?" he called out—with amazing calmness.

Kim knelt, too, to scoot the pillow under the girl's head. Heather seemed not to breathe, but then gasped and reached up with a powerful flailing. She struck Austin with the back of a hand, but then they held her down. Heather's breasts heaved and her eyes opened once, her dilated pupils like miniature black suns. The medics arrived and, clumsily but quickly, slapped oxygen to Heather's face and transferred her to a backboard. Kim dropped heavily to the couch outside.

Austin put an arm around her shoulders. "You were terrific," he whispered.

Kim looked up through her tears. "I was so scared. I—"

"Heather will be fine," he said, and kissed her forehead.

And with his kind face so near, Kim kissed his lips. Thinking back, she felt that he hesitated before kissing her, too. But who did what became unclear in her tears and rising excitement. She lay on the couch, while he pulled off her skirt and she peeled back her top. Then he was shirtless atop her, his chest slender but muscular. Such an elegant man, she thought. She clasped her hands behind his neck and didn't realize at first that he was inside her. Then she lifted her legs and tugged at him, and moaned, because never had it been like this with Blake. Meanwhile, Austin's face twisted with ecstasy, and regret.

In the days following, Kim tried out several sophisticated theories. Number one, it was meant to happen, as in one right person exists for you in all the Universe; number two, Austin was in reality a prince of darkness, hiding behind his almost-priesthood, preying upon vulnerable women; number three, sin was everywhere, among Christians, too, and if you dropped your guard even for a moment, it gobbled you up; and number four, this was how the world worked, people coming together not as perfect mates but randomly, with sex the inevitable byproduct.

She returned to the troubled teens once more, but couldn't find Austin. She resisted calling Austin's seminary, sensing his absence was a message, that she was as much trouble for him as he for her. Now, the correct attitude seemed to be that sex between them had been an accident, resulting from the stress of the moment. Of course, if she hadn't secretly been lusting after Austin, and he after her, the accident might not have happened.

This analysis, seeming true, profoundly depressed her, and she went about in a daze, not eating properly, almost speechless, unable to meet the eyes of her colleagues—all of whom, she was sure, stared knowingly. And of course she had to deal with Blake, who began to act self-consciously around her.

He'd leap up to do the dishes and sometimes brought home fancy steaks to grill. He bought her a series of books on the Amish that she'd professed an interest in. He bought her perfume, which she dabbed on religiously. With sex on her mind, it occurred to her they hadn't made love in weeks, and she took the initiative, climbing on top, sometimes. Blake seemed surprised and—she couldn't help but think—distressed.

The principles she'd adhered to in college returned to her, and Kim got her heart right with Jesus, sobbing and praying, and drinking wine, through a long weekend when Blake left for Boulder. Jesus forgave her, as always. He didn't judge her. She could lie with another man, with five men, and still He would forgive her.

But she wasn't free. Though it put her marriage on the line, she knew she had to tell Blake what she'd done. He was a godly man, and she hoped that he, too, would judge not, lest he be judged. She'd explain, somehow, that it had been an accident. Oh, yes, sin! But if you could even call it an affair, it was over as soon as it began.

Marriage was hard work, she'd say. Didn't people say that? She knew she could have been a better wife, and now she would be. She'd go along on some of his tournaments. Maybe they could take a motorcycle trip together.

That night Blake came home early, burst in full of false cheer, but with that look in his eyes. He knew. You couldn't fool a husband, at least *she* couldn't. She reached for the words: "Blake, we have to talk."

And he said the same thing: "Kim, we have to talk."

She sank to the kitchen table and watched in amazement as he drew a bottle of wine from his briefcase. He pointed to it meaningfully, but she shook her head. Her sweet Riesling. Her favorite label. He *knew.* He'd known all along, and now—

"There's just no other way to say this, Kim. I've found someone else."

She almost wanted to comfort him. As he talked, she poured herself a glass of wine and nodded understandingly, as wonder passed over his face that she didn't grow angry. He told of the many affairs he'd had, with students sometimes, risking his job, and with a coach down in Texas, and when she still didn't respond he grew more confident, because his unfaithfulness had taught him a lesson. Now he had the courage, you might even say the moral fiber, to make a stand with the love of his life, Alice, an art instructor right across campus. Of course, Kim, you're a wonderful woman. You're a wonderful *mother.* But we were so young, so much was ahead of us, and maybe, well, I'm not saying we made the wrong decision, but—

After a while she heard a door close. Alone with the truth, she gulped the wine Blake had so thoughtfully provided. For years afterward, she wondered how such an indifferent husband could have thought of the wine, the exact, German vintage she preferred, when never once had she drunk in his presence, when she carefully wrapped the empties in plastic sacks and buried them deep in the trash. She finished the bottle, leaving it on the table for anyone, for no one, to see. She looked in on Esther and staggered to bed.

Take the Man Out and Shoot Him

Birdy Blevins was New Jerusalem's best marksman. Guns felt as natural as hands to him, and he gave no more thought to aiming and firing than to hammering a nail or bringing down a hoe. Once, in time for Thanksgiving, he killed two turkeys with shotgun slugs. Not birdshot, but slugs! He messed up with the hen, hitting it in the breast. But he blew off the tom's head—incredible, people told him, because a turkey's head was never still.

Birdy had turned twenty and wanted to join the army, but Top claimed the army was a complicated place these days, that sometimes you didn't know if your orders came from your company commander or the United Nations. And the army had filled up with females. "I'm all for equal rights, but a woman just don't belong in certain situations."

"What situations?" Birdy asked.

"We was in Bosnia, don't personally see why but it ain't for a soldier to say; you gotta follow orders. I'm not suggesting most jobs, a woman cain't do 'em, only you put a man and a woman together under the stress of combat, what you thinks gonna happen?"

"What happened?"

"Close order discipline," Top muttered. "Cain't have no army without it."

Birdy suspected that Top just couldn't let him go. Maybe he didn't believe that Birdy could make it on his own, even though he was grown up now and had in mind a profession. Top was a wise old man, but some of his pronouncements didn't make much sense.

What was so wrong about having a woman in your unit? Particularly a woman Birdy's own age?

Sometimes, Top trusted him to run errands in Eureka Springs, and Birdy watched TV at Walmart. He stayed in the TV department so long that a clerk chased him off. But thanks to Top and his insistence that he study the Bible, Birdy could read better than he used to, and he walked right over to the magazine rack. Between the TV and the magazines he learned that the army fought wars all over the world. From what Birdy could tell, soldiers were mostly men, anyhow the ones carrying M-16s, though there were lots of girls who were nurses or even helicopter pilots.

The recruiter's office stood at the far end of a strip mall not far from the Walmart. Birdy sat in his truck studying the soldiers inside and sometimes walked casually by, but so far he hadn't gone inside.

One of the recruiters was a blonde female. She spied Birdy through the big window and walked toward the door—stepped onto the sidewalk, smiled, beckoned. She looked good, and she liked him! As if learning to walk, Birdy took a step forward, but then bolted up the street. Despite how it must have seemed, he wasn't afraid of the recruiter. He wanted what she wanted, but couldn't hurt Top. He owed him everything.

In the bad old days, to the extent that he remembered them, Birdy was high on methamphetamine most of the time. At last, over in Fayetteville, they threw him in jail for dealing crystal to some college kids, one of whom turned out to be a policeman. And it was Top, bringing God's holy word to prisoners all across Arkansas, who sprang him.

Birdy had learned about Jesus and being saved long before, at the Granderson Treatment Center. If you went on about religion there, they treated you better, and he came to think of Jesus as his ace in the hole. Sometimes, he forgot about it, but down deep still believed he could be redeemed. He said, "I'd rather burn in hell than go back to Shannon County."

Shannon County, Missouri, was where he and his Uncle Gabe used to live. When Birdy was twelve Gabe claimed him out of Granderson, but he was a cruel man. He wanted Birdy to do all the chores on his farm, while he cooked meth and entertained his girl-friends.

"Aw, son," Top said, and placed his big palm on Birdy's head and offered up a ferocious prayer. He said there was a place for Birdy in New Jerusalem, if he promised to study the Bible and never use drugs again. Almost five years had passed. They'd both kept their word.

Top fought in Vietnam. His army never lost a battle, but they lost the war nonetheless, because of the politicians selling out the soldiers. Standing up in Congress and calling them baby burners? You think that didn't have an effect? Morale dropped off the charts, black men fought white men for a place in the chow line, and new recruits were nothing but criminals and dope fiends.

Even so, America was a great country and Top was proud to serve. He liked army food, and long marches, and even the quiet Sundays, when the barracks emptied out and he sat reading Louis L'Amour out in the middle of the buffed green floor. Slowly, it occurred to him: he liked *peace,* not war. And during the peaceful 1970s he made grade all the way to first sergeant.

A fine achievement for a kid out of the hills, but after first sergeant the ranks became intensely competitive. Or maybe the word was "political." He performed adequately in service schools, but was always thought to be "outstanding," rather than "truly outstanding" or "exceptional." Somehow, the army had changed yet again. Pay increased, and the quality of the recruits, all of them volunteers, improved. These new soldiers were at ease with the fancy new equipment, with its digital displays, remote operation, and fussy maintenance. Precious few of them had even heard of Louis L'Amour. They didn't read much of anything. They played games on their telephones.

Many were family men. When more females came into the service, more marriages resulted, and more babies.

Top didn't hate women. He hated that when he pointed out obvious problems, people *said* he hated women. The official line was that you treated them just like men, but women befuddled him with their peculiar brand of valor, and their strange plumbing. He acknowledged women made good soldiers, but the army, at least among enlisted personnel, had always been a bachelor service. For Top, a priesthood.

He knew he was out-of-date. Deployed to Iraq near the end of a hitch, he didn't have anything to offer. In his opinion, only a weekend warrior such as George Bush, a drunk and a braggart, could think of war as holy. Top couldn't bear to see those pretty female lieutenants getting their legs blown off and their brains bashed.

It was his fault, not the army's. He'd grown soft and full of grieving for his old army. He declined his new hitch, hoping his thirty-six-year-old major would protest and beg him to stay. He stood at attention as she thumbed through a stack of papers. A parade of fine hairs, the ghost of a moustache, sprouted above her lips. He'd never noticed.

At last she looked up. "We'll miss you, First Sergeant," she said. "Thank you for your years of service."

That night in his quarters, in this desert so near the Holy Land, he began again to read his mother's Bible, which he'd carried from Vietnam to Ft. Leonard Wood to Iraq. He fell to his knees and had a long conversation with the Lord. And God said to him, these are the last days. You must go and prepare the people.

America was a Christian nation but had lost its way. Me, me, me, the people said, filling their fat faces at buffets. They worshipped football and beer, big trucks and big boats and semi-automatic rifles. And drugs! Dear Lord, you couldn't count the ruined lives. These people, these sad people, didn't even know the world was coming apart. Shrewd, worldly, *evil* men had purloined the government, twisting the words of the Founding Fathers to advance socialism. Who among the people knew? They knew what they saw on television, and nothing was on television except those Babylonian twins, money and sex.

Now the politicians meant to institute one-world government through the United Nations and the Council on Foreign Relations.

Quickly, indeed, the world moved toward Tribulation, that time of plagues and universal sorrow when the Antichrist ruled. Perhaps Arkansas, far from power, was not such a bad place to be.

"Home, Lord?" Top asked.

This time God was silent, and anyhow Top had lost confidence in himself as a leader. Like McArthur, he'd fade away. Unlike McArthur, Top would be happy in obscurity and maybe find true peace before he died. He'd raise chickens and vegetables and fruit and preach to those who had ears.

He bought eight hundred acres on a blacktopped farm road south of Eureka Springs. Trees and big rocks covered the land, and he had hardly any neighbors. He lived in a travel trailer without plumbing, using a portable generator for lights and, before he understood it to be a tool of the devil, his computer. He shored up the lopsided barn and established a herd of dairy goats. Goats could eat almost anything and pound for pound produced more milk than a cow. He learned the art of cheese making and found an organic market to stock it.

He grew a long white beard, an expression of freedom after his years of military grooming and wore the same olive drab T-shirt day after day, the same Tyson baseball cap. For days he spoke to no one, but he named his goats and berated and praised them like recruits.

One morning he woke and realized how lonely he was. Or more precisely: how much he enjoyed talking, and how badly he needed listeners.

He bought a defunct pottery studio in Eureka Springs. He renamed it "Top's Shop," and tried to sell geodes that he picked up on his place, along with goat cheese and produce. He sold Christian books, and that led to printing up tracts on the evils of taxes, the global warming hoax, conspiracies from Washington and Wall Street, and the Antichrist.

Men gathered on Wednesday nights, sometimes only two or three. They talked about deer rifles, maybe some politics, never women. All that changed one night after Top had settled into bed with his Bible, when he heard a rattling on the storefront door. Eureka Springs had little crime, but behind him his grandfather clock chimed midnight like a warning. Top opened the door with a baseball bat grasped in one hand.

She came right in, a stout woman with straight gray hair. "My name's Flora Barnett," she said. "My son's trying to get me tonight."

Flora cried, and Top never had known what to do with a woman's tears. He might have put his arms around her, but one hand still held the bat. "Your boy wants to hurt you?"

"Not his true self, but he uses meth-am-*phet*-a-mine when he cain't find work. Timmy's been in prison? I know him, he'll take money right out of my purse, he'll sell everything I own, and I'm just barely on my feet since Big Bob died."

"We could call the police."

"Speaking as his mother, I cain't bring myself to do that." Flora dabbed at her eyes with a Kleenex. "Don't you think I'm safe here in the house of God? With you protecting me?"

Top sighed. He didn't know what to say. "Maybe I could make us some tea."

"That would be wonderful."

Flora had heard Top speak several times, but never introduced herself. "I allus been a shy person," she said.

"Yes, ma'am."

"But where does a Christian woman go nowadays to seek out the truth? You cain't find a church no more where they preach the true gospel. You are a wonderful speaker."

"Well, thank you, ma'am. I just try to follow where the Lord leads."

"Amen." She patted his shoulder. "I can play the piano."

"Yes, ma'am."

"The Bible says, make a joyful noise unto the Lord."

"That's true enough, Sister. I play the guitar a little bit."

"You could join right in. Before you know it, we'd have a choir and a men's singing group like the Statler Brothers. I got a piano which the Lord has moved in my life to donate."

"That's awful generous. Only, I don't imagine—"

"I had it stored because I suspected Timmy was gonna sell it. That boy has broke my heart."

Flora's eyes welled again, and Top said, "Yes, ma'am."

"We could get some of these big, strapping men you got in the congregation and haul it on over here."

Turned out that Sister Flora and her piano was exactly what Top needed, at least if he wanted to start a church. Pretty soon, just like Sister Flora said, Top's Shop had a choir—and women, lots of women with their husbands, and kids crawling along the baseboards. Top's Shop couldn't hold them all.

So Top moved back to the hills, and the people brought in venison roasts and blackberry pies, and still more people came, until, with winter coming on, the leaky revival tent wasn't adequate, either. In just three weeks, the men erected a bright blue pole barn with a shiny, aluminum steeple. And Top preached and preached, because the multitudes hungered for the truth.

That's when Top had his big idea.

Every year in Eureka Springs the Helen Burkett Foundation ran a passion play, where literally hundreds of young people played out the tragic, glorious story of Jesus in a grand outdoor theater. It was extremely artistic and deeply moving, but it was also a profitable business. Pilgrims came from all over the United States and from Sweden and Japan. They paid the ticket price, bought popcorn and soft drinks, and took away a DVD and a coffee mug for their next stop, Branson, and its octogenarian warblers.

Top's great idea was a Christian theme park, which he called New Jerusalem. Soon his congregation carved out a road through the woods and fashioned replicas of the manger where Christ was born, the terrible hill of Golgotha, and even the Sea of Galilee.

The Sea of Galilee was really just a farm pond. Much work remained in God's kingdom.

A year after the great founding, Luke Muldoon drifted in. "Call me 'Lucky,'" he said, though he didn't appear to be.

Luke was a veteran, too, of the endless Middle Eastern wars. He'd lived in Denver and Tallahassee and Chicago. In Chicago, he had some trouble with the police, something about missing cash at a 7-Eleven, but he got off with community service because of his military record. He took a carpenter's job with the city of Memphis, but then his new record caught up with him, and maybe there was a day or two when he was too drunk to stay on a roof.

Lucky worked like the devil, seeing in Top's vision not only a way to spread God's word but a major role for himself. He knew something about construction and earth moving and put the men to work sculpting concrete walls and excavating holes for septic tanks. He supervised renditions of a typical Jewish home, Christ's tomb, strategic sites along the River Jordan, and an enlarged Sea of Galilee, stocked with white bass and hybrid bluegill, where tourists were welcome to fish. He paved the road, but still you wound your way under massive oaks and felt you'd dropped back in time. Then you pulled into a paved parking place entirely adequate for your RV and sought out one of Brother Luke's clean, modern bathrooms, complete with hot showers.

Lucky even found a place for Top's goat herd. They made fine props in the Ancient Jewish Village.

To Top's surprise, if not Luke's, tourists came in numbers that over a season rivaled passion play attendance. New Jerusalem even boasted entries in secular tour guides, and Sister Flora had to run a little office to take reservations. Luke bought a fine, air-conditioned bus to transport life-weary senior citizens, who made pilgrimages from as far away as Dallas, and he devised still more attractions to include the expulsion of two of New Jerusalem's more nubile young people (not actually naked, of course) from the Garden of Eden, and Top's own descent, bearing tablets, from Mt. Sinai. For this, Top shed his green T-shirts and donned a flowing white robe.

Sister Flora led worshippers into the tomb of Jesus, a damp, rock-and-concrete bunker carved out of the hillside with dynamite and a backhoe. She spoke in hushed tones, and even the brattiest children grew quiet. "Where they lay his *body*," she whispered, and wept in the silence, which went on so long others wept, too. Then Flora cried out, "And was gloriously resurrected! Oh, how long can He tarry?"

In one of his sermons, Top raved that everyone owned everything, and no one owned anything. The idea of property was meaningless when it all belonged to God, and when one's true home was in Heaven. Top held a lot of crazy notions; even those who loved him said so. But Brother Luke pinned him down on this one, drafting rules for new members regarding the surrender of their assets. They announced the new arrangement on a Sunday: Top, the patriarch, with his wispy white beard and blue eyes, looking upward to Heaven; Luke with his full black beard and dark eyes, opening wide his arms.

Over several months, working with a bulldozer and crew of men, Luke built a bridge over the River Jordan and cut a road north, stopping at the mouth of two shut-ins where springs flowed and where evidence remained of a homestead from more than a century before. Here he laid out his wilderness town.

Luke encouraged Top to place himself on high, in a fine cabin adjacent to the glass-and-cedar chapel overlooking New Jerusalem, a town of manufactured homes and rock-and-earth structures cut into the hillside. Cornfields, vegetable gardens, chicken coops, corrals of goats and milk cows and pigs, all testified to the rightness of Top's vision, and to God's infinite blessings.

In the dark hollow below, beneath an overhanging shelf of limestone, Luke took for himself a homesteader's cabin, rechinking the logs and hammering on a new roof of green sheet metal. Smoke issued from under the limestone, and at first people thought Luke brewed moonshine. "Sounds like a fine idea," he said. "But no, I'm smoking venison. Bring me your deer, and let's feed the multitudes!" Soon, Luke received offerings of calves and turkeys, and even a wild sow that Birdy Blevins shot and dragged through the woods. Luke asked nothing for his services, but men gathered around as once they'd come to Top's Shop, bringing their wives' biscuits and casseroles and staying to talk.

Men's and women's showers went up, a laundry room, and a great dinner hall. Everyone got along, because everyone loved Jesus—and maybe, too, because they came from jobs at Walmarts, tire shops, fast food restaurants, and franchise poultry farms. At New Jerusalem, they were building the Kingdom of God. New

Jerusalem was ordained, some thought, and quoted Bible verses to prove it. This was the very place where Jesus would return.

Luke posted work schedules every evening after worship, and it couldn't fairly have been said that he was a despot. He worked harder than almost anyone and took his turn at the worst jobs. Nor were the financial arrangements unfair. True, he required your initial assets, but for that you were awarded housing, food, and work. Some people took another job in town, from which they kept nine-tenths of their earnings, and if you needed time for your sick mother in Mountain View, that was all right, too. Brother Luke didn't even care if a bachelor headed off to Little Rock, for a no-questions-asked weekend.

Because he had no family, Birdy Blevins was consigned to the travel trailer Top had stayed in when he first bought the land. Like everyone else, he had electricity from the big diesel generators thumping in the distance, but the ground beneath the trailer was so uneven that Birdy couldn't make it level. He took the wheel off one side and dropped the springs to rest on flat stones, but still he couldn't find a place to sleep that didn't aim a little downhill.

And he didn't have TV or a computer, because Top, submitting to the will of Sister Flora, proclaimed them the work of the Devil. A TV wouldn't work anyhow, down in the hollow, but he bought a little DVD player that he watched under a blanket, drawing from his library of Salvation Army castoffs. His favorite actor was Sylvester Stallone, the loner, the ultimate soldier, true to the mission when higher-ups sold it out. Not in a lifetime could Birdy hope to match Stallone's muscles, but he could run just as fast. He was probably a better marksman, because Stallone never aimed at anything. He just shot off machine guns and threw grenades. But what a hero! In *Rambo III*, he cauterized a bullet wound with gunpowder. Even though he was Rambo, he screamed in agony. *Oh, no,* Birdy thought. *I couldn't do that.*

Birdy owned a battered Dodge pickup he'd been able to buy his third summer in New Jerusalem, when Top hired him out as a carpenter and sometimes as a face in the crowd at the passion play. Much of the time his truck was commandeered for New Jerusalem work, and if he headed to town on a Saturday night for the adventure of eating hamburgers and seeing a movie, Top chided him.

"I know you're restless," Top said. "I was, too, when I was your age. I'm on your side, but we're *both* on the Lord's side. If you have a dream, if you have a vision, if God calls you to the army, I sure won't get in your way. But you know where we stand. You know we made a bargain, Birdy."

"I don't want no drugs!"

Top hung his head. "I understand, son."

Top couldn't protect him forever. You couldn't avoid temptation even at the passion play—especially there. Some of the kids smoked marijuana in the parking lot; he'd seen them. He almost turned them in, but forgot to when he fell in love with the blonde playing Mary Magdalene, Trish Barber. Birdy thought it was love. All day long he wandered in a trance not so different from religious ecstasy.

Trish was a senior at Central Baptist College in Conway. Because she had a major part, she hardly condescended to work on the set. She trounced about in shorts so short and tops so tight that surely she violated some Baptist precept, but no one said anything. After all, Mary Magdalene had been a fallen woman.

Loving Mary, or Trish, only made Birdy miserable. He broke into a sweat around her and couldn't talk. He was conscious of his old clothes, the fact he'd never been anywhere, taken courses such as Advanced World History, or seen any of the movies Trish raved about. He managed one word: "Rambo . . ."

"Rambo!" she said. "You're kidding!"

These were the only words she ever spoke to him, but he loved her all the more. She was a flower, a delicate scent. Everyone—every man, at least—perked up when Trish breezed through, trailing good cheer, wholesome Christian fellowship, and the promise, counterfeit as it must have been, of athletic sex.

Birdy stood in the shadows, summoning courage simply to enter her golden aura, when he heard her say to another girl: "So far

back in the hills he scrapes his knuckles on the way to the outhouse."

She might not have meant him, exactly, but a chasm opened before Birdy, as gloomy and unfathomable as Hell. He felt he could
go to college and take courses called Trish Barber, and Trish Barber
II, and Advanced Trish Barber, and never understand her in the least.
He felt he had no place in the world. He wanted to kill himself.

Soon after, he had the idea to shoot John Stone.

Three red cedar crosses, weathered and split, seemed stark enough
to represent the agonies of Golgotha, but then Top decided that
Birdy should play Jesus. Birdy's hair reached to his shoulders, and
when he took off his shirt he looked emaciated. Certainly, he evoked
sorrow, if only because he so hated being on display. He wondered
why Top sought to torture him.

Word came on the cell phones—that only those very close
to God were allowed to use—that a bus was soon to arrive, and he
hurried down from work on "The Defense of Masada." Masada,
where every Jew committed suicide rather than yield to Roman
tyranny, was the perfect metaphor for Top's view of the world, that
he was the leader of a gallant few soldiers standing against impossible odds.

The project involved moving great slabs of limestone to erect a
fortification wall, not to mention hauling up water for the concrete
of the garrison and city street. Luke, the foreman, could be a cruel
boss, and often the men complained. Pulling duty on Masada made
you feel like a convict breaking rocks, but still Birdy preferred it to
playing Jesus.

Miserably, he stripped, tied half of an old sheet around his
genitals, climbed up on the foot pegs, and slipped his wrists through
two leather straps. He closed his eyes and allowed his head to slump.
If a fly lit on his belly, he ignored it—or he shivered, as the long
summer at last turned to fall.

The rendition was realistic enough that tour guides had begun
to warn parents they might not want to bring along children, because Birdy and the two thieves frightened them.

On his right Brother Ronald squirmed, and moaned dramatically. He was a thin, worried little man who'd brought a worried wife and six children to New Jerusalem. Ronald never said much, never looked you in the eye, and maybe he was the one who taunted Christ. Birdy couldn't remember which thief was on the right, which on the left.

"How'd you get elected for this?" Luke Muldoon asked—from the cross to Birdy's left. Brother Muldoon had truly been a thief. Maybe he was the one whom Jesus forgave.

Birdy sketched his sad story. "I'd do anything for Top."

"He's a great man, but it don't mean every idea he has is divinely inspired."

"He's made a place here, almost a city."

"Him and lots of other folks. I give him credit, sure, but he's just a man, Birdy. Not God! Dressing up in Bible clothes and playing pretend, what kind of work is that? The world out there is coming apart at the seams. Some of us think we got to fight back."

Birdy didn't know how to respond. "I get awful bored, sometimes."

"Why don't you come on down to the cabin tonight, Birdy? You like beer?"

"Sure, I like beer, Brother Muldoon. Only Top—"

"Call me Lucky. We're friends, ain't we?"

"Top would say—"

"Nothin' wrong with a beer now and then." Luke laughed harshly. "For the stomach's sake."

Men gathering at Luke's cabin had become an institution, another sort of church where you didn't need to scrub up or show reverence. The humble aggressions of pitching horseshoes made every man gleeful, and even Top joined in the fun one evening, sniffing the chill air of the shut-in like an old hound.

Over time, horseshoes had given way to bows and arrows, then crossbows. This proved a practical amusement, because several men were skilled enough to kill deer.

Crossbows evolved to target practice with Luke's many rifles, which made sense, too, because guns were a more efficient way to bring down game. Firearms contributed to the camp's attempt to be self-sufficient, important because nearly everyone believed that soon you wouldn't be able to find fuel or food or clean water. Others thought that the federal government would force people into ghettos and that the only farms would be gigantic corporate enterprises such as Tyson.

"I want no part of *that,*" Luke said.

"No, sir," said Dale, another of the bachelors. He was a rangy, middle-aged fellow who lived in a trailer not much larger than Birdy's, though more level. In Springfield, Missouri, he'd tried to make a living selling junk copper and steel. New Jerusalem was a great improvement, because now he was a sub-foreman. You always knew what Dale would say: whatever Luke said. "Like Masada! We'll defend ourselves to the death!"

When the men began a regimen of calisthenics, wearing pieces of uniforms, running their obstacle course, and marching in a haphazard way, this seemed if not natural exactly then at least possible. And they didn't always practice war games. Most of the time they sat behind Luke's cabin and talked politics until midnight, as they drank beer and blackberry wine. Alcohol, combined with free talk, was the chief attraction for most of the men, who had long since exhausted whatever charm they had for their wives.

Top chose to ignore the beer drinking like the wise old sergeant he was. Possibly, he'd preach a sermon on the subject one day, but Luke had become a powerful force in New Jerusalem, almost as powerful as Top. You didn't challenge him on the small stuff.

Birdy, admitted to Luke's circle because of his marksmanship, held the men in deep awe, particularly Luke, who sometimes leapt to his feet and paced, gesturing wildly.

"One world," Luke declared.

"We know it's coming, Lucky!" called out Dale.

"The Tribulation! The world of the Antichrist, when men will cry for the mountains to fall upon them! It's coming, and here we, we . . . *sit.*"

"What would you have us do, Brother Luke?" asked Ronald, the other thief, the one who wouldn't meet you in the eye. "You know what Top thinks. He thinks we are on this earth a brief time. He thinks we live the best life we can and leave the rest to Jesus."

"I don't care what Top thinks!"

This was sacrilege, and Birdy gasped. The circle fell silent. No one stirred.

"He's a great man," Luke allowed. "But naive."

"What you mean?" Dale's voice sounded phony. He was loyal to Luke, but maybe not if it involved risk. Criticizing Top was risky.

"He mounts no defense against the enemy. And when you are outnumbered, the best defense is—"

Laughter broke out. But now Ronald whispered nervously, "Timothy McVeigh. He's your hero, I suppose."

"No hero of mine," said Tom, an Oklahoman, a mixed-blood Cherokee whose arguments with his wife could be heard all over the camp. He crunched his beer can in his fist. Tom was always angry. He was angry if you smiled or frowned or cleared your throat, and Birdy avoided him.

"Timothy McVeigh was a fool," Luke said. "I knew him at Ft. Riley."

The faces, all on the border of darkness, poked toward the fire like a ring of ghosts. Their breath steamed in the November air. Brother Ronald said, "You knew Timothy McVeigh?"

"Tim understood one thing: there's a war going on. It's a war against your families, your right to speak, your right to worship, to send your children to a school where they ain't afraid to pray. They want to take your guns, people! It's a war against Satan, against the Antichrist. Timothy understood that we must fight. Brothers—" Luke paused. "—do *you*?"

"Killing little babies," muttered Tom, rising, stumbling, and kicking a bucket into the darkness. "What kinda war is that?"

"That's why he was a fool," Luke agreed. "He got the FBI chasing after Cub Scout troops—you *cain't* operate on the internet no more. We all had to go underground because of Timothy McVeigh, because the idiot killed babies . . . but listen to me, brothers. Looky here." Luke passed around copies of a flier for John Stone. The man looked something like Luke, thought Birdy: the same piercing dark eyes, radiating the same toughness and confidence. He looked like Sylvester Stallone, too, except that he was bald and wore a tic. An educated man?

No, Birdy thought. John Stone didn't look like Luke or Sylvester Stallone. He looked like—

"Who's this, Brother Luke?" Ronald asked.

"Name's John Stone. Running for governor up in Missouri."

"So?" asked Tom.

"I knew him in the army—"

"You knowed everybody in the army," Tom said.

"They shoulda taken him out and shot him. Worst example of a man ever walked the earth."

"Should qualify for governor, then," Tom said, and once more kicked the offending bucket and staggered into the darkness.

This brought more laughter, and Luke broke out another round of beers. Birdy grabbed one, his third. The beer slaked some deep thirst inside him and he drank it all at once, then studied the arrogant face of John Stone. He knew this man.

"He could be the Antichrist," Luke resumed. He told the story how, the day he headed home from war, he'd drawn the detail of escorting two dead Iraqis to the army's morgue. "I was hoping I could get this thing done and find a flight out. I was running for the airport when I realized I still had this big envelope full of effects in my hand.

"So I looped back and went right on in and wasn't nobody there. I put the envelope down on John Stone's chair and started to leave again, only then I heard this panting and scraping, kind of. And I took a few steps and looked over a file cabinet, and Stone was pumping away—"

"With a dead body?" Tom asked. "This is some vampire movie you saw. I won't listen to this trash." He strode up the hill, cursing, and in his wake a restlessness ran over the men, and several more stood.

"With a female," Luke said quickly. "A live female. Pretty blonde female."

Birdy believed it. His Uncle Gabe liked blondes most of all.

"But they were going at it with them dead bodies all around 'em. I know this man. He's—"

"Pure evil," Ronald said quietly.

"Evil!" Dale chimed in loyally. "Evil!"

"Yes! John Stone is an evil man. He wants to take away all the guns up in Missouri. All the guns!"

"That's bad," Ronald said. "But I don't see where it makes him the Antichrist."

"It's the first step!" Luke cried. "What A-dolf Hitler done! And the idea is, see—you're not hearin' my *idea!*—is that you come out of nowhere, you have this target, a plan, you *assassinate* him. You strike that blow, and the whole war starts! Like the Archduke, the Archduke of—"

"You don't know him, so they cain't trace you afterwards," Dale said, nodding. "What an idea, Lucky! One less evil man, subtracted from the Devil's bank account."

"That's right!" Luke said. "The world a little bit better place, and they don't even know who done it! This is *war*, men, and in war—"

Ronald stood. "Thou shalt not kill."

He spoke softly as he always did, but every man, even subforeman Dale in the end, followed him away from Luke's cabin. Luke had gone too far, not so much in advocating violence in the abstract, perhaps, as in the melodrama of his story, which seemed at best an exaggeration and might be an outright lie. There was more. To the best of their abilities, these were godly men. For the first time, it seemed clear that Luke was not.

"Didn't mean *him*, exactly," Luke called after them. "Maybe not John Stone specifically. But it's an *action*. A thing we could do!"

Only Birdy lingered. His Uncle Gabe, up in Shannon County, had beat Birdy until he ran at sight of him and half-lived in the woods. One time, he sat up on the bluff with his single-shot .22, watching his uncle put it to a blonde woman on the stainless steel table where he cut up pigs. The women came to him for meth. He had women all the time, all of them blondes, and they paid him with sex. Even from the bluff, even with a .22, he could have killed his uncle. But just as Ronald said, you weren't supposed to kill.

And yet what if the man were *so* evil that the world improved with him gone? With his trousers around his ankles, the skinny blonde woman writhing beneath him, his uncle's face took on a convulsive expression—as evil as Birdy could imagine. He stared at the flier of John Stone. He saw the face of his Uncle Gabe, the face of the Antichrist.

He could do it. Cold and dispassionate, an assassin as in the movies. Like Rambo, he'd slip in, fade away, without a trace. One spot of evil vanquished forever!

Luke's status in the camp quickly fell. All through the week he tried to be a model worker, invoking the blessed name of Jesus every second sentence. But he sat near the back of the chapel on Sunday morning, his head low, and no one doubted to whom Top referred in his sermon.

"These are the last days. There are vipers everywhere around us. But brothers and sisters, *this* is our weapon of choice—"

Top held up his mother's worn, leatherbound Bible.

"—not *this.*"

He held up an AR-15. And there might have been a distant amusement in the old soldier's eyes, as he raised the assault rifle and the Bible skyward. Maybe he'd been waiting on the dissenter to make a false move. In any case, toward midafternoon, Luke climbed the mountain for a final audience with Top. Perhaps the two prayed over the matter before Top settled some money on his fallen angel.

By evening Luke had packed his truck. He taxied slowly down the rough road, and no one but Birdy came to say goodbye. No doubt, men and women stood behind windows, watching, but the camp had gone soundless except for the steady chug of the generators and the wind rattling the oak leaves. It was the middle of November. The nights were cold now.

Birdy held his shotgun. Just that afternoon he'd killed three squirrels. "I'm sorry to see you go, Lucky."

"Lucky? Hah!" Luke narrowed his eyes. His very face seemed violent, and Birdy took a step back.

"You was the only one understood," Luke said. "Just a kid."

"It's an idea," Birdy said. "You was talking about an *idea.*"

Luke's face relaxed, and he almost smiled. "A principle. John Stone's an evil man; I don't know if he's the Antichrist. Probably ain't. What they don't get is, we're locked in battle. They think they're safe here, but they'll come a time, not long now, you ain't safe nowheres. Here you go, son."

He pulled a rifle from behind the seat.

Birdy was awestruck. The rifle was old, with a polished walnut forestock, and a strange, wire stock that folded forward. He raised the rifle and pointed toward Golgotha, bringing down the telescopic sight on the crosses. He knew he couldn't miss with such a weapon, but he said, "I cain't accept this."

"Oh, it's an antique. Can you believe it? I bought it at a garage sale. M-1 carbine, commandos used 'em in World War II. For close quarter combat or maybe you're behind the lines, need something short you can conceal. I put that scope on it and makes a pretty fair deer gun, don't drop long range like a .30-30. Take it, Birdy. I got lotsa guns."

Humbly, Birdy lowered his head. He would carry on. "What you gonna do, Brother Luke?"

"I know an ole gal down to Ft. Smith." He laughed. "I believe tonight I'll do the devil's work."

Finally, Birdy slept, only to dream of Trish Barber floating above him, her hot hands stroking his chest. He woke and masturbated violently, as if casting out evil spirits. He felt sad but calm, defiled and simultaneously washed clean, and slept on deeply until the howling coyotes woke him.

The armory was locked but Birdy knew where Top kept the key. He needed buckshot for his shotgun and rounds for the carbine. He hated stealing, but you couldn't just walk into Walmart and buy ammunition, because you had to sign your life away and then they could trace you. Assassins left no trails.

He'd parked his truck strategically, so that now he could push in the clutch and coast silently from the camp, guiding himself on the moon, bumping roughly over the flint rock, the gnarled oaks hunched to either side of him like trolls. The lane emptied onto pavement near Golgotha, where he shifted into second, flipped on the ignition, and released the clutch. The engine sputtered to life and he turned on the lights. A 'possum froze ahead of him, albino white, alien.

"John Stone, you're a dead man," he said, so fiercely he surprised himself.

Birdy reminded himself that John Stone wouldn't make his speech for five days, in Springfield, one hundred miles north. He had time. He could stop in Branson and play miniature golf and eat a big meal at a steakhouse with ice cream afterwards. He could play video games and look at girls. He could even buy some clothes. His jeans and T-shirt were so tattered they attracted attention. An assassin should look like a tourist.

He pulled over at a Burger King in Eureka Springs because of how his hands shook. He ordered a bacon and egg sandwich and a Coke. Even after five drug-free years, Cokes reminded him of meth. You were always so thirsty, and you longed for sugar, and Cokes were the best. He watched the pretty black-haired girl behind the counter, who glanced at him once and slowly smiled. He smiled, too, and she laughed and shook her beautiful hair but then turned back to the window and said something into her microphone.

He could have that girl, couldn't he? She wasn't prissy or mysterious like Trish Barber. He could work at the big hotel, where the honeymooners came, and clean the pool and mow the grass. He closed his eyes for a moment, trying to pray. *Lord, I don't know my way. What should I do?*

When he opened his eyes, it made no sense at all to drive up to Missouri and kill the Antichrist, because no one could do that. The Antichrist was a matter of prophecy. You needed him so that Jesus could return. What's more, John Stone couldn't possibly be his Uncle Gabe.

Except that both men were bald. Had Gabe been in the army? He never said so.

The main thing was that no matter how you fancied it up, killing was killing. Brother Ronald was right about that.

And even if John Stone really was the Antichrist, Birdy could never see through such an important mission. *I am not Rambo. I can't even be in the army, because I didn't finish high school.*

Back in his truck, sipping his Coke, he rounded the parking lot and glanced through the service window, but the girl had retreated to the counter. He reached the street and meant to turn south toward the hotel and apply for a job. Heavy traffic clogged the lane, full of tourists in their mammoth RVs.

He turned north. He seldom cursed, but now he needed to.

"Fuck it," he said, and drove ten miles, growing steadily more agitated. He leaned forward and beat the dash with his palms. Shaking again, he pulled up a grassy lane to an old, fenced-off fire tower and sat listening to crows and blue jays. He lay on the truck seat, thoughts racing. How could Top expect to keep him in New Jerusalem? Playing Jesus! Wasn't that—the big word—sacrilegious?

He remembered the rush of meth and how powerful he felt, how he could stay awake for days.

Then he set tin cans on a stump and practiced several hours with the carbine, taking firing positions at various distances around the tower. With the scope, he was accurate even at four hundred yards. And compensating for his weapon's kick was satisfying. He dialed the carbine to automatic for a few rounds, yelled, and charged the cans.

He'd drive to Springfield. That didn't mean he'd kill anybody. He'd saved almost three hundred dollars and could have a good time for once. Maybe he'd buy a last hit of meth before he joined the army. He wouldn't mention that he hadn't finished school. They'd take him because he was a great shot. They'd probably turn him into a sniper.

On the state highway again, Birdy missed a turn and found himself nearing Berryville. The truck climbed feebly up the big hills, but then Birdy coasted recklessly, his tires screeching around the curves. At a summit, he glimpsed the blue waters of Table Rock Lake, then dropped off low. Down in the hollow, it was almost dark. Where did the afternoon go? Cold air surged past him, and he realized he'd forgotten his ragged coat.

Glinting off the high mirror of an RV, the westering sun blinded him. Birdy hit the brakes and bumped onto the shoulder, but the highway climbed a high ridge here and the grade fell sharply on either side. He veered jaggedly onto the highway again, then sat in neutral, foot on the brake, heart racing. Four RVs rolled slowly ahead of him; he was the fifth driver back. He didn't understand until he saw the tall state trooper, tipping his hat to the driver of the first RV, motioning him on. The RV in front of Birdy slipped backward, then lumbered forward with all the grace of a tank.

A roadblock. In the middle of nowhere. What for? They *know,* he thought.

The cops didn't know anything. What was there to know? Had the Antichrist already taken over and placed transmitters in people's brains? No! New Jerusalem probably wouldn't miss him until the evening service, and then Top could only conclude that his little slave had finally showed some backbone and joined the army. They might notice the armory had been raided, but Lucky Muldoon could have done it as well as Birdy, and anyhow no one would say anything. So what was going on? *Think,* Birdy!

He turned his head, hoping to squeeze the truck from behind the RV and turn back south, but the car behind boxed him in. It was a sleek, top-of-the-line Toyota or maybe one of those fancy German cars, but he caught only a hint of the woman driving and couldn't signal her to back up. Clouds sailed by in her windshield and he saw only a nose, sunglasses, and wisp of blonde hair.

He could crimp sharply, back up, and make it on his second try, but that would take so long the officers surely would corner him.

The second RV lurched north and he eased the truck forward. Oh Lord, the shotgun! His carbine lay on the floorboard, wrapped in a big, pink towel, but anyone could see the shotgun. Birdy reached low and pulled shop rags and fast food sacks from under his toolbox. He had no time for artistry, but he tried to spread things around naturally, making it look as though he were just another slob.

The last RV hardly stopped, and Birdy rolled up slowly, smiling, hoping the officer would simply wave him on. Farm boy in a pickup, feed sacks, a shovel and length of chain in the bed; what could be more natural? The trooper stared hard, pointed a finger, and Birdy gulped. He hit the brakes and the tires squealed, the frame rocked.

"Li-cense," drawled the trooper. "Proof of *in*surance." Birdy handed the officer his license and reached across to the glove compartment to search for the insurance card, though he'd never had one. Top gave him the money but Birdy kept it.

The trooper seemed bored. He stepped back and looked at the tailgate, glanced over the truck bed, and lifted his hand as if to return the license. Then the radio squawked up the road, and the trooper's partner motioned.

The trooper handed over Birdy's license to the man inside the car, and the radio squawked some more. The seated man pointed to something, and the two men waited, until the time grew long and someone in an RV shouted impatiently. Birdy's trooper grew stern and asked a question that had the word criminal in it. "Criminal" floated on the evening air.

They'd found his record: the dubious time at Granderson, the ninety-three days in Washington County Detention Center he'd served before Top sprang him. He was on drugs then and didn't know what he was doing. The entire story was on their devil computer, and they'd find the guns, and he'd be back in jail because he had a record and no insurance. Maybe Top couldn't get him out this time.

Top said that cops were good men, just doing their duty in a decadent world, but Top had never been in jail. Around big men who wanted to turn you into a girlfriend.

The first trooper spun about and began walking toward Birdy, hand on his sidearm. As he walked, and Birdy reached for the shotgun, the entire scene slowed down.

The trooper ducked from a bumblebee. The bee must have smelled something sweet about him, and circled, and again tried to land. The trooper took two quick steps, shooing away the bee. He ducked again, and when his head slowly rose there was the merest snarl on his lips. He had time enough to understand what was happening, though in no amount of time could he have understood why, except the kid in the truck was terrified.

Birdy screamed as he pulled the shotgun from the seat, pushed it through the window, and pulled the trigger. He screamed because it was as though he were the one being hurt, and he simply reacted. The world had always been this way. You meant to do a right thing but did a wrong thing, and nothing right remained. The trooper fell soundlessly with the explosion and lay on the pavement, his chin torn away as if a panther had clawed him.

Then things happened so quickly Birdy didn't understand, but he knew he had to move. He heard the bumblebee buzzing. Something exploded, and glass fell all over him. He crawled across the glass and opened the passenger door, yanking along his carbine in the towel as if this were combat and he had to return fire. He dropped to the road as the trooper from the car opened up, and the blonde woman in the fancy car screamed and banged on her horn. Somebody dropped from an RV, and Birdy heard footsteps.

He rolled into the grade and clung to a little pine. Then he plunged down the loose rocks of the bluff, cradling the carbine even as he realized he'd left behind the box of ammunition. He slid for fifty feet and grabbed a cottonwood, cutting his hand. He bled from an ankle, too, and his sock was wet with blood. He let go the cottonwood and skimmed the muddy bank, dropping his feet neatly into shallow water.

Darkness surrounded him. He heard engines, and shouting, like voices calling from the faraway pit of Hell. He half-walked, half-slid, down the swift creek, until he looked out upon the long lake, set afire by the dying sun. Mosquitoes swarmed around his ears, but he hardly noticed. He heard his heart thumping and turned his head oddly, spasmodically about. His cheeks stung with tears. He'd killed a policeman, the worst thing you could do, but he couldn't take it in. It was as if he'd seen it in a movie.

Stars reflected off the water blindingly, but slowly he grew aware of a glowing to his right, and laughter. A marina pushed out only a few hundred feet to his east, with a restaurant behind it a little up the hill. Wet, shivering, he at last realized that the only way he could cross the lake was to steal a boat.

Rambo began his rampage because of police brutality. They arrested him, a Medal of Honor winner, for vagrancy. They threw him in jail and beat him, when he had done nothing except look for food. Like Rambo, he'd be shot on sight, wouldn't he? And by God, he still had his mission, to rid the world of the Antichrist.

The blood from his hand had stopped flowing. With his pocketknife, he cut a strip from his shirt and bound it around his ankle.

He couldn't swim. But he waded into the lake waist-deep to avoid passing the restaurant and the marina's office directly. He had no bayonet to clinch between his teeth, then to rise with his hair slicked back in the starlight, but he felt as though the restaurant were full of Nazis or heartless drug runners. He heaved onto the dock and crouched low as he examined the boats, most of them too fancy even for him to operate. At length he found an open, fiberglass boat in which the engine didn't look much more complicated than a lawn mower.

Several minutes passed before he found the pull rope, the choke, the throttle. The engine started with his first crank, and he clunked into a gear and ran out ten feet before a rope yanked him back. He looked up frantically toward the restaurant, then cut the rope, but the little boat ran toward the dock. At the last moment he understood that the engine itself was the rudder and split the difference between the two dark shores.

He shoved the throttle into its fastest notch, but his progress was slow. Any moment now, a fast boat, full of angry policemen, would bear down on him. He could take them out with the carbine if he had the nerve.

At last the marina's lights winked out from his wake. He passed houses, a village, anchored boats, and then the lake turned north, and east again, as channels forked off confusingly. He reasoned that the right shore was always south, the left always north, no matter how the lake turned. With no watch, he couldn't judge how much time passed, but surely he traveled two hours, and maybe that equaled ten miles. He stuck a finger into the tank and pulled it out dry. He turned up a branch that ran due north. When he spied a long, flat place reaching far into the woods, he beached the boat.

He disliked harming it. It belonged to someone. He imagined himself living along this lake in a little house, every night bringing in bass and catfish, packing them into a smoker like Lucky Muldoon. He imagined eating fish with the Burger King girl, settling down on the couch with her head leaned against him as they watched zombie movies.

No. Tomorrow the police would be all over the lake with their helicopters, and like Rambo he had to hide his trail and conquer some distance.

Unless he gave himself up. Rambo tried in *First Blood,* but they wouldn't let him. Because he'd killed a cop, they'd shoot him on sight.

At the edge of the woods he sharpened a hickory sapling with his pocketknife and brought it down like a pike against the bottom of the boat. After a dozen blows, the stick went through. He found a jagged rock and kept pounding until water flowed in. The boat still refused to sink, so he threw in every rock he could find, tied off the engine, and pointed the boat toward the middle of the lake. In two hundred feet the prow tilted up, until the engine itself went under and died. Now he heard frogs and whippoorwills. Mosquitoes attacked his face and neck, but he watched the boat until he couldn't see it anymore. He wasn't certain it sank.

Birdy waded through weeds, and his feet fell into stinking little pools, filling his shoes with slippery gunk. He found dry land, pulled off his ruined socks, wrapped a fresh cloth around his ankle, and collapsed. His lungs heaved. He sneezed and began to cry again. He had no hope. He pushed the barrel of the carbine into his mouth and held his finger poised by the trigger for a long time. He tried to pray, but he'd never been able to talk to Jesus.

Finally, the mosquitoes grew so insistent that he ran from the shore. Cold as it was, this must be their last night on earth, and they made the most of it.

The flat place was a forest service road that stretched out northward through the woods until it disappeared under power lines. He ran small distances, flailing his arms and trying to warm up, while the wires above hummed menacingly. He expected to see aliens over every rise. He'd live on their planet. He didn't belong on this one. He felt so lonely that crying overcame him again, but his crying was partly rage and he screamed at the woods until the whippoorwills quieted, though nothing could silence the trilling, the mockery of the coyotes.

Snow whirled around him, and his ears numbed. Cold and hunger conquered tears, and he bent forward determinedly. Toward dawn, the high wires crossed a blacktop, and he saw the lights of a town.

Top slept unconscionably late and shuffled about for ten minutes— brewing coffee, splashing water on his face, combing his beard—before he remembered that New Jerusalem had changed. Brother Luke always had men hammering by seven, and not long after you could hear his backhoe grumble to life up on Masada, but Top had banished Brother Luke from the kingdom. Stepping onto the deck, Top's bare feet melted through a patina of frost, but he endured the cold to look over the misty camp. He heard voices at the dining hall. From on high they had the character of soldiers in combat, whispering hoarsely.

Without leadership, your army became a mob. Top was too old to defend Masada, but he could appoint a new leader and get the men working again. Ronald was a good man, though perhaps too gentle to make a foreman. Dale would do. He was not entirely a sycophant. He had some fire about him.

Top heard a knocking on his door and drew on his white robe and shower sandals. Sister Flora marched in like she always did. Top was always a little afraid she'd pin him to the wall and propose marriage, but she brushed past and turned on his radio to the Eureka Springs FM station. Ordinarily, the station carried little news, but now featured a high-pitched woman's voice, full of anguish. Top couldn't tell if the woman was a reporter or a victim, but slowly he understood that she talked about Birdy.

"Just a safety stop," the woman said. "Turn signals!"

A trooper gave the boy's name, said he'd killed an officer, that he was "armed and dangerous." Stay in your homes, the trooper advised. Top and Sister Flora sat at the table, staring at each other, as if they were brother and sister and had learned their mother died.

Top said, "He didn't mean to."

"It don't matter. They gonna come after us now. There's people in New Jerusalem, they got records."

"He wanted to join the army," Top said. "Wait, I said."

"What did he *do?*"

Top pulled on his shirt and pants in the kitchen, but Flora rounded the corner, wringing her hands. She didn't care he was halfnaked, and Top didn't, either, and went on dressing. He said, "I'll go down there, I'll make some sort of announcement—"

"Sweetheart, they already know."

He nodded at her endearment. It was all right, and he folded his arms awkwardly around her. "Maybe I can help a little. Offer a prayer for Birdy. For us. Then, you know, we have to cooperate, Flora. You and me, we need to go to town."

"Before they come here," she said.

A little distance into Shell Knob, Birdy realized he couldn't carry the carbine in public, even inside the towel. He stepped into an alley and hid it behind a rotted piece of siding, panicking, looking toward the street, calming himself.

A cafe was open, and the barbershop beside it. He crossed the street and in a vending machine read the headline: "Officer Killed; Highway Patrol Widens Search." He dropped change into the machine and read his name, his address—Route 4, Eureka Springs, which meant that soon they'd descend on New Jerusalem. The strangest thing was to see his photo on the front page, but it was the wrong photo! They'd taken it from his driver's license, but he didn't look anything like that.

He sat in a booth to avoid the men at the counter. They all wore orange vests and hats with earflaps, and several had propped rifles by their stools. Sight of the rifles alarmed him, but at the same time he could hardly keep his eyes open. From above, a heater pushed warm air over him, and he wanted to lie down in the booth and sleep forever.

The waitress, a thick, middle-aged woman, said, "You're a sight! Been mud-wrassling with a deer?"

Birdy tried to smile. "Pretty cold out there."

He ordered ham and eggs and potatoes. The waitress kept bringing him coffee and plying him with questions, but every little town was like that. They wanted to place you, because you might be a drug dealer or rapist. "Yes, ma'am," and "No, ma'am," he said, as he bolted his food, but then the waitress whirled with her coffee pot and stood transfixed. "Jesus Boy Still At Large" trailed across the TV screen, and photos—from tourists? from their cellphones?—showed long-haired Birdy without his shirt, agonizing on the cross. Then the scene shifted to a reporter standing on the highway above Berryville, grim-looking troopers behind her, their patrol lights flashing.

Birdy dropped money at the register and headed for the door. He didn't believe anyone noticed him, intent as they were on the television. He turned sharply into the barbershop and a bell tinkled, startling him. He'd never been in a barbershop. He'd never had a real haircut. His Uncle Gabe sheared it off, sometimes, making such a sorry job of the chore that both of them gave up.

The bald barber pointed impatiently, and Birdy climbed into the chair. A cape settled around him, and the barber said, "I oughtta charge double."

"I—"

"Just messing with you! Only listen, you got a lotta split ends. There's this special shampoo, in fact I got the franchise on it, that'll take care a that problem."

"Can you cut it short?"

"Army style? A number one?"

"Like, like—" Birdy pointed to an old black-and-white poster.

"Beaver Cleaver? Sure thing, son. You're the doctor."

The barber snipped, occasionally lifting his shiny scissors high. He sang "I Walk the Line" not too badly. The door tinkled again as the barber turned on his electric clippers, and Birdy tensed in the chair at whom he thought was a policeman. Then he realized the newcomer was only an old man in a shop uniform.

"Gonna snow, Carl?" the barber asked.

"They're saying Wednesday."

By the time Birdy left the two men paid no attention to him. A kind of talent he had: people never saw him. He walked down the street to a thrift store, where he bought a green shirt that looked almost new, and jeans that were worn at the knees but didn't have any holes, and a stocking hat that said "Tigers." He found a fur-lined leather coat, in perfect shape except for a tear on the shoulder, and even some gloves.

What about the carbine? In movies, assassin's rifles were precision instruments that the hero, or the villain, snapped together with great authority. The carbine wasn't like that, but still he had to hide it. Sylvester Stallone seemed to walk with him down the aisles of the Dollar Store, and together they selected a green backpack with a SpongeBob SquarePants logo. Improvise. That's what Rambo did.

He'd hide in the woods for the next several days. Maybe he'd kill a rabbit with one of his precious bullets, but to be safe he bought crackers, pudding, canned soup, and plastic spoons. And matches. Some gauze and surgical tape for his ankle. And a small flashlight. He thought he was done, but then went in search of a map of Missouri.

As cars swished by on Main Street, he wrapped the carbine in Dollar Store bags and the magazine in a separate bag. He had only eight rounds, but that was enough. A little dog trotted up the alley, yapping at Birdy as he drew on the backpack. He bent to pat the dog, but it lost all its courage and ran away howling, as if he'd struck it. "No harm. No harm," Birdy called after it.

He couldn't handle much more. He had to locate Highway 39, which would point him north and into the hills again, toward Springfield. Then he'd find a safe place to sleep. He walked south three blocks and turned east along the lake, waving at people when they waved at him, a tourist, a friendly college boy. He reached a bait shop and in the window, under a flashing Budweiser sign, saw his Uncle Gabe, the Antichrist.

The strength ebbed from his legs, and he could scarcely walk. As if approaching a god, he drew slowly near the poster for John Stone. Unquestionably, the candidate was his uncle, though how could it be? How could the man have covered up his sordid history? How could he be dressed so fine?

Missouri Representative John Stone, Democrat, running for governor from Shannon County. Shannon County! Where his uncle kept him locked in a shed and fed him the same slop he gave his pigs.

- FRIEND OF THE FARMER
- FRIEND OF THE VETERAN
- FRIEND OF SMALL BUSINESS
- WILL TAKE GUNS OUT OF THE HANDS OF CRIMINALS
- WILL CRACK DOWN ON DRUG MANUFACTURE
- COMMITTED CHRISTIAN

Committed Christian! Exactly how the Antichrist would present himself.

"Cold morning, ain't it?" said a man with massive wrinkles around his eyes, wearing a floppy, fur-lined hat with one flap down, one tucked up into his hair. Birdy read it in his eyes. Birdy knew, when a policeman might not. Such men parked near liquor stores and all-night laundromats, and they could spot their marks from a hundred feet. Oh, Birdy knew.

The man sat in a massive truck with toolboxes and ladders, marked "Bishop's Pole Barns." Everyone had a disguise. Maybe Mr. Bishop even built a pole barn now and then.

Birdy stepped near the truck. He opened his leather coat and let three twenties show.

Mr. Bishop stared, then flipped his cigarette onto the parking lot. "I believe we should go somewheres."

"Out on 39? North?"

"Anywhere you want." The man revved the truck engine, a big diesel. It seemed to growl as Birdy came around to the other side. The man lit a cigarette from the one he was smoking and began backing out, but then he stopped the truck and stared meaningfully. "Seat belt."

"Oh. Sure."

They turned north on 39. Mr. Bishop drove with his window half down and never stopped smoking. "What's your poison, young man?"

Birdy sniffed at the smoky air. "Powder," he said.

Black officers were often suspicious of Top, a southerner, though Top could work past such feelings, and they could, too. In fact, the army was the only place Top had been where you ignored skin color, at least some of the time. One crisis, one man killed, and you forgot to think, *he's black*.

Still, Top wondered why they'd put Commander Terrell, a black trooper, in a zone as stubbornly white as northern Arkansas, rather than down south among stubborn blacks. All his military life he'd marveled at dense bureaucracy, even as it rolled right over him. Not that it mattered. He no longer had a place in the big world, or an opinion anyone would heed. He had some facts.

Terrell was a major, interesting because troop commanders were ordinarily captains. He was still a young man and wore his uniform well, even fussily: the old-fashioned Sam Browne belt over the shoulder, the stiff-brimmed hat with its precisely dented peak. A fine uniform, though maybe the epaulets were a bit much. "This is Flora Barnett," Top said. "And Dale Biggs. Major, we believe Birdy Blevins is in Missouri."

Terrell took off his hat and looked up wearily. His eyes were tinged with red. "We know that."

"Headed for Springfield. To kill a man, we think. I'm going that way myself, sir. I want to help."

"That's right," Dale said. "We just wanna help."

"Maybe you can." Terrell nodded and looked up at the wall clock. He rubbed one eye, then came around from his computer and took a folding chair, so that the four sat in a circle. "Get you folks anything? Coffee?"

Sister Flora said, "Wouldn't mind some coffee. We been traveling so fast—I swear, we was so shocked by the news, Birdy was allus such a quiet boy—we didn't take time for breakfast."

The major tried out a smile. "I think I can find some doughnuts for you."

Top explained how he'd rescued Birdy from the Fayetteville jail and how the boy had been a faithful apprentice but lately had grown restless and wanted to join the army. He tried not to characterize New Jerusalem, because he knew how nonbelievers thought and still hoped that God's work, and his own utopian experiment, could be preserved.

Dale spoke like a backwoods kid forced to address the school board. Top knew he had a record, and before all of this was over that record would probably come forth, but Terrell waited patiently, and Dale grew calmer. He told how Luke Muldoon and the other men had met in the hollow and shot off weapons and talked politics. Muldoon spoke of John Stone, the gubernatorial candidate up in Missouri—the Antichrist, Muldoon claimed, who should be taken out and shot. It was reckless talk, but that's all it was. This was America, where you still had the right of free expression! None of them would ever have done such a thing, not even Lucky Muldoon. "But that kid was bat shit, sir. Excuse me. I don't wanna say it. Birdy took that wild talk *serious.*"

"Where is this man, Muldoon?"

Top broke in. "Brother Luke left the community."

"No chance they're working together?"

Both Top and Dale shook their heads, but Dale said, "Only, I saw 'em both right at the end, and Lucky, I mean Mr. Muldoon, he give Birdy a gun."

"The shotgun? We retrieved that on scene."

"I just barely seen it, it was almost dark, but some kind of rifle. Lucky oughta knowed better. That kid—"

The major turned to Top. "So the boy's armed."

"And he can shoot," Dale said. "I seen that myself."

"I told him, 'Don't watch them old *vi*-lent movies,'" Flora said. "My son, Timmy, that's all he ever did, and look what happened to him!"

Top frowned and grasped Flora's hand. "Major, I hope—I hope you can—"

Terrell sat back. "I thank you for coming in. It's a huge break."

"Birdy was *scared*," Top said.

"Scared, but determined to kill a man." Terrell stood, squared his shoulders, and donned his stiff hat. "More than ever. What's he got to lose?"

"I don't know," Top said. "I thought of Birdy like a son, but—"

"He killed an officer of the law, one of my men. Byron served two tours in Iraq. I know his family."

Even as Top thought, *he's so calm,* Terrell changed. His face clinched tightly and his eyes grew fierce, almost cruel. He jabbed at the air as if Top were the murderer. "*You're* ex-military. *You* know how it goes."

Top nodded gloomily. "Even if you can take him alive—"

"Yes, sir," the major said, already subduing his anger. Cool again, his face almost inscrutable, he punched a number into his cell phone. "Exactly, sir. That's how it goes."

The dealer dumped him in Jenkins, a nowhere town with nothing in it, forty-six miles from Springfield. A car passed, then a school bus; two little blonde girls stuck out their tongues at him. They were probably twins. Somebody had told them how cute they were. They couldn't know he was Jesus Boy, could they? Anyhow, he had to escape the open, the daylight, and he jogged from the highway across the stubble of a cornfield, turning every few steps to observe passing cars. He ran through a thicket of wild plums and ducked into a hay barn, where he crawled up near the metal roof and fell asleep between two round bales.

When he woke, shivering, snow swirled across the field, not so much it would accumulate, but he felt still colder. He slid down to a vacant place in the middle of the barn, raked away loose hay, and built a small fire between an old Massey-Ferguson tractor and a dump truck. He heated soup, then stood with his feet to either side of the coals as he ate. He climbed into the truck cab and pulled a rough tarp over himself. The windshield pointed east and caught some sun. He grew warm and slept nearly six hours.

He woke to the *whoop-whoop-whoop* of a helicopter. His heart leapt, and he imagined himself running toward the wooded hills as Black Hawks swooped down, their yellow rockets pluming, just as they'd pursued Rambo.

They can't see you here, Birdy.

What if there are soldiers on the road?

Not yet. It takes a while to call them out.

Mightily tempted, he was proud of the discipline he'd shown to wait. Now night descended, and he snorted a hit of meth. They gave it to soldiers in World War II, and Birdy, too, was a soldier, and meth was a weapon. Meth wouldn't let you sleep. It pushed away the cold. It lent you the strength of Superman.

Birdy crossed the field and climbed through the woods, until he reached a bare ridge that ran crookedly north. Immersed in the cold starlight, he jumped from rocks to rubble, tireless and strong. He leaped in the cold air, floating like an astronaut. He almost touched the moon.

He fell, scraped the gauze off his ankle, and inside of him armies collapsed, cities burned. He sat, gasping, and bound the ankle again. He ran on, but now his face twisted wickedly, and he forgot where he was, that men searched for him. He journeyed back to that time in Shannon County when he didn't feed the chickens.

"I hated the chickens!" he yelled to the hills and far valleys.

Every day the bus went down Highway M, but Gabe wouldn't let him go to school. "Don't want the attention," he said. "Got to stay off the radar, Birdy!"

Well, then he wouldn't feed the damn chickens. Gabe didn't even know until the man from Tyson came and said why are there so many dead chickens? They got a disease?

*A neighbor had found them in the gully where Birdy threw
them. The neighbor hated Gabe. He meant to cozy up to Tyson.
Thousands of dead chickens, and the man said he had no choice. He
was forced to bring in the health department or maybe the agricul-
ture department or maybe just more Tyson people, but anyhow this
was the end. Don't expect any more little chicks! The farm was number one on Tyson's shit list.*

*The man went up to the house where Gabe slept off a drunk and
talked to him a long time. Birdy knew how angry Gabe would be
and hid in the barn loft. He should have fled to the woods, because
Gabe came after him with that piece of rebar, snorting, snarling, his
black eyes red as a space alien's. Birdy rolled up like an armadillo,
and Gabe hit him again and again with the rebar. He nearly put out
an eye, and Birdy couldn't see for the blood.*

"I couldn't get up!" Birdy screamed, as his powerful legs
pounded the top of the world, and the moonlit hills swept out to either side of him like an ocean.

*For a long time he'd lain gone from the earth, racing through
the stratosphere, dimly aware of doors slamming and one of Gabe's
blondes screaming, then wild music blaring, fading, dopplering as
the truck rounded the curve along the bluffs. Birdy sank to earth
again but didn't want to, because the earth was a terrible place.
Sometime in the night, he limped toward the house and packed
twenty pounds of his uncle's product into a little suitcase. He was
sixteen. He'd head for Oklahoma Territory, like an outlaw in a
western.*

Calmer now, Birdy slowed to a walk. He licked his lips, visual-
izing a six-pack of cold Cokes and a tall bottle of Orange Crush.
After that, he'd eat ten cheeseburgers and French fries and a bagful
of hard candy.

The bare ridge descended into oaks, but because he had super
powers, he saw over the trees to a crossroads lit with red and yellow
lights. Police, but they didn't like to leave their cars. He was supposed to walk right into them. He unwrapped the carbine and
looked through the telescopic sight down Highway 39, where more

police sat in the dark. Behind them soldiers milled around two army trucks. Those guys weren't afraid to walk, and dawn neared.

They'd found the boat, because it didn't really sink. They'd discovered his tracks on the shore. Maybe even they found the dealer who drove him to Jenkins.

Did they know about the Antichrist coming to Springfield?

Birdy snorted another hit and couldn't focus. The lights at the crossroads grew fuzzy, then multiplied and became like stars, darting all around him. Head reeling, he ran east, down hill, up hill, away from his pursuers and into the woods again. He stumbled into a creek, drank his fill, but the water wasn't sweet like Coke. He vomited, drank again, and plunged into the swampy, scary woods full of serpents' hisses and the red eyes of demons. The demons clawed at him, but with his colossal strength he shook them free and pushed down his legs, which were strong as elephant's legs, relentless as pistons. He rose out of the dark and climbed tirelessly to the peak of another mountain.

Staring into the rising sun, he beheld a red-rimmed face among the clouds, like one of those solemn men of history, Abraham Lincoln or Moses, but the face grew brighter until he couldn't look anymore.

He knew he had seen God, and now a beautiful valley opened before him. Maybe it was Heaven. The sun lit the red oak leaves, the yellow hickories, the purple sumacs as Birdy descended. Full of wonder, he ran through the brown corn, following a grassy lane tinged with frost, flushing turkeys that feasted in the stubble. It was all so beautiful!

A solitary man, riding behind a massive, red horse, harvested corn a row at a time. He wore a blue shirt, but everything else about him was black: his full beard, his long coat, his suspenders, his trousers. Birdy waved as he passed, but the man didn't turn his head. The horse and man made a lot of noise as they crashed through the corn, but from a distance Birdy no longer heard them, and they seemed motionless, as if their task were suspended in a painting.

Something was wrong in the beautiful valley. Smoke rose. Not quite human screams carried from over a little hill. Birdy looked around at the farmer, who'd reached the end of his row, turned, and now pulled back his reins. The farmer lifted his head, sniffed, and stepped down from the metal seat, moving quickly for an old man. He began unharnessing the red horse.

Birdy flew like Superman. He topped the hill and saw the old man's narrow little house, his dying vegetable garden, some trousers and socks on a clothesline—and the barn. The old, sagging barn was on fire, and the screams came from inside. They were shrill, bewildered, reproachful. They were unbearable, and Birdy never stopped. Smoke poured from the barn, he could see naked flames up high, but he grabbed a towel at the hand pump and plunged inside.

He found little smoke, but the air was so poisonous that every hot breath seemed fatal. Wood in the stalls glowed red. Flames licked at the low ceiling and forked like lightning, and when part of the far wall fell, beams crashed across a feed barrel and the barrel burned blue. His shoes burned, and Birdy danced into a pan of steaming water and at last saw the mare. She'd hunched against the wall, banging it with her head because her mane was afire. She saw him, bared her teeth, and screamed.

Birdy found the latch. He shouted hoarsely, but couldn't hear his own voice in the roar around him. The mare snarled at Birdy, though not really at *him,* he thought. He dove to the wall, pushed her, beat her. She twisted her head, her great eyes terrified, but then bolted from the stall and leaped through the collapsed wall.

A timber fell after her and for the first time Birdy was frightened. He veered left and right in the spongy, smoking stall bed. Mustering all his strength, he pushed, fell back, pushed again, and the wall gave way. He stumbled into the sunshine, threw down his leather coat, and the grass caught fire around it. He yanked off his burning shoes and ran to the pump. He pulled pure air into his seared lungs, coughed, and looked blearily at the old man, who stood hatless, his patchy, black hair pointing up straight.

Birdy whispered, "Where's the horse?"

The old man lifted his hand slowly and pointed.

Maybe she was a black horse, but her skin had burned away, leaving the red muscle and puckering blood. The mare didn't scream anymore. She lay on her side, heaving, lifting her eyes in resigned pain. Birdy worked the pump and held his head under the spout, thinking of the policeman's blown-away jaw, and how for an instant the man pushed his head and heels into the pavement, lifting his hips. The old man stood over the mare with a rifle and spoke to her. When he pulled the trigger, Birdy thought he was the one being shot.

From fifty feet away, the red horse whinnied and trotted up to the mare. He dropped his head near hers, then backed away and whinnied again.

"Maggie was twenty-four," the old man said. "Haven't worked her for five years. Funny thing, I us'ly take her out to pasture, only today, she was feeling low, I said, 'Just you sleep, Maggie.'"

"I'm so sorry, I—"

"No, no, not your fault! That's the way of it, sometimes, you try to do good and it don't work out. I allus treated her right. I give Maggie food sometimes when *I* was hungry."

Maggie's eyes were like those of all the animals he'd killed, angry or fearful or threatening in that last second, expressionless the next. Birdy was amazed how quickly her spirit fled. Again he thought of the dead trooper. Mostly, he visualized the blown-away jaw, but the man's eyes had also lodged in his memory, not filled with horror, simply vacant.

They watched the barn roof fall. It was only a small building, and already it had turned to coals. "Why didn't the fire department come?" Birdy asked.

"Oh, this place is pretty far out. Lost in time, I do believe," the farmer said. "Is your feet burned, son?"

"No."

"Never seen nobody run so fast! Burnt on your legs, your back? I got some salve."

Birdy lifted his eyes skyward so he couldn't see the carnage on earth. "I don't think so."

"Well, it's a miracle. What say you wash up there at the pump, and I'll heat some soup, and fry some spuds. You like fried potatas?"

Blinking back his tears, Birdy nodded.

"I got a coat I bet you can wear."

Up in Springfield, Top and Major Martin Terrell sat at a little round table, on stools perched so high Top had to brace himself to climb up, but they could watch the elevators from here. They listened to a woman play "Tea for Two" and "Moon River." Flora's piano was tinkly, and she wasn't skilled. This piano was rich in tone, and the pianist seemed accomplished. "Are we in a fancy hotel?" Top asked.

"Not very," Terrell said. He took off his stiff hat and eyed it critically, then swallowed some beer. Top took a gulp of his, too. It tasted bad, but brought to mind the Black Label they flew out to field troops way back in 1970. That might have been the last time he drank beer. "I gotta wonder," he said.

"What's that?"

"What sort of MOS you'd need to bid on beer."

Terrell laughed. He'd done a tour in Afghanistan, and one near Addis Ababa, before joining the police. He spoke into an imaginary phone. "'I'll take three million cases.'"

"We don't have to stay, Marty." Maybe it was a futile trip, because Birdy Blevins had become a Missouri problem. "By now the man knows all that we know."

"Well, we drove up here. We don't know all that *he* knows."

The elevator swished open as the pianist launched into "Strangers in the Night." They both stood and Top felt nervous, like a boy on his first date except that Top had never been on a date. Like a job interview, he thought, but from across the lobby John Stone didn't seem intimidating. He wore a cowboy hat and tooled boots, a blue work shirt, jeans. He carried a guitar.

You hardly saw him, suffused as he was in the aura of the tall, blue-eyed woman beside him, wearing a black evening gown, her blonde hair parted precisely in the middle and flowing halfway down her back. Top willed himself not to look at her, and indeed he wasn't lustful, not even deep in his heart. As an enlisted man, he'd learned he was too gauche and poor to interest such creatures and had overcome lust like a debility. Now that he was old, such a woman seemed part of a rare species, as if she'd dropped in from New York City or Hollywood.

But Major Terrell was young. Immediately, the woman came to him, her eyes tender and intimate, as though she had known and trusted him for years. He stepped back in confusion, but she took his arm and guided him toward two overstuffed chairs and leaned toward him over a small coffee table. She nodded, she smiled, and Terrell began to talk. "Byron," Top overheard. "*Why?*"

"Just doing his job," the beautiful woman agreed, crying softly. "So senseless."

"So empathetic," said John Stone. He wore a wide black belt with a brass buckle. It was an old cavalry buckle with crossed sabers, and Top remembered that Stone had been in Iraq. He stared. He couldn't speak.

"You're Top, correct?"

"Yes, sir." Why did he say sir? The man was a politician, a Democrat, but, no question, he had an air about him. Top had once seen a news item of President Clinton in Florida, in which his black SUV got stuck in sand. Clinton stepped out to help push, along with six big Secret Service agents in their dark suits. Clinton joked, just one of the guys, but you could see an awe approaching worship in the men's eyes. Stone was like that. He'd carry you away if you weren't careful.

"Well, you're a good soldier, Top. Coming forward as you did. I'm very much in your debt."

Top nodded. He met Stone's eyes. They were not the eyes of a crazed prophet. They were full of appeal and even empathy like his beautiful wife's, but Top also had a sense of the man's arrogance, and his indulgence because Top had worked with the police. Stone was the sort who would dole out sympathy, get you talking, then dismiss you with a curt nod. Like county commissioners, surgeons Top had known, and many an officer. "Not much to say at this point—sir—but there's one thing I need to know. Birdy claimed he knew you."

Stone looked incredulous. "This I hadn't heard."

"He claimed you made methamphetamine in Shannon County and enslaved him to do your chores."

Stone threw up his hands. "What can I say, Top?"

"Somebody, somebody from Shannon County, made drugs."

"And somebody in every other Missouri county. It's a scourge. This . . . *pitiful* young man also thinks I'm the Antichrist."

"*Some*body was his uncle."

"And some poor woman was his mother. What was she thinking, to name a kid 'Birdwell?' What do you suppose the little boys and girls called him? Not Birdy, not *Birdwell,* but Birdbrain. It's tragic, of course it is, I'm sorry for the kid even though he wants to shoot me, but he's a dope fiend and a birdbrain! And—it breaks my heart, Top—a murderer. It's what happens when guns float around without any controls whatever, which apparently they do in the great state of Arkansas."

Top lowered his head. It was a radical leap, but he agreed. "Are you canceling your rally?"

"No!"

"You're making a lot of police work overtime. You're costing taxpayers a great deal of money."

"You do see the principle, don't you, Top? Right of assembly. Free speech. Refusal to yield to terrorism."

"What I see is that Birdy's going to get you elected."

Stone sighed. "They'll find him, Top. They'll find him and kill him. Let's change the subject."

Stone sat on an ottoman, positioned his guitar just so, and played a riff of "Malagueña." The piece was standard enough that Top recognized it, though it was beyond his skills. All he knew were a few country chords he'd learned in Vietnam.

As if on cue, the pianist left off "The Shadow of your Smile" and stared wistfully across the almost empty lounge. A dollar and two quarters lay in her tips jar.

Now Stone played softly, and Top knew this song, too:

Only believe, only believe,
All things are possible, only believe.

Top closed his eyes. He returned in time to the country church of his boyhood, where Brother Jonah Jones played the saw. His voice was so mournful, so paired with the saw, so broken that even as a child Top cried. He carried the words with him all through his army career. When they brought in the mutilated, the dead, he kept up a front and showed no weakness, except for the small one of murmuring the words:

Only believe, only believe,
All things are possible, only believe.

"Isn't that wonderful?" Stone asked.

Top fought back tears. "Yes."

From across the room, the major and the beautiful blonde applauded.

"It's going to be my campaign song." Stone nodded at his wife. "It was Katrina's idea."

Katrina smiled tenderly at Top. Her ring, her bracelet, her tasteful necklace gleamed in the subdued lights. She came from a world Top couldn't fathom. "Like a pastor's wife," he murmured, speaking his thoughts aloud. "But too beautiful."

Edginess crept into Stone's voice. A fire leapt in his eyes. "How can a woman be too beautiful, Top? Listen. You and I, we could talk all night. You were in Iraq? Vietnam? Bosnia?"

Top stared. Stone was a phony, his wife too good to be true, but it was just show business. Everyone above the rank of major was a performer. "Yes."

"We'll get together sometime. I promise! But right now Kat and I have a soiree. With people who have lots of money."

"Thanks for meeting with us."

"Thank *you*. I don't exaggerate, Top, when I say you saved my life." Stone rose, and put his neck through his guitar strap. "On the matter of the Antichrist."

Top nodded gloomily.

"New Jerusalem. Isn't that what you call it?"

"Yes."

"Where you've constructed a facsimile of the Holy Land and posed as Bible figures. Maybe—of course, it hasn't occurred to you—maybe *you're* the Antichrist, Top. One of hundreds."

"Just a minute, sir! The difference is . . . the difference is that we are truly God's children. We are . . . sincere."

"That's the best part of John the Beloved's whacked-out fantasy." Stone laughed. "The Antichrist is *sincere*."

Top and Terrell watched as the beautiful pair strode confidently through the glass doors. Two jolly, clumsy couples came in, stood openmouthed at sight of the celebrities, and took seats in the lounge. The pianist returned with "Some Enchanted Evening," and the drunks sang along.

Terrell pulled on his hat. "What you think, Top?"

"I don't know what to think." Birdwell. It must be Birdy's given name. How did the man know? "I think I'm in a regular town and haven't had a pizza for ten years."

"Let's get a pizza," Terrell said.

Birdy bought a bicycle at a yard sale and rode into Springfield on back streets, two days ahead of the rally. He swished past police, and the army beat the bushes behind him, searching for Jesus Boy. But now Birdy wore the black coat, the suspenders, the straw hat the old man gave him. They should look for "Amish Boy."

And he'd entered the dimension of dead things. People stared at him, even cops, and didn't see him because being dead made you invisible. Being dead, he didn't care if they killed him, but he knew they wouldn't for two days. It was as though, when they killed him for real, he'd stop being dead and people would finally see him. God or the Devil, or maybe both of them together, had it all worked out. He wouldn't die in these fancy neighborhoods.

He loved the bicycle because it was fast and had red tires. He could ride it forever. He made wrong turns, but knew that the First Christian Church sat on a side street not far from the university. In the afternoon, he rode by the platform where Stone would speak, across from a park with a stream running through it. Yellow sycamore leaves sailed in the wind.

From a picnic table back near the creek, he could easily take out the Antichrist, but how might he get past security in the first place? Today only one cop stood guard, parked in his cruiser in front of the church. But barriers and fencing were about to rise at both ends of the street, and on Sunday, for the rally, fifty policemen might assemble. With all of Missouri looking for Jesus Boy, armed and dangerous, no weapon would get through.

A construction project was underway parallel to the tennis courts. The crew had gone for the day and probably wouldn't return through the weekend. They'd scraped the ground bare down to the creek, and it had rained recently. Between the mud and a strong odor of sewage this seemed an unlikely place to congregate.

His eye on the police car, Birdy pushed the carbine into a drainage pipe, itself bound into a banded stack leaning against the tennis court fence and draped with a plastic sheet. Branches hung low here, so he'd have some camouflage, and he stood only one hundred yards from the speaking platform at a slight elevation. He could fire right over the crowd.

Would they station cops on the *other* side of the creek? Not as many. He'd have to wait and see, but he didn't believe Rambo could have made a better plan.

Birdy found a motel on a wide street directly east and slept for thirty-five hours. Then he staggered into the world again, ravenous, and weak because he no longer had superpowers. From his bicycle, through the drive-up window, he ordered five cheeseburgers, double fries, and a huge fountain Coke. His Last Supper!

Back in his room, he sat dozing to *Gilligan's Island,* but at 5:00 a.m. snapped awake to an interview with his uncle, the Antichrist. Birdy didn't remember if the reporter worked for CNN or CBS, but knew the man was famous. He always seemed to show up after shootings, but this was different, of course, because the shooting hadn't happened yet. The consensus seemed to be that the Antichrist would live and Jesus Boy would die. The cameras were in place.

"First, I want to say that I can't imagine the stress you must be under," the reporter said. "Are they any closer to finding this disturbed young man? Jesus Boy?"

Once again, Birdy-on-the-Cross filled the screen.

Stone smiled thinly. "They know where he's headed."

"Because of an informant. But that brings up an interesting question. Why give him a target? Why not postpone the rally?"

"Who knows if he'll show up?" Stone lifted his eyes, then dropped them slowly into the camera. Birdy shrank in his chair. "Let me say this: I am running for public office. What kind of candidate—what kind of man—would I be if I let fear interfere with the voters' right to know? Their right to assemble freely? I fought for this country in a foreign land. We cannot allow terrorists—and that's what this delusional boy is—to subvert the sacred practice of democracy. If I die, it will be because—"

The reporter cut him off. "Representative Stone, you are a religious man."

Stone nodded. "I am a committed Christian."

Exactly what the Antichrist would say, but not his Uncle Gabe, and Birdy was confused.

"What do you make of this young man's—to many Americans, bizarre—motivation to kill the Antichrist? For the record—" Lives were at stake. A good man had already fallen. The famous reporter managed to keep a straight face: "*Are* you the Antichrist?"

Stone smiled condescendingly, then caught himself and tried to smile for real. Birdy remembered that about him. "Isn't it sad that people have so lost faith in government that they retreat to the hills, they take up guns and wall themselves off—"

"You're referring, of course, to New Jerusalem."

"I refer to the fear so many have of their government. And is it justified? Are not the halls of power farther and farther from the people? And is not that remote power sometimes oppressive? Obviously, this young madman fell under the influence of some very radical thinking. Oh, how I grieve for the fallen young trooper, who died bravely in the performance of his duty and leaves behind three beautiful little daughters!"

"So you're *not* the Antichrist."

Stone sighed. "The Antichrist is spoken of in the Book of Revelation and also in Daniel. Some say he was Nero. Some say, Hitler. I don't believe the Last Days are yet upon us. This so-called Jesus Boy is just a cop-killer."

He never answered the question, Birdy thought. He didn't understand all that Stone said, but he did know the man was a phony who could talk fancy.

They were all that way.

And yet, what if Lucky Muldoon was wrong? Birdy wasn't certain if Stone was the Antichrist, or even if he was his Uncle Gabe. He looked like him, but almost six years had passed. The TV might be riveting, but it wasn't really real. Sometimes, Stone's voice chilled him exactly like his uncle's, but also the voice veered into tones he couldn't recall. Birdy needed to stare into the man's face.

The guards made a great fuss over his pocketknife. We'll have to keep that knife, they said, and seemed sorry but also contemptuous, because who was so stupid as to try to take a knife through security? Birdy smiled and said he was sorry, he *didn't* know, and maybe the diversion of the knife kept the guards from any further inquiry. After all, Birdy didn't look much like the Jesus Boy, whose picture had been blown up into large, grainy, frightening images that hung on the fences, even as if Birdy Blevins were the Antichrist he had resolved to kill.

Off to the right, two men in navy blue suits eyed him suspiciously, but they eyed everyone suspiciously. Birdy offered another stupid smile and swam into the crowd—a large crowd, more than a thousand, standing all along the street before the church and bulging into the park. No one noticed him, and Birdy felt sad. He knew it wasn't because he was dead. He was alive, and no one had ever noticed him. No one noticed even when he, Jesus Boy, paused to eavesdrop:

"Stone was nobody. Should never have gone to Jeff City. That old boozer Collins ran unopposed for thirty years, till they caught him with his little floozy."

"Those floozies get 'em every time. Can anybody stop him?"

"Not now! I bet he *hired* that idiot kid."

A dozen or so police stretched out before the platform, keeping the crowd ten feet back. Men with cameras moved freely, following reporters who danced about, pushing their microphones before likely faces. Birdy slipped behind to the stack of plastic pipe, then stood by the picnic table. The smell of sewage had grown stronger.

Two policemen stood together on the other side of the tennis courts, their line of sight cut up by the chain-link. None were positioned across the creek.

Was that how it was? Chasing after the Antichrist, he'd insured his rise?

He only wanted to kill his Uncle Gabe. The trooper was an accident.

Accident? He'd pulled the trigger.

A hymn Birdy had always liked, "Only Believe," rose and fell. John Stone jogged up the steps to the stage, the old, limestone church centered behind him. He pointed left and right, grinning. Birdy's eyes followed the direction of Stone's fingers, and no one waved or called out. He did it for the cameras!

As the applause died, Stone donned a sober face. "Thank you. Thank you for coming out under these distressing circumstances. Before I begin, could we bow our heads in respect for our fallen first responder, Lieutenant Byron Moore? If you are a Christian, pray for his beautiful wife and three precious daughters. A moment of silence. Ladies and gentlemen, please."

So soon. Birdy wasn't ready! But most of the policemen had bowed their heads.

He thought of the trooper with his dead eyes fixed on the treetops. What a gun did was instant. You weren't allowed a great speech as in the movies. Birdy leaped backward and tucked the carbine under his black coat.

Birdy could hardly hear John Stone as he eased forward, eyes on the cops. He moved slowly, in order not to attract attention, because he was about to be visible. Which cop should he approach?

Top stepped before the podium, glancing left and right anxiously. Yes! Birdy didn't need to deal with the police; he'd give *Top* the carbine. He caught the old soldier's eyes, which were full of alarm—and fear! Why was he so frightened? Didn't he realize that Birdy could never hurt him? He brought out the carbine with one hand, then held it with two hands before him, like an offering. Hardly a second passed, only a heartbeat, and the eyes of John Stone descended upon him with hatred so pure, so vile, so vicious, that it was like a blow. And Birdy knew.

He pointed the carbine like you'd point at something on the horizon. He shouted, "He's a drug dealer!"

Top lunged for him as the crowd split, letting out a collective gasp. A woman screamed. The policeman to Top's left, and one to his right, brought up their revolvers almost formally, as if they were on a firing range. The screaming grew so shrill Birdy couldn't hear the weapons explode, but as with the trooper his death was instant. Or almost. He knew he was falling. He thought, *like the horse.*

The police of two states regarded Top as a hero. A minor hero, but he spoke to veterans groups and police unions now and again. He didn't enjoy the attention as much as he'd thought he might. Several folks in the Eureka Springs Chamber of Commerce urged him to run for state senator, but he was too old for crusades and didn't trust government enough to become part of it.

Even before the feds raided and made their showy arrests, many from New Jerusalem had fled. Several found work in the gas fields near Ft. Stockton, Texas, and gathered around a full gospel church. Dale Biggs opened a bait shop in a bend of the Piney River, near Cabool, Missouri. Luke Muldoon died in a knife fight with a Mexican in the parking lot of their employer, a pork processing plant in Guymon, Oklahoma.

Worried Brother Ronald was the only one to remain in New Jerusalem. He set up a sawmill and made oak and walnut furniture. Top sold him most of his land for a dollar. He had no need to lay up earthly treasures and disliked paying property taxes. And Ronald had been the first to say, "Thou Shalt Not Kill."

John Stone lost the election to a lawyer from Cape Girardeau. Birdy's last words were never quite substantiated, but the papers said they led to the defeat. Stone had served in Iraq with an MOS in Mortuary Affairs. He owned a nice farm in Shannon County, and he attended church regularly. He was even a lay preacher, but almost four years in his past were hard to account for. Maybe he'd hauled Birdy out of Granderson then and enslaved him. Manufacturing methamphetamine *might* have been how he financed his run for governor.

Flora and Top married and moved back to the highway, where they built a small house and reopened the pole barn church. Flora played her piano and organized a lively men's quartet. If the people insisted, Top preached, but after a while he turned things over to newcomers. "I run outta words," he claimed, laughing a little.

Flora found him in the strawberry patch after his stroke. He lay there most of a day, studying pure white clouds in the blue sky, and afterwards it was difficult to translate his fast, but garbled speech. On Sunday mornings, he sat in a back pew and nodded off. He snored, but the sound was no more intrusive than a cough or a child crying, and no one complained. Sometimes, Top jerked awake, and Flora rubbed his arms and eventually could calm him, but she didn't understand why he seemed so frightened or what he meant to say. It sounded like "Be well," and she said, "You be well, too, Sweetheart."

Top shook his head a dozen times, and at last Flora made out, "Birdwell."

"Birdwell," she said. "You mean Birdy? Birdy Blevins?"

His eyes glistened.

"Honey, it's all right," Flora said, stroking Top's thin hair. "You don't have to make sense."

The Book Club

On the morning of April 19 Audrey Delacroix claimed her backpack at Inmate Property. She found a ten in a secret compartment, and also her pack of Marlboros, though only two remained. She knew the pack had been unopened twenty-one months before, but where did you lodge your complaint? With the governor?

She assumed they'd give her money at the gate. It was the right thing to do, after what they'd put her through. In all the old movies you got at least fifty dollars, but no longer, not in Arkansas. She'd earned almost four hundred dollars working in the kitchen, but she'd have to find a bank, and fill out God knew how many forms, before it was hers.

It wasn't fair.

And that Puerto Rican woman at the gate wasn't *human.* No "Good luck, Inmate," or "Don't wanta see *you* again." Looking skyward, the woman droned, "Transportation is available for the newly released to the point of arrest," which was such a complicated way of talking that for an instant Audrey didn't understand. When she did, she thought that Arkansas had gone crazy. Her point of arrest had been the police station in Berryville, but why would she return to the county jail? The Salvation Army had offered her a job in Eureka Springs, hardly five miles away. She was a free woman. She'd walk.

Happily, the day was clear and sunny, with wild plums blooming alongside the road, and dogwoods joined like white lace in the understories of the oaks. Hazy green hills stretched as far as she could see, making Audrey feel like she was part of something big and important. She walked briskly at first, the scent of lilacs around the farmhouses filling her with joy and nostalgia for her childhood with her grandparents.

She grew tired after a mile or so and stopped to smoke one of her cigarettes. She discovered she had no light and, with a brave shudder, crushed both cigarettes and dropped them into the grass. Nicotine was the gateway drug to just about everything. She was beginning her new life, and she WOULD NOT SMOKE!

This seemed like a victory, the first of many to come, and her resolve carried her for a while longer. But by the time the Walmart came into view—two miles, still, from the Salvation Army—she was worn out. Her feet were sore and she wanted new shoes, but at least she'd buy something to eat. An apple, perhaps. They never gave you fresh fruit in the prison.

It wasn't her fault. Oh, she couldn't claim to be innocent, but Larry was the one who manufactured meth. The state of Arkansas didn't make any allowances. No such thing as "gradations of guilt"—a phrase some lawyer used, somewhere between jail cells. And then claiming she was a bad mother!

By the front entrance, three women sat at a long table with baked goods and a few early vegetables. They all wore long, pale blue muslin dresses, with black stockings and black shoes and thin white hats with cute little chin straps. They seemed so pure that Audrey was ashamed to approach them. Head down, she bought a rough, beautiful loaf of bread and, inside the store, an apple and piece of cheese. She was left with only a little change, but she needed strength to reach the Salvation Army.

She sat in the sun to attack the bread and cheese, but though ravenous, she held back half her plunder. She might need it this evening. She sat with her Walmart bag and backpack beside her, trying to look as though she were awaiting a ride. A girl of four or five, the age Catelynn would be now, crawled up on the bench.

"Are those new blue jeans?" Audrey asked her.

"My mama bought them."

"They look really, really nice. And you're very pretty with all your blonde hair. What does your mother call you?"

"Faith."

"Such a pretty name." Audrey reached inside her Walmart bag. "Would you like a piece of cheese, Faith?"

The girl held out her hand, but from nowhere a woman rushed up, grabbed the girl, and hurried into the parking lot. Head on her mother's shoulder, the little girl waved goodbye, closing her fingers in a soft fist like Catelynn used to. Audrey couldn't hold it in. She began to cry.

The youngest of the women selling baked goods hurried to Audrey's side. "Are you all right, Sister?"

Audrey hyperventilated, and the young woman stroked her back tentatively. Gasping, Audrey said, "I just got out of prison."

"I know."

"You . . . know?"

"How lonely you seem, for one thing. And your old clothes."

Audrey wore sweatpants with a cigarette hole at one knee and a purple T-shirt with a Razorbacks logo. She liked the pure young woman and tried to check her tears.

"It's all right," the young woman said. "A lot of us got law trouble."

"Not you nice Amish ladies!"

"We may be plain, but we're not Amish. We're the Book Club."

Audrey sat at the table with the kind ladies and almost relaxed, though jail time had put in her head the idea that someone was always watching you. Beth Nunnally, the young woman who'd befriended Audrey, and Laura Abbott, the plump one, both said that they had been in prison. And Laura also had a daughter somewhere in the foster care system. Her eyes were red, as though she herself wasn't far from tears.

Martha, the gray-haired woman, took them in no matter what, Beth said. "We grow all our food. We have a fishpond. One girl shoots deer."

"Men?" Audrey asked.

Beth smiled, and Martha finally spoke. "No men," she said neutrally.

Audrey had to think about that for a moment. Inmates could talk of nothing else and flirted with even the homeliest guards. But after being married to Larry, Audrey thought the idea of doing without men somewhat daring. You'd only see them at Walmart, as in a zoo. "No men, and you work all day. You read . . . *books?*"

"A book a week," Laura said.

"What about TV?"

Martha almost snarled. "They *spy.*"

"Yes, ma'am," Audrey said.

"*Look,*" the old woman said, holding out an arm, and Audrey lifted her eyes to the eaves of the building, where a camera had been mounted. Cameras were everywhere in the prison, even in the shower nozzles, inmates said. The Walmart camera, its red light blinking, pointed directly toward them.

"The TV's just like the internet," Laura said, though she seemed confused.

"The internet is *worse,*" Beth put in. "They know who your friends are, and if you say things against the government."

"And cell phones," Laura said, daubing her eyes with a Kleenex and sniffling. "That's how they find you."

"They say it's for your own protection," Martha said. "But you can't trust them. They spend their days dreaming up enemies. *You're* their enemy."

Audrey stared at the blinking light.

"Martha worked for Homeland Security. She knows everything," Beth said.

"My goodness." Audrey didn't understand what the women were talking about, but at least they were serious women, unlike the flighty types, the bullies, and the sickos in prison. "I want to come with you," she announced.

"What about your parole officer?" Martha asked, her blue eyes suddenly fierce.

"Don't have one. I served every last minute."

"Carrying any electronics? Tablet? Laptop?"

"No."

"DVD player, iPad, camera?"

"No, ma'am."

"Cell phone?"

"*No.*"

"You're sure," Martha said. "No cell phone. Don't lie to me, Audrey."

Audrey held up her wrist. "Just this old watch."

At the weekly convocation Audrey ate more of the delicious bread, this time with strawberry jam, though she could have had venison and pork, potatoes, even morel mushrooms. The bread and jam, with mint tea, made her feel like a little girl, nestled by her grandma's woodstove.

Martha spoke. She cautioned how everyone needed to seem meek when in town, so not to arouse suspicion, then dropped into a harangue about electronics and government spies, citing stories of how the government had hauled away innocent families in New Jersey and Arizona. Audrey didn't perfectly comprehend, except that the world was monstrously unfair and dangerous and that she was lucky to have blundered into this safe place.

Where they even had cigarettes. She shared one with Beth as Clubbers gave boring reports on how well the field corn was germinating, the health of calves and goat kids, and projections for the muscadine yield. Finally, they broke into small groups for book reports. Book reports? Just like in junior high.

Audrey didn't read well but it wasn't her fault. She grew up with her grandparents, kindly people, though not much for books. She never knew her dad, and her mom jerked her from school to school before she herself went off to prison. Some example! No, Audrey never had the advantages, but she got hold of Laura Ingalls Wilder and read about pioneer life in the fearsome north woods. What Wilder described was pretty much like life at the Book Club—except for the lack of men.

"We work like pioneers, and there are no men!" She didn't mean this as a joke but everyone laughed. It seemed she'd made a good book report.

Plump Laura Abbot just opened her Bible and read, "Blessed are those who mourn, for they shall be comforted." Silence followed, rather than discussion. What could you say? Laura wept, and everyone was embarrassed, or maybe contemptuous. Audrey hadn't read any rules, but she sensed you were supposed to be strong in this place and not cry over a Bible verse.

"Why do we do this?" she asked.

"They've allus done it," Beth said. "Though lotsa folks wanna drop it. Who reads anymore, right? Or you see people out in the world, they read on their phones, and you know we won't be doing *that*. I believe, back when they started, Martha thought it would be kinda inspiring, and relaxing for the girls."

"It's both of those," Audrey said. She liked that the books didn't have to be profound, or even sensible. Most women read tattered novels from the Book Club library: Gene Stratton-Porter, Grace Livingston Hill, and Peter B. Kyne. Girlhood trials, Christian example, and adventure stories from a hundred years ago. People rode around on horses then.

Levelheaded Beth read a romance, *The Beautiful Entrepreneur*, about a smart young businesswoman who was pretty dumb when it came to men. She fell for the handsome, slick guy—like Audrey's own Larry, who, when he was twenty, promised her the moon. Meanwhile, the heroine hardly noticed the shy fellow who set up the business, and whose hard work made it succeed. She didn't appreciate him until almost the end, when the slick guy was revealed as an embezzler. He was a cheater, too, when that flashy, big city woman breezed through town. Finally, the shy fellow won the heart of the businesswoman. Of course, you knew he would on the first page.

"Beth," Audrey said. "Life ain't like that."

Beth's blue eyes flashed. "It's a *fantasy*," she said.

After the readings, Clubbers gathered around a bonfire and drank muscadine wine. Wine? Yes, the Book Club made wine from elderberries and dime-sized muscadine grapes. After convocation, conversations grew intimate.

Audrey stared into the flames and once in a while slapped at a mosquito. She lit her third cigarette of the day. If she drank wine, she might as well smoke. Cigarettes soothed her soul. "Were you married, Beth?"

"You could say. Charles was hardly never there, but we had a little boy together, Norman."

"Where's Norman now?"

Beth shrugged. "I had to give up my rights."

"That's so unfair!"

"I wasn't no fit mother, Audrey."

Near midnight, while Audrey and Beth hugged and cried and drank sweet wine, someone slipped out of the darkness, raked the coals, and threw on more wood. A woman in a long dress, whom Audrey assumed was Sister Martha though she couldn't see clearly, read from an old book. The fire, the dark, and words she didn't comprehend thrust Audrey backward into her vague, sometimes pleasant childhood, when her grandparents took her to prayer meetings. The meetings ended with tearful altar calls, and drunken Audrey cried to Martha's words, too, and would have gone forward had this been a church service, had she been called. Out of the smoke, women's voices rose, chanting and sobbing. Hers, too.

"Bless you, Sister!" women cried, and now they did come forward, in triumph rather than sorrow, to feed the bonfire with bags of cell phones, DVD players, even TVs. Though her old watch didn't seem like much of an offering, Audrey approached the fire and was startled to see a long keyboard, still in its box, slowly curling with bluish, poisonous flames. Her tears came from a deeper place, as she remembered how she'd wanted to learn the piano when she was seven. Her mother couldn't afford the lessons.

"A brand-new keyboard!" she said to Beth. "Some little child— my Catelynn—"

"Shh," Beth said, holding out cigarettes. She poured more of the sweet wine.

A diesel generator churned enough power to light the meeting house and pump water to sinks and toilets. Sister Martha didn't object to electricity, only electronics. Still, you went to bed in the dark, unless you had candles or could find kerosene for a lamp.

Audrey was too weary to care. Being new, she drew the most demanding work, hoeing three-hundred-foot rows of beans and potatoes and, every third day, washing soup kettles in the steamy kitchen behind the cafeteria. Her calves swelled and her feet grew numb from shuffling across the concrete floor.

But even from her deep sleep, she'd sit up at two in the morning and see shapes creeping about in the darkness and hear doors closing softly. Only half-awake, she assumed the women were climbing into one another's beds. She'd witnessed such behavior in prison, and it didn't trouble her, because if you were poor and lonely, love was all you could hope for. Any kind of love. If Beth had asked, Audrey might have said yes.

She dreamed of Larry, who by the time the police dragged him away, had grown menacing and ugly. She woke again in terror, but then almost willfully dreamed of him when he was twenty, and she seventeen. They swam in the Piney River and afterwards lay on a blanket, on a high bluff that caught the breezes. She laughed, threw off her bra, while Larry pretended to be a hound dog, sniffing her toes, licking her. She woke at dawn drenched in sweat and for a moment looked about for Larry. But only the women were there, most of them snoring, one or two padding about with toothbrushes and combs.

Having proved herself a steady worker, Audrey drew easy duty, a week up at the store. Martha had broken her own rules to deal with the state of Arkansas, jumping through every hoop to make Book Club wine legal for public sale. Of course, customers stopped for noodles, jams, bread, eggs, and heirloom tomatoes, but muscadine wine, with its peculiar, earthy flavor, was the big draw. Occasionally, one of the more comely sisters climbed in a car with a man, never to return, but Martha allowed that such liaisons were overhead.

Late in the afternoon, the flow of customers dwindled, and it began to rain. Audrey had been reading her book for convocation, *Little Women,* but the store had no electricity, and light faded with the dark skies. She napped, then was startled awake by a man standing across the counter, dripping. He wore a foolish grin, as many men did when they were attracted to you, and Audrey raised her guard. Immediately, she dropped it. The man was Howie Spire, her boyfriend before Larry happened along.

"How are you, Audrey? I ain't seen you in . . ." He met her eyes and paused. "You're pretty as ever."

She might even have blushed. Anyhow, they were shy. They'd been high school sweethearts—almost. How long ago? Ten years? Twelve! Howie was a senior and maybe a little ashamed of her because she'd dropped out to work at the Dollar Store. She figured that's why they never had sex, because for a guy like Howie, sex meant commitment. She was cute back then, if she did say so, and could have seduced him if she'd tried. He went on to college up in Missouri, but she couldn't blame him for the breakup. She started running with that ignorant hillbilly, Larry Delacroix, and *his* wild crowd.

Even in the soft light, Howie didn't look like much, but he was the sort you brought home to Mama. If you had a mama.

Life was so unfair!

"What is this place, Audrey? I saw the sign on the highway, never stopped."

"Kinda hard to explain. It's—it's rare. Bunch a women, Howie."

He grinned. "What you do for entertainment?"

"Read books."

"You're not telling me the truth."

She laughed. She hadn't laughed much lately, and it felt delightful. "You and Suzie doing all right?"

"Oh, we split up three years ago. I got on with the federal government—"

"Howie! What do you *do?*"

"Secret stuff." He brought a finger to his lips and rolled his eyes. "Have to kill you, if I told you."

She stroked his wrist. "Howie. Always such a clown."

"I'm kinduva investigator, you might say. It's amazing what goes on back in these hills."

"Allus has been. Meth, and before that, all the bootleggers."

"I heard what happened to Larry. And you, just caught up in the thing, so unfortunate. You had a little girl, didn't you? Know where she is?"

Audrey bit her lip. "I don't."

"Life ain't over, Audrey." Howie brought out a fancy little computer, frowned, made some entries, and finally turned the screen so she could see.

"They're offering her up for adoption," he said.

Audrey studied the photograph. Catelynn had grown taller, and they'd cut her hair short. She looked sad, and she'd always been such a happy little girl!

"Here," Howie said, passing a cell phone over the counter. "You can call her up at that place."

"I cain't take your phone, Howie."

"It's old. Got a few minutes on it, that's all."

The rain had stopped. Sunlight broke through the front windows and spread out on the bare wooden floor. Flies that had gathered on the screen door began to stir.

"We ain't allowed—"

"To talk to your own daughter?" Howie snapped shut the little computer and walked toward the door. "None a my business, but what kinda place you living in, Audrey?"

"Oh, Howie, you don't need to go!"

He opened the screen door and stood half in sunlight. Flies took off in every direction. "You take care a yourself, Audrey," he said.

When she could steal a moment, she stepped down a path in the woods and punched in the number for the Granderson Treatment Center, but mostly she was out of range. If she turned the phone left or right, sometimes a mechanical voice spat out a menu. Once she reached a live person whom she could swear was that Puerto Rican woman at the prison gate.

"You will need to make an appointment."

"Is she there? Is Catelynn there?'

"When you arrive, please have available proof of parentage. Visiting hours are nine through two."

"Lemme me just—"

She lost the connection. She thrashed through the woods, terrified by the hoots and yips around her, but determined. She climbed toward what she thought must be a microwave tower far to the east, but now the phone didn't work at all. That night she crept out to the Book Club's barn, and climbed the stairs, and over the hay bales, to the dilapidated cupola. No answer from the Granderson Treatment Center, but she left a message for her old boyfriend. "Howie, I need to see you!"

In several days Howie didn't answer, and when she tried again, the number he'd given her had gone out of service. Audrey supposed that he'd learned the truth about her, that she'd done time. Then again, he already knew about Larry, and Catelynn.

Why had Howie shown up, just to tell her about Catelynn? He was a nice guy, but why would he care?

She grew tearful as Laura and couldn't get through her report on *Little Women.* The women were silent, judgmental somehow, and later she had nightmares. She dreamed Larry came at her with a crowbar, and Catelynn cried out, "Mama! Mama!" Audrey woke, and Beth looked down on her with a face so kind and full of love that Audrey knew she must still be dreaming. She woke again and heard her child's voice, crying, "Mama!" from the backpack. She grabbed it and ran out into the darkness, away from her nosy roommates.

She didn't hear "Mama! Mama!" again and knew she'd imagined everything. She'd broken Book Club rules for nothing. She carried the phone for several days more, like a dead baby, and then accidentally dropped it into the sudsy water with her pots. She reached down, all hope gone. Almost happily, she smashed the evil thing with a hammer and threw it in the trash.

That evening she discovered that someone had ransacked her bunk. She owned nothing worth stealing, but her blankets and sheets had been thrown to the floor, and the contents of her dresser spilled: her two long dresses, her underwear, her stockings. A wave of fear passed through her, as she realized something *was* missing: her one photograph of Catelynn, which she kept in a small brass frame atop the dresser. She sank to the bed. "I've been such a good worker," she wailed. "It's not fair."

Someone in the dormitory had done it. Or several someones. Absurd to think so, but in a way she'd been raped. Of course, she'd been around rough men all her life and knew what rape *was*. No, not rape, but she felt violated. And she realized now that everyone had grown wary of her, averting their eyes when she neared. She jerked her head around wildly. Where was her one friend, Beth?

She stumbled through the next day and still couldn't sleep. She lay awake until two, then wrapped a blanket around her shoulders, intent on making it to the Salvation Army. Maybe there was no job by now, but she knew they'd take her in.

She was worn-out in fifty steps, and the night confused her. She didn't know her directions and heard coyotes. She retreated again into the dark barn and slept fitfully, reaching out for the pillow she didn't have.

She was an hour late to the kitchen, but no one said anything. She'd forgotten to go out with her hoe, coming to the kitchen like it was truly her job, like she was a robot. Of course, no one would complain if you volunteered for the hardest chore there was.

Why would anyone raid her little corner and steal her picture? Where was Beth?

She vowed to spend one more night in the barn and at noon the next day, when everyone was eating, slip out the back way through the woods. The highway was only a mile off, and someone would give her a ride. Asleep on her feet, she visualized Howie in a flashy, new car. Her hair would blow in the wind. She'd make eyes at him.

Again she woke in the small hours and looked down from the cupola to see shapes moving about the Book Club's old truck. The women were dressed in dark pants and shirts, rather than powder-blue dresses. She thought one shape resembled Beth, but couldn't be sure. Three women climbed into the cab, and another four into the bed, and the truck moved off slowly, without lights. It seemed like another nightmare, and she fell back on the hay, shivering.

At noon the next day, as women filed in for lunch, she hurried out the back way. Nothing seemed changed. The Book Club tractor churned along, and three women, their bonnets bent low, picked green beans. On the clotheslines, thirty powder-blue muslin dresses fluttered. But she couldn't flee through the woods, because women were digging potatoes at its edge. She'd have to brave the night again. She knew the direction now and where she could find a flashlight.

She turned her head. A van with tinted windows sped toward her from the highway, fast as firemen or policemen, responding to an emergency. The van stopped abruptly, sat idling for a long moment, until three men wearing suits stepped out and strode purposefully toward the office.

In moments Martha emerged, staggering down the walk, wearing her blue muslin smock over slacks and no bonnet. Her straggly, gray hair made her seem impossibly old, a relic, a pioneer who'd wandered into the hills a century before and now emerged through a portal of time. She seemed confused, like a captured animal. As the side door of the van slid open, the old woman held up her head briefly and looked over the grounds. Then the men pushed her inside, and Audrey couldn't see anything but the van speeding away and disappearing down by the store.

She stood frozen. She thought of the day they came in a van for Larry, and how a week later they came for Catelyn, and how she'd sat in that rental house that stank of meth, watching soap operas, smoking cigarettes, until a van came for her, too. When she finished the pots, she washed every dish she could find, and mopped the cement floor, and cleaned out the grease trap, as though working harder made her more virtuous.

At dusk she tried to reach the woods, but women stood in every path—more women than she recognized. A group of them had gathered by a bonfire, even though convocation was three days away.

Now she saw Beth! She'll tell me what's wrong, Audrey thought, and where they took Martha and what the women, Beth among them, did in the middle of the night. We'll have this out like friends do. She'll tell me why they rifled my little bedroom and scared me so. And if they wanted her to leave, well, it wasn't as though she hadn't tried.

Beth wore her full Book Club dress, stockings, and shoes. Slowly, she raised her head under her white bonnet. Her chin straps were untied and fell forward. "I cain't help you, Audrey," she said, and reached out gently to place something in Audrey's hand.

As Beth drew back, the women began to gather, slowly encircling Audrey in the near darkness. "What did I do?" she asked. "What did I do?" She lifted one hand to shield her eyes from a sudden, sharp light. She realized that she held a brand-new package of cigarettes. "Thank you," she said, logic deserting her.

And then she whirled in panic, as hands plucked at her dress. She knew she must run. As her blouse ripped, Audrey saw an opening between two of the oldest and ducked through. Even as she did, a rock struck her head, and she stumbled. More rocks rained down.

"It ain't right. It ain't fair!" Audrey screamed, and then they were upon her.

Mariposa

Antonia, her cruel mother, demanded even the little that Portia made from babysitting. She couldn't buy new clothes and school was only a week away. Portia went to her father, Esteban, a gentle and fair-minded man whom she could always count on for ten dollars.

"There is no work," her father said, with great sadness. "We must go home, niña."

Work had been so easy to find, until it wasn't. After years of steady carpentry jobs, her father could secure nothing but part-time meat processing—fast, dangerous work, slicing hogs in two with a heavy saw. His old arms couldn't endure it, and he was fired.

They couldn't pay the rent for the trailer.

Portia liked her teachers, and they liked her, a quiet, imaginative student eager to learn. At fourteen, she dreamed of attending college and becoming a famous writer. She was an American girl! The idea of Mexico terrified her.

Then some drunken white boys threw a bomb into the trash cans, and the Mexican boys said they'd get guns, and people began to leave.

In Durango, they stayed at a rundown motel without air conditioning and where the showers didn't work. The place had filled with Indians from the mountains, and they didn't act like what Portia thought of as real Mexicans. The women were hostile, while the men staggered in the parking lot and bragged and argued.

Antonia warned her to stay clear, but Portia crept out as her mother slept, her curiosity overpowering her fear. She looked on in wonder when her father bought liquor in brown bottles and offered it to the Indians. He sat on a rickety bench and talked to them in a peculiar Spanish she couldn't quite follow. He laughed and drank several bottles, and it had been a long time since he'd seemed so relaxed.

Mexico, Portia decided, was a foreign country.

In the gas station, she found love. That is, love stories—comic books, or graphic novels, with flimsy bindings and weepy, lurid covers. They concerned beautiful, proud women who owned great ranches, and dashing men in black who rescued them from drug lords who looked like the Indians in the parking lot. The stories were ridiculously cheap, and Antonia seemed to approve, so Portia bought several to practice her Spanish. They proved easy to read, demonstrating that she was brilliant in two languages.

Sprawling in the back seat, she wrote:

At last rugged Irishman Brad O'Reilly owned his own shrimp boat. It couldn't have been easy for him, thought Miranda Mendez, brushing a tear from her dark eyes and bringing her engagement ring to her lips. When Brad sold his first catch, he mailed her a one-way ticket to New Orleans with the words, "I will love you always." "I love _you_, Brad," Miranda whispered, as the bus drew into the flamboyant city of New Orleans, with its rich Creole heritage, founded in 1718.

Many great women writers wrote love stories. Just consider Jane Austen, but after staring at her words for half an hour, as they entered Mexico City and then turned west, she ripped out the page and tore it into pieces. What she'd written wasn't like Jane Austen, or even the ranch romances. She didn't know where the story came from. It seemed juvenile.

After a long climb in the high country, they looked down on a valley, and Angangueo.

"Home," Antonia said, crying a little.

Portia cried, too, for different reasons. "I was born in Arkansas!"

"Hush, girl," Antonia said.

Angangueo lay at the head of a rolling valley surrounded by treeless, sage-covered foothills streaked with reddish gullies. Patches of agave dotted the high slopes, while on the valley floor, tall, dusty palms bunched along a gushing, brown creek.

"Where little Mattito drowned," Antonia said, crying again.

Concrete houses spilled over each other, some small and flat, hardly more than tin propped up on stones, some reaching three stories and brightly painted, some with orange tile roofs, some—their owners having run out of money, Esteban said—topped off with rebar like a bad haircut. In the cluttered back yards and stretching into the sage, turkeys and goats and sad-looking horses grazed alongside rusted boilers and drills and ore cars from the old mine—Angangueo's reason for existence, and decline. The mine had closed by Esteban's time, else he'd never have journeyed north.

Ford and Toyota pickups, diminutive Chevys made in Mexico, and ancient school busses brought down from el norte rattled up the stone street, hauling citrus, strawberries, peppers, potatoes, and plastic jugs of pulque. Plaintive ranchero ballads trailed from the trucks as they twisted upward into the foothills.

Portia shrank in the back seat. She longed for Dardanelle, so quiet and orderly.

A colonial Catholic church stood in the center of town, in a square called the Zócalo, which her father told her was a Mayan word. In late afternoon disco music blasted from the church courtyard—the devil's music, Antonia said.

"Then why do they play it?"

Esteban smiled. "They want to reach the young people."

Terrified of the music, the church, the street—even of the wind with its alien scents of bougainvillea, ripe fruit, and manure—Portia fled to her tiny upstairs room. She closed the curtain and read through stacks of romances.

In great flourishes, using colored pens on a thick yellow tablet, she began writing her new romance, imagining her longhaired heroine a prisoner in the church's high tower. Her prince rode up the crooked street on a white stallion, except that he wasn't a prince but a leader of the Revolution, though still he was very handsome. Later in the story he would bear her away toward those smoky volcanoes that Esteban claimed were active. Maybe that's how the story should go. Her heroine would work to save the children from the volcano, and *then* the Hero of the People would bear her away. Together they'd battle the federales and save Mexico from relentless tyrants.

By such paper daydreaming she mustered sufficient confidence for her first venture down the hill, while her mother slept, and her father trudged the mountain roads, looking for work. Brown foreigners gaped from doorways, and her knees grew weak. She managed one hundred steps when her progress was blocked by a battered truck filled with cantaloupes. She lifted her head to meet the angry eyes of a young man, arms full of melons, who *kept* looking.

She bolted for her room, fell on her bed, and sobbed until she grew sick, even as she came to the admission that the cantaloupe boy hadn't been hostile or even flirtatious but merely curious.

Why couldn't she adapt to this place? Was it the scabby dogs, stumbling in the sunlight? The babies crawling on the sidewalk? The broken cars and trucks, their parts strewn everywhere—sometimes turned into decorations? This part of Angangueo wasn't so different from the trailer park—Dardanelle's Mexican town—that her family had called home.

Maybe it was the girls—the ripe girls, some younger than she—strutting in tight jeans. They were hillbillies, while she was a smart American girl, college bound. Oh, how could she hope to attend college in poor Mexico, with parents as poor as hers? To embrace this culture spelled doom, and she wept, as her mother had wept in el norte. "I *can't* live here," she announced.

Her cruel mother seemed happier now. She'd returned to her proper role, in a proper house and country. Because she understood the proper role for her daughter, her sympathy grew thin. "Ye—ess," she said. "You *can.*"

On their fifteenth day in Angangueo Antonia lumbered up the narrow stairs and yanked back Portia's sheets, throwing her to the floor. "There is work to do, lazy señorita," she said.

For two days Portia cleaned a brick wash room at the back of the property, filling plastic bags with cans and bottles and foul-smelling rags—shrieking when she uncovered scorpions. She brushed the ceiling and walls, and as she scrubbed the board floor, men delivered a washer. A drain and electrical outlet existed, but no water until her father ran a line. Portia carried buckets from a neighbor's cistern, enough to fill the tub three times, before Antonia released her. "Stay out of that room until bedtime," she said. "Or you can paint the porch."

Portia swept her long hair into a ponytail and pushed herself down the street toward the church. No dogs chased her. No leering young men accosted her—no cantaloupe boy, whom by now she wanted to see. A bent old man tipped his hat.

The church courtyard wasn't as large as she'd imagined, but featured a bandstand and a dry, hard-packed soccer field. Statues representing saints Portia had never heard of looked down from cracked pedestals, as if about to topple.

On the second floor, down open halls that faced the courtyard, were classrooms—her school, she thought, daring to hope. She drifted in the quiet courtyard, head down, hands tucked behind her back, peering into the church's inscrutable, dark doorways.

"Hola, Señorita," said the old man from the street, only now catching up with her. Smiling sadly, he disappeared through one of the doorways; she heard the soft slap of his sandals on stone steps. Puzzled, but somehow less frightened, Portia turned toward the street again, when bells rang out deafeningly. Simultaneously, a nun appeared out of the dark interior, motioning.

Portia bolted, thinking, *what a fool you are. Shyness will be interpreted as rudeness.* The nun meant to be friendly, but still Portia could not bring herself to return. Breathless, chastened, she paused in a little market where old women hawked butterflies—ceramic, brass, wooden—to tourists.

Behind them, on both sides of an alley, stood a mural painted on adobe, telling the story of Angangueo. First, it was a tranquil place where sheep dotted the mountains and butterflies filled the air.

Then the rapacious Europeans—they wore top hats but didn't seem to be Yankees—discovered silver. They exploited the poor workers, until one day many of them were killed in an accident. The workers united, bought the mine, but soon the silver played out. And yet all was well somehow, because in the bright final tableau butterflies filled the air again, flitting and flopping their way to a welcoming Jesus.

"Could you explain?" A tall, blonde woman stood by Portia's shoulder. "What do the butterflies . . . and Jesus . . . mean?"

She almost answered: "I'm not from here." But for a moment she desired to be and felt a fleeting pride that this angular suburbanite could mistake her for a native. For a Mexican.

"She doesn't speak English. Why would you expect her to?" This from the woman's husband, a man shorter than Portia, wearing those multi-pocketed safari pants such as you saw in catalogs.

"I'm sorry, dear," the woman said, and reached out as if to pat Portia but then seemed to think better of it. She turned to her husband. "Should I give her a little something? She's pretty."

"Whatever."

"I mean, they don't have *anything*."

This was too much, and Portia hurried down the alley. Round the corner, she broke into laughter. All around her, people smiled and laughed, too. Almost, she belonged.

Esteban told her that the Purépecha Indians believed monarch butterflies—*mariposas monarcas*—were the souls of the dead, returning from the Underworld to be reborn. Finally, their purpose on earth fulfilled, they joined Jesus. It was a pretty story, he said, though unacceptable to a good Catholic.

Portia wasn't religious enough to understand heresy. "The who?"

"Your ancestors, hija. The Purépecha."

"I'm an Indian?" Like the Indians in Durango?

"Indian, Castilian, African, German—we are Mexicans, Portia."

"Mutts."

"Mestizos. Be proud."

Her father sought the counsel of school friends, many of whom also had gone to the United States, only to return when the work dried up. Some opened tiendas under awnings in their front yards, displaying their pitiful goods like a census of poverty. Other friends waited for carpentry work or hired out as guides, though the tourist business, too, was in the doldrums. Some drank pulque, so cheap it was almost free.

Rumors of work seldom resolved into substance. One man took a job building a hotel near the great Zócalo in Mexico City, but the bosses lost their financing and laid off the man before he began. Her father's friend Victor undertook the long journey to Hermosillo to work for the Ford Motor Company. True, Ford was hiring, but for every job, two hundred applied.

No work for her father, and no education for her. The nun she'd fled from told her that because she was halfway through the ninth grade, the school couldn't help her. The diocese had no money for secondary school. You could go to Hidalgo, but the tuition was costly and so far away you needed room and board as well.

Christmas passed, cousins and aunts cycled through, and everyone said how pretty she was, that she'd drive the boys crazy. But driving Mexican boys crazy led only to babies and then her life, like her mother's, would end. No, no, she was college bound. All her teachers said so.

Antonia tried to show her how to make tortillas but Portia couldn't master the art—just the right amount of water, the quick turn of the wrists. "Why not buy them in the tienda?" she asked, and Antonia slapped her.

"You're fat," Portia said. "You're fat from all that grease and cheese. I hate Mexican food. I hate *you.*"

Antonia tried to strike her again, but Portia ran upstairs and locked her door. She wrote furiously in her romance. The girl in the tower had the worst parents in the world, and they lived in the worst town, in the worst country!

At dinner, she asked Antonia about school in Hidalgo, but her glum mother said only, "You are old enough to find work."

"What work is there to find?"

Her father hung his head.

She no longer feared the street. Mexicans were much like the people of Dardanelle, she concluded, though with even less money. She walked along carelessly in her tight jeans, sticking up her nose when boys whistled. She danced with them at the Catholic disco but only with the little ones, some still in their school uniforms. This was hardly a disco at all. Where were the older boys?

One night the cantaloupe boy came. Both he and Portia stood a head taller than los niñitos. As in a romance, her eyes locked with the cantaloupe boy's, and when he drifted toward the street, she followed.

A hand from the alley grabbed her arm and pulled. Fear leapt out of her stomach, and she swallowed bile. She twisted past the boy, then found herself pinned to the adobe church wall, panting. A cat yowled, fighting off a tom, as Portia tried to find the boy's eyes. He thrust hard against her as he lifted a pipe stem to her lips. He struck a match and held it to the bowl. "Inhale."

She knew she shouldn't, and she understood, more or less, what the boy wanted, but at last she'd found something exciting in Angangueo. She breathed deeply, coughed, and breathed in more. She reeled from the wall as if the boy had struck her, but with a mighty resolve she turned her stumbling into a sort of pirouette. She whispered, "Your name?"

"Diego."

"I saw you in the market, Diego."

"I saw *you*, Señorita."

He held the pipe again and she drew deeply, coughing not as violently. Meth differed from marijuana, which merely turned you stupid. Meth made you confident, and fearless, but she had learned at Dardanelle High School that it was false confidence, and false courage. Toothless, emaciated meth addicts lined up at assembly, telling the kids not to do what they had done. Meth not only made you stupid, they said, it ruined you. Just look at us.

She couldn't use drugs and write. On the other hand, she thought, writers needed to gather experience, as Diego unbuttoned her blouse, and undid her bra, so quickly she hardly felt it. He demonstrated more efficiency than other boys she'd experimented with, but no more finesse. He put his mouth on her breasts.

She giggled. "That tickles."

He pulled hard at her arm, but meth lent her the strength to hold back. She knew that Diego meant to draw her deeper into darkness, perhaps into that ramshackle little garage at the alley's end, but he was only a campesino, while she was a princess of the high country.

The princess filled up with laughter like fuel and tore away her arm. She ran and ran, and laughed and laughed. No, no. She didn't need a prince to be saved.

She crept to the kitchen in the wee hours and drank from her father's jugs of pulque. Fermented maguey, a kind of agave, she learned. In Mexico, where winters didn't amount to anything, you could cultivate your cactus—or properly, succulent—year round and stay eternally drunk. If you couldn't find work, why not drink?

Pulque looked like milk but tasted like cider. Intoxication crept up slowly until you fell down the stairs. She liked pulque too much, and one night met her father at the refrigerator. He took the pulque away and smiled knowingly. "Come along with me, niña," he said.

In the chilly dawn they climbed into a discolored Volkswagen bus with three silent fellows clutching shovels and axes, leather-faced, deeply brown men who stank of tobacco. They nodded to her father but didn't look at her—out of shyness, she thought, rather than rudeness.

The bus jolted its way up the mountain, crawling over rises of baked mud and stony rivulets cutting away the road's surface. Climbing through clouds, they burst into clear sky and briefly hung as if on a precipice, before the bus ground into a lower gear and veered around the rock face. Two thousand feet below, Angangueo stretched out, a coppery green, gleaming magically in the morning sun.

They came to a muddy parking place surrounded by tall, straight trees.

"Oyamel," her father said.

"What?"

"The trees are oyamel firs. Home for the mariposas."

Butterflies? Her father had a surprise for her. She smiled and took his hand as if she were a little girl again.

The trail to the summit curved steeply ahead, and they had to ride horses—tame, defeated animals with tenders. "I will help you, Señorita," said the young man from the alley, the cantaloupe boy, but he didn't meet her eyes.

"Another job for you, Diego?"

Portia, aspiring princess, was prepared to forgive him, but he stared without recognition. She stuck her nose high, trying desperately to seem sophisticated and graceful, but she'd never sat astride a horse. Her legs veered out awkwardly, and she felt certain she'd fall. Eyes held low, Diego adjusted the stirrups and pushed in her feet.

She felt she'd snap like a wishbone. Bravely as the bravest heroine, though in growing pain, she cried out, "Don't you remember me?"

He didn't answer. And she couldn't say, *I am the girl from the alley.*

Diego led her horse by a rope halter, while she dropped the reins and clung to the pommel. She tried to sway with the rhythm of the horse, but the trail was rocky, and fir branches slapped her face. Her father, separated by three plump tourists, turned in his saddle, grinning. She smiled in reply, masking the throbbing of her thighs.

She believed she understood. She wasn't a princess to Diego, but a privileged American girl, a vague foreigner who melted away with daylight. He was working now. By definition, she could not enter his world, and in a sense he didn't see her. She wasn't consequential enough even to be snubbed.

In her pain, she murmured, *I do, too, matter!* All the time she'd looked down on these hillbillies, they looked down on her. They were all like Antonia. Maybe, *maybe,* she could fight for a proper respect, but—

Now she saw the monarchs, flitting among the oyamels, clinging to rocks, and puddling in low, damp places. The trail leveled out and Diego stood stone-faced, holding the horse steady as she dismounted. She scraped her stomach across the hard leather, dropped stiffly, and staggered backward on her numb legs but managed to stand erect.

Diego was about as romantic as his sad little horse. As romantic as the benighted little town he hailed from. Imagine having babies with such a jerk!

With her father and a dozen tourists she climbed another one hundred feet, then descended into a long gully. Holding his index finger to his lips, her father motioned for her to sit beside him on a great, overhanging boulder. It was cool beneath the firs but warm on the boulder. As the tourists busily, importantly snapped pictures, setting up fancy equipment, fighting for angles, finally she saw: thousands, no, millions of black-and-orange monarchs. They clung to branches and each other, piled so deeply they obscured the trees. They were like leaves, like the brown crepe paper she'd folded into butterflies in the second grade.

"They come from Canada," her father said. "Right through Dardanelle. They mate and die along the way, four, even five generations of them."

"How do they know? How do the young ones . . . remember?"

"Only God can say." He shrugged. "But they must journey to this place, to these trees. Sometimes, it is too cold, and they freeze. I came here when I was a boy, and you could scoop them up with a shovel. And they say there are fewer now, because farmers spray the milkweed. But on a day like today, when it is warm on the mountainside—"

A streak of sunlight burst through the trees, and the monarchs awoke two and three at a time, fluttering up, resting again. Then they all awoke and the sky filled with darting specks of orange and black, stabbing the air like embers from a campfire, like multicolored leaves fluttering away, dully golden in the sunlight. Their wings whispered by her ears. She lay back, and they landed on her stomach and down her sore legs, two of them, then fifty.

"Oh," she said, closing her eyes. The sad town of Angangueo, where you could not find work or go to school and the boys behaved like dogs, could boast one romantic thing. And she, to whom God was only a hazy absence, would never draw nearer to Heaven.

At last her father broke the silence. "Portia, we must return to Arkansas. Your mother will stay—"

She sat, and the butterflies flew away. Ungainly, really, not built for flying, but so beautiful. One monarch still clung to her shoe. "Home," she murmured, as the monarch fluttered up.

"Where there is work again," her father said. "And school for you."

The Hidden Kingdom

I had the kind of job, throwing crap into boxes and slapping on addresses, where clearheadedness was overrated. That is, the night before, I'd tied one on, and now I muddled through. Once or twice, I nearly sliced off a finger on the tape machine, and Sam Olney, the supervisor, threw me a look. By morning break I was doing all right.

Monica Bowser, my girlfriend of four months, had dropped me cold. So I drowned my sorrows, or celebrated my freedom—take your pick. Anyhow, I woke up alone, and my head hurt.

"I made a study of it, Eddie," Monica said, when she dumped me. "I took a poll with my many Facebook friends. Your modern-day romantic relationship—you and me, Eddie—lasts just about four months."

How cynical can you be, I said, the voice of the trusting public, of the television audience, but I feared she was right. In the beginning, everything Monica said was brilliant, and we both had promising futures. We saw some serious movies, attended some serious concerts, and agreed on many vital subjects. She cooked her one, special recipe, just like her great-grandmother in Italy. It goes without saying that the sex was fantastic.

After four months we grew bored. I hoped for a secret compartment, an exit that we both could duck through, where we'd find ourselves holding hands in a field of daisies. My timeless new world never appeared. Always, my hopes glowed bright, then faded, and Monica—and Olivia, and Kayla—dissolved into memory.

Meanwhile, I shifted my route to work, and changed where I bought burritos, and spotted a cute redhead named Jessica. Ever the optimist, I was convinced Jessica was the one. In four months it was over—well, we had a pregnancy scare, and stuck it out for five months. By then Jessica and I were screaming at each other.

Newton's Fourth Law of Motion: a relationship spins for four months, until gravity pulls it to a stop. Any woman you can think of: four months. Four months with the most beautiful woman in Georgia, or anyhow Valdosta, or anyhow the south side of town encompassing several fulfillment centers, strip malls, and franchise eating establishments, and then it's over.

So what the hell am I doing here, I asked myself with a clear head, as the little hand inched past eleven on that strange, white clock big as a wading pool. Shouldn't I plan for years, rather than months? For marriage, for kids? Oh, the curse of a world in which everything is known! Where there's only sex and bad food, jobs you sleep through, and people you wear out in four months. Surely, there's more, but I can't see it! Organic farming, or saving the polar bears, or a career in law enforcement. Something that means something. Maybe, for God's sake, God.

Just as the little hand reached 12:00 noon, Sam Olney squeezed my shoulder. You can't talk on the line, with those conveyor belts whipping off northwest and sideways. Sam motioned to our break room, a glass cage over in the corner. I had a call on the landline.

Which usually meant somebody had died, but my mom had already passed, and there was no one else in my life except those four-month women. It was my old girlfriend, Monica Bowser.

"I thought you hated me," I said.

"Oh, you're a good guy, Eddie, but our four months are done. We're helpless. It's a force of nature."

"Okay, Force of Nature. So why'd you call me?"

"I saw the numbers."

"What?"

"On TV."

Well, the damndest thing. I'd won the lottery.

You've heard the stories, how suddenly you have relatives you didn't know you had. Monica didn't call again, but Kelsey did, and Jane, and several more, I'm ashamed to say, whom I didn't remember. Men I'd hardly spoken to at work wanted to get together for coffee. A realtor offered a tantalizing proposition in Cherokee Hills. Insurance people, car dealers, worthy causes all made their pitches. I grew depressed and almost called back Kelsey, from whom I'd rebounded to Monica. Then I remembered the arguments we'd had in our fourth month, and my head began to throb all over again.

I yanked out the phone and walked to the movies, where no one recognized me. Walking back, I saw my face through a store window, on the evening news, with "Winner!" and "Mystery Man!" flashing. Mystery man, because I had yet to deal with the media.

I went down to see my landlord, Maria. Unfortunately, we'd had an affair long ago, lasting approximately four months. She invited me in, threw her arms around my neck, tried to fix me something to eat. This was how it was going to be everywhere, I thought, but Maria was a good sort. I paid the rent, bought out my lease, and wrote her a generous check in addition, to handle my calls. "Where you going?" Maria asked.

I said, "Somewhere they won't call."

By the end of the week I fixed things with the lottery folks, signing papers, routing payments, posing for pictures. I was your ideal winner, explaining to the media all the good deeds I'd do, and meaning it. I'd do good deeds, if I could find any worth doing.

The reporters and bloggers filed out, satisfied for the moment. I waved to a last camera and excused myself. I counted out fifty thousand dollars in one-thousand-dollar increments and wrapped each pile in butcher paper. I used the restroom, poured a mug of coffee, and hit the road for Alabama.

Little towns, big cities. Vast, abandoned parking lots, busted up with Johnson grass. Empty motels, gas stations, big box stores, still standing amid piles of bricks dropped by the tornadoes. Tall buildings, dead or alive, with shiny windows that blinded the blackbirds. They crashed into the glass, killing themselves.

Old black men, some of them blind, sat in wheelchairs and sold boiled peanuts. White people, eyes protruding, teeth lost to drugs, stumbled along the highway in hopes of a free meal. White trash, we used to call them, from the wrong side of town—before they showed up everywhere.

As I drove through the night, I grew confused. Bank of America, Walmart, Sonic, Lowe's, McDonald's, General Baptist Church, T.J. Maxx, Sprint, Burlington Coat Factory, La Quinta, Denny's, Sam's Club, Edward Jones, Red Lobster all flashed their colors at me, and when I topped a hill there they were again: Better Burger, Comfort Inn, Applebee's, stretching onward, for all I knew, straight to hell. This was Birmingham, but I thought I had returned to Valdosta, that I'd never left—until at last those lights went out, and I whisked through a deep blackness.

Then far to the west, at dawn in the highlands near the Piney Woods, I almost escaped. I saw no one, or no one who mattered. Just good old boys in rattling pickup trucks and some dusty vans delivering potato chips to diners and convenience stores. Maybe here you could buy a little house, I thought. You could grow vegetables, go fishing every day.

In that country you looked out for twenty miles, until the horizon dissolved into blue-green nothingness. I watched a potato chip truck as it made a turn down a narrow blacktop, then fluttered from sight, as if a great curtain dropped from the sky. I drove the same rolling blacktop, chasing the truck, but I couldn't overtake it. I parked beneath a rusty water tower that poked out of the woods where once there had been a town. Broken machinery lay on either side of me, and deer grazed under the limestone bluffs.

Maybe you came to this woebegone, dreamy place before entering Heaven. You walked through the deserted town and topped a hill. You looked back and couldn't remember where you parked. You walked on, free at last, toward the singing.

Four a.m. I'd fallen asleep with the TV on, and now Mr. Ed was busy making a fool of Wilbur. For a moment I couldn't remember where I was.

An anonymous motel in South Memphis. A stone's throw from Graceland. Where you'd hide out after you robbed a bank, at least in the movies.

In the movies, I'd find a reason to return. People knew me in Valdosta. Obviously, I had money, and could do good deeds. I'd give my ill-gotten gains to the Salvation Army, and then I'd counsel the poor. I'd say to them, buy a lottery ticket every week.

What were my piles of money good for?

For escaping. Hadn't I escaped?

I carried my bags to the car. It had rained, and oil slicks gleamed dully on the King's Highway, also known as Elvis Presley Boulevard. I hadn't locked the doors, but my butcher paper stacks of money were untouched.

Turning north, I spied the blinking neon of a Piggly Wiggly—the King's own grocery. Never again would I visit Memphis. I parked and stumbled through the doors, surely the only customer. I grabbed orange juice, grapes, and then stood as if paralyzed, my half-awake brain studying the display of cookies.

Me, an ordinary, unworthy jerk. My life a meaningless bore. Even with money, I hadn't truly escaped.

Elvis, the most famous hillbilly of them all, didn't escape, either. All that fame, all that money, all those women, and still he lost his way.

"Help you, suh?"

I hadn't pulled on socks or shaved, and my hair needed combing. The clerk didn't know I was rich and bound off on a mission to find the meaning of life. He probably dealt with crazies every night.

I reached for molasses cookies. "I was thinking Elvis must have come in here, sometimes. Bananas, cookies—he loved 'em. Late at night, see, he wouldn't cause a stir. Molasses cookies. Poor kid, maybe he grew up on molasses. Don't you think?"

The clerk stared.

"Some people think Elvis is alive. And if he is, like any other guy, he's gotta eat. What more likely place to run into him than right here by the cookies?"

"Shee-ut," the clerk said, backing away.

"You've heard of Elvis, haven't you? 'Hound Dog?' 'It's Now or Never?'"

The clerk stopped by the frozen fish. "Everybody heard of Elvis," he called back. "They say He *did* come in here, sometimes. But he'd be eighty, man. He's dead!"

"Maybe he's alive," I said. "He's alive if you—"

A woman turned abruptly on heel and marched up the aisle. Her image, her briskness hung on in the air and seemed to accost me; involuntarily, my eyes followed her pretty legs and fastened on her swaying hips. So little was nonetheless all it took, sometimes, to begin sleeping together, and regretting it. Generally speaking, as documented by my friend Monica Bowser's scientific study, it took four months to disentangle yourself.

I caught her face in profile as she paused to select a bottle of wine and some fancy cheese. She glanced back as if seeing me for the first time, then jerked her head toward the wine again. She must be desperate, I thought, to leave such a hot trail at such an unlikely, though prescient, hour. A lawyer, perhaps, in that gray—slightly rumpled—suit. Went from work to a party, and the party had just broken up. Or was drinking wine how she greeted Saturday mornings?

I ran my hands through my sweaty hair. She was my age, which is to say, no longer young. Formerly, before I became rich—before I became a pilgrim—she'd have been out of my league.

Beside her, I began an inspection of the imported beers. "You like Elvis?" I asked, somewhat innocently.

She wheeled away and waved at the clerk, who put down his mop and joined her at the register. She laughed merrily at his chatter, but I knew it was a diversion.

I stood by the magazines, near her once again. Her eyes drifted up to mine, but not flirtatiously. She merely seemed weary, and I must have looked homeless. Suddenly, she was gone, and I faced the empty day, my long and imponderable journey, by myself.

Maybe I'd catch her in the parking lot, I thought half-heartedly. *Hello, Miss. Don't be misled by my slovenly appearance. I'm rich.*

Chasing money, chasing sex. What happened when you caught them? Four months went by and you never remembered. You did it all over again.

The clerk began ringing me up, but as if responding to some silent signal, we both paused and turned our heads toward the parking lot. I bolted toward the exit. The lawyer stumbled endearingly.

Out of the shadows, a great white limousine, its long, dark windows reflecting the Piggly Wiggly neon, drew inexorably near, and the farthest door opened. A silhouette leaned forward, and one sequined white leg dropped to the pavement.

"Shee-ut," the clerk said. "It's *him*."

The electric doors whirred half-open, and closed, behind me. The woman stood transfixed, hands fluttering, as if she awaited the rapture. A big, turbaned chauffeur came around the long white hood and motioned to the open door. Then he stood with his arms folded and his feet apart, like a cartoon genie.

The woman pointed toward her chest. *Me?* her lips said. *Me? Me?*

The chauffeur nodded.

Elvis wasn't dead. Every night, he descended from Heaven to haunt the Piggly Wiggly.

No. The man with the sequined leg was an imitator. That ridiculous car was some kind of Memphis joke.

The woman slipped into the black interior, and the chauffeur closed the door. He turned, slid behind the wheel, and the great car plunged down a side street toward a dark grove of trees. I blinked, and the limousine vanished into the wall of blackness.

Munching molasses cookies and slurping coffee, I crossed the Mississippi as the sun rose behind me. I played the King's gospel: "Peace in the Valley" and "So High," and I thought, there's a hidden kingdom on the Alabama line. And in Memphis, in the Piggly Wiggly parking lot. And maybe in the West, that land of pure air and infinite horizons.

As the day heated up, I dropped into the lowlands of Arkansas. What a sad place this was! Burnt-out cars and gutted trailers and sharecropper's shacks with caved-in roofs. Then nothing, nothing in that flat land I can remember until I reached Jonesboro and turned up the great thoroughfare of Caraway Road.

I thought my journey had been a dream and that I had awakened in Valdosta. Stretching to infinity were McDonald's, Papa John's, Pet Palace, Walmart, Manny's Chiquita, Paesano's, Mattress Land, Home Depot, Kroger, Walmart, Baptist Church, Culver's, Bank of America, Verizon, Checkers, Target, Comfort Inn, Wendy's, Jack in the Box, Dickey's—wait a minute. I was hungry and I'd always enjoyed Wendy's. When our allotted four months expired, Monica Bowser and I met there for a sentimental last dinner.

The traffic was too fierce to make a turn, so I continued over the hill, and what did I see? Petco, Quiznos, Second Baptist Church, Bank of America, Walmart, Sonic, Lowe's, McDonald's, General Baptist Church, T.J. Maxx, Sprint, WhataBurger, Burlington Coat Factory, Denny's, Sam's Club, Edward Jones, Affordable Mattress, Red Lobster, Freewill Baptist Church—and finally, at the end of the highway and bordering a great swamp, the end of franchises, the very last Wendy's.

In the parking lot, a man stood in the bed of a high-wheeled, mud-splattered truck, holding up the Good Book, shouting out his message even as he tossed loaves of white bread to a writhing crowd of homeless. Who was I to judge? This prophet helped the poor, the hungry of Jonesboro, and I had vowed to do good deeds if I could find any worth doing. I took one of my butcher paper stacks of money and held it out. "For you, sir, and your noble effort. I am a pilgrim who has lost his way. Can you give me directions?"

The prophet's fierce blue eyes bore down on me, and then he pointed up the long four-lane of Carraway Road, toward T.J. Maxx and Affordable Mattress. "Broad is the way that leadeth to destruction."

"Don't I know it, Brother. Mammon has led to my undoing."

"Indeed," the prophet said, as I handed him two more butcher paper stacks.

"Also the delights of the flesh," I said.

The prophet tore off the end of one of my bundles and thumbed the bills. "No doubt about it."

"Is there an answer?"

The prophet looked up thoughtfully and pointed toward the swamp. "Take the narrow gate, Friend."

I hadn't seen it. An old, rusted stock gate, and I opened it and drove down the muddy road, ever deeper into the swamp. The road twisted through groves of stunted oaks, then seemed to disappear. My wheels sank deeper as cypresses rose tall and pressed around me. A shallow lake stretched ahead and I didn't believe I could get through. I wondered if the prophet had conned me, or if he was a prophet at all, but I couldn't turn around. I had to have faith even if I drowned. I gunned the engine and kept on and on, almost floating. Far on the horizon, I saw green hills and blue sky.

I entered a sort of town where hollow-cheeked men stumbled toward me, stared up with puzzled eyes—I threw them packets of money. Beautifully painted, ravaged women called out to me of love—and I threw them money. Young men stood on the narrow road, angry young men who cursed and threatened me with their guns. I threw them money. They pounced on it like meat.

The road lifted up. I drove toward the misty horizon, climbing, sleepless, into a land of high hills where the air smelled of grapes.

Clear rivers rushed around me, and tall pines marched on for miles, into valleys broken up by pretty little orchards. Maybe I dropped back in time. Maybe you had to.

I followed a blacktop under the trees, crossing and recrossing the Piney River, and bought a cabin by what long before had been a grist mill, near the village of Dadeville.

Time passed.

I cannot account for it.

I found I had become a businessman, renting canoes and kayaks to tourists who discovered us by accident, who had taken a wrong road, who were almost out of gas, who needed a place to rest and a simple meal. I studied them to see if people had changed. I listened to their tales of the great world, and it seemed just as implausible as when I lived in it. I found solace in the words of a great poet: "That's all right, Mama. Any way you do."

I grow vegetables and apples, and every day I fish. I am well liked by my neighbors. Little Dadeville has recovered from poverty: a drug treatment center set up shop in an abandoned church, and a hardware reopened. We have a new winery and a shop for making dulcimers. All our hopeful entrepreneurs draw from a fund managed by our savings and loan, itself established by a mysterious benefactor.

A schoolteacher, Laura Dale, laughs at my jokes, and on Friday nights she cooks for me. She, too, is from somewhere to the east, as are many here. She, too, dreamed of a better world.

We have been together for several years, but Laura says, "Jimmy, it has only been five months!" And sometimes, when a few days have passed, it seems as though we are meeting for the first time. I believe that this anomaly can be explained. It is necessary to begin again, and again, and again, and again, until we get things right.

Sometimes, I climb the high hill behind Dadeville and then the old fire tower atop it. From there my eye follows the Piney as it trickles out of the hills into a great inland sea. Fierce storms rage out there, and watching the lightning play across the blue-green water fills me with a sense of danger, and comforts me.

Laura and I have a good life in Dadeville, but still we are curious—what lies over the water? I have yet to meet anyone who has sailed all the way across, and returned. In my barn I am sanding and planing cedar boards for a lightweight, sturdy boat. One fine day, this summer or the next, we'll float down the Piney and onto the sea, toward that brand-new world we dream of.

JOHN MORT'S first novel, *Soldier in Paradise*, won the W. Y. Boyd Award for best military fiction. He has published seven other books, including the story collections *Tanks*, *The Walnut King*, and *Dont Mean Nothin: Vietnam War Stories*. John Mort served in Vietnam with the First Cavalry and afterwards attended the University of Iowa, receiving MFA and MLS degrees. He is a member of the Western Writers of America and in 2013 won a Spur Award for his short story, "The Hog Whisperer," included in this volume. He lives in southern Missouri where he raises vegetables and fruit.